DUNCAN PRYDE SERIES

LONE OPERATOR

JAN DOMAGALA

Contents

Prologue   1
Chapter 1   7
Chapter 2   17
Chapter 3   23
Chapter 4   29
Chapter 5   35
Chapter 6   39
Chapter 7   43
Chapter 8   49
Chapter 9   55
Chapter 10   61
Chapter 11   67
Chapter 12   71
Chapter 13   77
Chapter 14   83
Chapter 15   87
Chapter 16   93
Chapter 17   97
Chapter 18   103
Chapter 19   109
Chapter 20   115
Chapter 21   121
Chapter 22   125
Chapter 23   131
Chapter 24   139
Chapter 25   145
Chapter 26   149
Chapter 27   155
Chapter 28   161
Chapter 29   165
Chapter 30   171

Chapter 31   177
Chapter 32   181
Chapter 33   187
Chapter 34   191
Chapter 35   197
Chapter 36   205
Chapter 37   209
Chapter 38   213
Chapter 39   219
Chapter 40   225
Chapter 41   233
Chapter 42   241
Chapter 43   245
Chapter 44   249
Chapter 45   255
Chapter 46   259
Chapter 47   265
Chapter 48   269
Chapter 49   273
Chapter 50   279
Chapter 51   285
Chapter 52   291
Chapter 53   295
Chapter 54   299
Chapter 55   305
Chapter 56   311
Chapter 57   315
Chapter 58   321
Chapter 59   327
Chapter 60   333
Chapter 61   337
Chapter 62   341
Chapter 63   349
Chapter 64   353
Epilogue   359

About the Author 367

Also by Jan Domagala 369

Prologue

Cronus III, 2287ce

The convoy was moving slowly but with purpose through the countryside. Four vehicles in all, the lead vehicle was smaller than the others. It held two soldiers in front, Captain Hanley was in command of the convoy and he sat next to Sergeant Johansson, his second on this mission.

Behind them was the first armed vehicle, which held four armed soldiers who manned the weapons platform; behind this was the payload, followed by the rear armed vehicle with the same complement of soldiers.

The payload was a complement of experimental missiles being transferred to a testing site for the final stage of testing before deploying to the military around the galaxy. The testing was nothing more than confirmation by the military's highest echelon, putting a rubber stamp on their approval, which meant the weapons could then be used.

"Approaching last kilometre of the op lads, we're almost there so that means we keep our vigilance. This isn't the time to get lax, heads on a swivel, let's not screw the pooch at this late stage," Hanley said through the comm link they all shared.

"Area is clear in front and to the rear, no threats detected, your way is clear," said the pilot of the forward aircraft, providing air support for the convoy. Both jet copters were variants of the old Osprey, tilt rotor V-22 aircraft. Each had the ability to keep pace with the vehicles below, to hover over them or speed off if the need arose, and were armed with a variety of weapons—rockets, missiles and pulse cannons.

Hanley glanced at Johansson, his driver, to say, "We're on the home stretch now. We should be free and clear in just over an hour."

Johansson was about to agree when the sound of an engine rocked their vehicle.

"What the fuck was that?" Johansson said as he peered up through the windscreen at the aircraft that had suddenly come into view. It had appeared from nowhere, or so it seemed, passing over the two air support aircraft to position itself in their path, hovering thirty metres off the ground facing them.

"What is that?" Hanley said, looking at it. He had seen nothing like it before. Shaped like a flat egg with a weapons pod popping out from under, where he assumed the pilot sat at the front, two pulse cannons appeared from inside the hull at the side aiming right at them. Bright lights shone from these weapons and twin beams of particle energy fired right at the leading aircraft. The beams struck the aircraft, slicing through like a hot knife through butter, cutting it into three slices which then erupted in explosions as critical systems were destroyed. A fireball lit the sky up as the aircraft was destroyed and then fell to the ground in front of Hanley's vehicle.

"Incoming," he shouted, and Johansson steered the vehicle around the burning wreckage that had slammed into the ground blocking the convoy's path.

"Light that thing up," he shouted to all support craft. The trailing aircraft acquired a target lock immediately and opened fire with missiles which were blown out of the sky before they had travelled more than a few metres from the pods holding them. The armed vehicle behind the payload truck opened fire with its large calibre pulse cannon; it's major weapon then followed it with its full complement of rockets.

The attacking craft turned slightly, then targeted the smaller ground vehicle with its twin particle beam weapon. In seconds the rockets had all been destroyed and the vehicle sliced down the middle, killing all on board.

The last remaining aircraft fired more missiles and opened fire with its pulse cannons as well. The missiles fared no better than last time and the pulse cannon blasts struck shields that stopped them without causing any damage. Another burst from the particle weapon sliced the aircraft into pieces as it tried to turn and evade further attacks. As it erupted into a huge fireball it lost all power, then slammed into the ground seconds later.

Hanley had seen all this and wasn't sure what else they could do. He was staring defeat and possible death in the face. Johansson had pulled their vehicle up to a halt and both of them were outside firing up at the strange vehicle attacking them with as little effect as the last aircraft had. They watched as their bullets bounced off the shield erected around it.

The forward armed vehicle had pulled up, allowing the soldiers to deploy to add their firepower to that of the pulse cannon on board.

A blast from the particle weapon sliced through the pulse cannon and vehicle, destroying it in seconds. The soldiers spread wider, looking for cover from the trees that lined the road they had been travelling along when the attacker had struck.

Taking a stand behind stout looking tall trees, both Hanley and Johansson used covering fire to help the four remaining soldiers to join them. Spraying bullets from their rifles at the shielded craft, Hanley saw the bullet strikes impact the shield.

The hovering craft fired the twin particle beams into the trees, severing them just above where their heads were. The massive trunks were sliced through, felling them, toppling them over. Bodies went scuttling as their cover suddenly disappeared.

The huge trunks fell down, crushing two of the soldiers like rotten fruit. The others were more fortunate to reach the cover Hanley and Johansson had found.

As the craft hovered, lines were dropped that soldiers rappelled down to the ground from. As soon as they were on the ground, they began to spread out, targeting anything that moved with rifles. One of the soldiers who had escaped being crushed put his head out from behind a tree to see what was happening and received a bullet through the forehead for his curiosity.

"This is looking worse by the second," Hanley thought.

Most of the soldiers who rappelled down from the strange craft congregated around the payload truck. They began to offload the missiles and ferry them over to below the craft.

Hanley and Johansson, along with the last remaining soldier, came out from under cover to fire on the soldiers walking in their direction.

Bullets slammed into all three of them the moment they emerged, knocking them all off their feet.

Hanley lay on the ground and pain filled his senses as he managed to turn his head to see the soldiers walk over to them all. A bullet to the head killed Johansson, then the other soldier. He lay there unable to move as blood pooled on the ground from all his wounds. Beyond the approaching soldiers he could see the missiles being hoisted up into the craft and he knew his mission had failed.

He looked up into the face mask of the soldier standing over him just before a trigger was pulled and a bullet through his brain turned out his lights for good.

Chapter 1

Praxis, 2287ce

Duncan Pryde breached the surface of the water in the bay to see the moonlight glinting off the waves tops as he looked toward the shore.

He had swum the distance underwater using a rebreather so as not to give his position away with bubbles from a scuba tank breaking the surface. Now he was able to touch bottom as he remained where he was to survey the area before moving in.

The refinery was quite plainly visible even at this time of night, close to midnight, because of the lights illuminating the huge silos that reached up to the sky as if demanding someone take notice of them, crying out for attention. Which was strange considering their purpose, which was to store vast amounts of the narcotic known simply as Dust. You would have thought that an enterprise of this nature would want to be kept a secret, or at least to have more stringent security than what he was witnessing.

Duncan was an agent of the Ministry of Intelligence; it was the government agency that ran intelligence gathering within the Coalition Of Planets. The section he worked for was MI7, which was classified as SecOps, or Security Operations. This had a broad scope of operations and most of the time they dealt with covert operations such as this one. They had been alerted to this operation by an informant who wanted to remain anonymous but also wanted to get out from under the clutches of the criminal organisation running this endeavour, hence his presence here. He had been sent to investigate and, if the intel given to them proved to be correct, he was to shut it down.

Taking out a scanner from his belt, he aimed it at the silos. Within a short time, he had readings from them. Inside each silo was a huge amount of the narcotic. The chemical analysis conducted by the sensors proved the intel to be correct.

It was time to move on to the next phase of this operation.

He swam ashore silently and walked up the narrow beach to the promenade wall that surrounded the facility.

Looking both ways, he couldn't see anyone nearby. Guards patrolled this wall periodically, but at the moment they weren't anywhere in sight. Climbing over the wall, he kept low as he assessed which direction he would need to go.

He was wearing a wetsuit that also doubled as a stealth suit. The material it was made from refracted light so that anyone looking directly at him would see a dead spot, as light was bent around him. As long as he remained absolutely still, he would be invisible to the naked eye.

The silos were visible from the wall and he walked over to the fence surrounding the area. A quick scan with the small device told him the fence was not powered in anyway. From another pouch on his belt, he took a small laser cutter and proceeded to cut a hole into the mesh fence large enough for him to get through. Once inside, he ran over to the nearest silo. Each of the three silos stood over three hundred feet high and was at least a hundred and fifty feet in diameter. They could hold millions of tons of Dust inside. Taking out a small round disc device, he placed it at the base of the first silo and pressed a touch screen, which activated the timer. An LED visual showed the timer ready to start counting down, which would begin as soon as the last device was set. He then repeated this action with the other two.

The bombs he'd placed there would destroy them and all the contents inside, curtailing the criminal group's ability to supply the narcotic to this sector.

As he set the last device, he saw the countdown begin. He had four minutes to get to a safe distance or be killed in the blast.

He ran for the fence and went through it and sprinted for the promenade wall. As he reached it, he became aware of two figures converging on him.

Guards, they had come as part of their routine patrol and were about to see him. Having no time to stop, he continued toward the wall. His stealth suit wouldn't matter now as he was moving too fast for it to be of any use. At the wall he heard one of them shout a challenge to him, ordering him to stop and surrender. He had no intention of following that particular order or any others they might issue as he leaped onto the wall, then vaulted over it to the beach beyond.

Inside his wet suit was a sidearm he'd brought with him, just in case. It was a Walther Q9 fitted with a suppressor—a standard sidearm for the MI7. As he landed on the beach, he withdrew the weapon, turned and aimed at where the guards would appear. As soon as he saw the two of them, he fired. Four shots, two double taps each, all of them making no more noise than a slight coughing sound. Each guard's head exploded in a red mist as the bullets struck their target.

Turning, Pryde ran for the jetty he had seen on his approach. Tied to the end was a small boat, sleek and trim; it appeared to be a fast speedboat. He ran down to the jetty and jumped aboard. He released the tether holding the boat in place, then started the engine. A deep throaty growl affirmed his suspicion and he steered it away out into the open sea.

He hadn't gone far when he heard the sound of two other engines on the water from somewhere behind him. A glance over his shoulder told him everything he needed to know. Two other fast boats had appeared from around a curve in the coastline and they were headed after him.

"Things are about to get interesting," he thought.

To make matters worse, an aircraft appeared in the night sky, lights blazing as it too chased after him. A spotlight lanced through the dark sky, spearing him in its brilliance, showing the two chasing boats exactly where he was.

"Brilliant," he thought.

He couldn't quite see what the aircraft was through the intensity of the light shining down on him but he suspected it was an old Sikorsky chopper fitted out with the searchlight and possibly a weapons rack slung on either side of the pilot's cabin. Which meant, if the chasing boats didn't get him, they could blow him out of the water. Seeing as how they hadn't done that so far meant they wanted him alive, probably to see who he was and what he was doing here. His internal clock told him the second part of that question would be answered momentarily.

Aiming his pistol at the spotlight, he fired three shots, taking out the bright light, plunging him and the boat back into the sheer darkness of the inky black night.

Bullets zinged past his head as the chasing boats opened fire on him. It was clear by how they were missing deliberately that these were nothing more than warning shots. That would change soon enough when it became fully clear that he was not going to stop.

Swerving his boat to give them something harder to hit, he saw bullets strike the water as their shots went wide of the mark.

Knowing their warnings were falling on deaf ears, those chasing him tightened up their aim and bullets began to hit the back of his boat, sending up splinters from where the shells hit the woodwork of the boat.

Because he was moving in a zig-zagging pattern, he was giving the others more of a chance to catch him up. Before long, he had a boat coming up on him on either side.

He felt the thud as the nearest boat slammed into the rear of his, which rocked when two men jumped aboard.

Duncan turned to face this new challenge. He had to evict them if he wanted to get to his exfil position. The first man came at him, snarling through gritted teeth, only to have them smashed when Duncan struck him in the face with the butt of his pistol. Blood and shattered teeth sprayed out in a red mess as both his hands went up, instinctively to cover his face. A foot in his chest sent him sprawling back to collide with his colleague, and they both fell to the deck. Duncan finished them both off with a coup de grace, splattering their brains over the deck below them.

Returning to the controls, Duncan sped away from the boat at his rear only to have the other ram him from the starboard side. The collision sent him off his feet momentarily. He struggled to his feet, clawing his way off the deck, pistol still in his hand. Seeing another boarder climbing over the rails near the collision point, Duncan raised his pistol and shot the man in the face. The man following him screamed out in shock and pain as the bullet passed through the head of the man in front to graze the side of his face too.

Duncan was on his feet by this time and he grabbed the dead man at the rails by his shirt front and pulled him into the boat, then shot the man behind him as he too was climbing aboard. The bullet took out the top of his head in a red jet of gore that would stain the water beyond for several feet before dissipating in the moving current. The dead man fell back into his own boat, preventing anyone else from following.

Duncan steered his boat away from the other two as they came to terms with the chaos he'd caused, which had caught them all flat footed. Using this confusion, he opened the gap between them even wider.

As he cleared his path away from the other boats momentarily, he breathed easier for a second only. Large calibre shells tore up the prow of his boat as the chopper above opened fire on him.

As he was just thinking about how to deal with this new development, the silos exploded. The night sky was lit up in a display any firework supplier would be proud of. Flames flew high into the air, throwing debris outward, scattering shards and flaming debris over an area that covered the entire facility. The fireball reached as high as a skyscraper and covered an area at least as large as two football fields placed end to end.

Nothing close to this cataclysm would survive; buildings that stood next to them were flattened in seconds as the shockwave tore through them. Flames spread out as the flaming debris landed, catching fire with everything it touched.

From out at sea, all eyes naturally turned to view this spectacle, giving Duncan those extra precious seconds to escape.

Before moving off, he turned his pistol to the chopper and fired at the cabin. He smiled as he saw his shots strike the pilot as he slumped over the controls, dead. This sent the aircraft into a spiral towards the surface of the water it would be unable to return from.

Duncan then set course for his exfil location because he knew the boats would forget about their pursuit of him in favour of returning to shore to see what they could do to salvage anything from the blast. Their friends and comrades were in that blast and they would do what they could to help, and all thoughts of him were lost in the shock of seeing the explosion.

Seeing the other two boats turn back, he continued on to where he needed to be. Alone now in the vast sea, he checked his coordinates on his wrist pad. When he was in the correct location, he switched off the engine, replaced his pistol inside his wetsuit, then vaulted over the side of the boat into the water. With his rebreather firmly back in place between his teeth, he dived for the bottom.

His arms stroked as his legs kicked, powering him deeper into the dark depths of the sea until he saw lights flickering in the distance.

His ride had arrived.

A ship had held position off the coast waiting for his arrival. He headed for it, entering through one of the three escape hatches—one fore, one amidships and the one he used, aft.

As the water left the hatch and the door opened, he entered the sub.

"Okay ship, take us home," he said. The ship he had entered was a small starship that was run by an AI. This entire operation was a covert black op, so the fewer people who knew about it, the better for everyone.

Stripping off his wetsuit, Duncan got dressed in his normal clothes, a shirt, cargo pants and soft leather boots before returning to the flight deck. As he sat down in the command chair, he saw the water far below as the AI steered him high into the air toward the upper atmosphere and the space beyond.

"A message came in for you from Terra II," the ship said.

"Okay, play it for me please," he replied. There was no need for privacy here; he was the only human on board.

He recognised the voice as soon as the message began playing, but the content of it hit him harder than anything he had experienced before. Seven words ripped his entire world apart.

"Your parents have died, I'm so sorry," the voice said. It was the voice of William Chambers, the man who had sent him on this mission, his immediate superior in the MI7.

Once the message had been consigned to his memory, he said, "Ship, set course for Terra II."

Chapter 2

Terra II

P ryde was still at his parents' home. The funeral had taken place months ago and he was finalising the details of selling the family home. He had no need for it; he already had an apartment where he was comfortable.

Grief over the loss of his parents had passed—in fact, being able to compartmentalise things had never been a problem for him. He was able to dial down emotions or dial them up if and when needed. It made him an ideal covert agent. He could dial down empathy and dial up aggression all the while remaining calm and detached.

Some had called him a psychopath but in actuality he was a functioning partial sociopath, which meant he could control his emotions better than most normal people. Psychopaths generally were said to have a personality disorder that had impaired empathy or remorse, exhibited antisocial behaviour which displayed in low fear, high stress tolerance and narcissistic tendencies. It was sometimes synonymous with sociopathy, but in Pryde's case, although he exhibited a high tolerance to stress and could dial down his empathic response to certain situations to perform certain tasks, it didn't mean he was devoid of these emotions, only that he could control and contain them until they were needed.

Having dealt with all the family's details, he was left with a considerable amount of money which he had never even considered before. He was wealthy enough now to live a life of luxury, wherever he felt or wanted. He would never have to work again if he so chose, which faced him with a problem. He loved his job, not the killing part, however suited to it he was, no he loved feeling that he was making a difference. He was doing jobs that normal people could not or did not want to face because they were the kinds of things normal people didn't want to dirty their hands on. It was a moral dilemma for them—they hated that these things needed doing but did not want to do themselves. It had long been a soldier's lot to fulfil that need and he was one of the few who were absolutely suited for the task.

He was just about ready to wrap things up and return to work when his comm link buzzed, informing him he was being contacted.

The comm link was a small device implanted inside his ear. With a touch he could activate it and speak, and the tiny mic would pick up his voice easily.

"Pryde here," he said.

"There has been a situation that's developed that needs your attention. Are you available?" Chambers' voice said clearly in his ear.

"I was about to contact you, sir. Yes, I am ready to return to work," he replied.

"Good, be at Station Five for your briefing in an hour," Chambers said, then the call ended.

Station Five was the headquarters of the MI7 on Terra II. Situated near the coast of the largest city on the planet, it had entry points from both land and sea.

To an untrained eye, it was nothing more than a boat shed—a long, low structure constructed of local timber that had a jetty attached that boats could tie up to when visiting. At the other end was a landing pad for small-scale craft that arrived either by land or air. In reality, it was none of this.

Inside the building that had been reinforced with more modern materials, it was a hive of activity. It had offices, a communication section, and an armoury. This was MI7's SecOps HQ on this planet and Pryde arrived soon after receiving the summons from his boss, Chambers.

Every agent in MI7 had a chip implanted in their arm. This monitored their location as well as their vitals. It also allowed them access to certain things, such as bank accounts so they could pay for things, and it also acted as their ID, which could be altered when needing to go undercover with an alternate identity.

As he approached the dilapidated door that was the entrance to the boat shed, he placed his right wrist against a concealed sensor in the wall by the side, which opened it so he could enter.

The entrance was an air lock of sorts. It opened into a small cubicle which allowed him inside while he was scanned for any evidence of tracking or sensory devices unknowingly planted on him. He was also scanned for toxins and explosive devices he might be carrying. When he had the all clear, the inner door was unlocked and he entered the building.

The short corridor led to a door at the far end which, once he walked through, opened out into a wide open-plan space with cubicles filled with people all working on computers monitoring different areas of interest. This was the communication section.

He saw a friendly face at the end of this room smiling his way. Dressed in a white blouse and pencil skirt, she was the epitome of class. Deep auburn hair framed a face that was open and friendly with eyes that had a mischievous quality to them that seemed to smile all on their own.

"Afternoon, Goodchild. I got here as soon as I could," he said as he closed the gap between them. Stephanie Goodchild was Chambers' secretary, an old-fashioned arrangement that harked back centuries but seemed to work. Chambers couldn't function without her valuable organisational skills, although he would never admit to that.

"He's waiting for you Duncan, go right in," she said as she opened the door to her outer office. The two of them entered and she operated the intercom on her desk to inform their boss of Pryde's arrival.

He thanked her, then entered, closing the door after him.

"Come in Pryde, take a seat," Chambers said. Inside the Ministry, Chambers was known simply as C. This was a direct homage to the British Secret Service of decades ago when the head was called C for Control; now it was simply the initial of his surname.

He was a small man who had a liking for pin striped suits of a dark colour—todays was a dark navy blue. He had a head of wavy brown hair that was cut regularly by his personal barber. Eyes the colour of caramel looked out on the world with the knowledge that not everything was as it seemed. Some thought him to be cynical, but in reality he was a pragmatist; he had seen enough death and destruction during his military career to fill several lifetimes.

"Thank you, sir."

"I'll get right to it," C said, "a couple of days ago an armoured convoy was attacked on Cronus III. It was carrying some experimental missiles to a base there to be tested before giving the all clear for deployment to the various systems that could carry this munition."

"Attacked, sir? Do we know by whom?"

"It is a bit of a mystery. The craft they used to perform the act was able to carry troops and was incredibly manoeuvrable. It was unlike anything we've ever encountered before."

"I take it the footage from the soldier's body cams has been rescued then and analysed?" Pryde asked.

"It has. The tech labs edited all the footage from each soldier's body cam together, and this is what was revealed," C replied, turning to look at a wall mounted flat screen monitor behind him. The screen came to life with all the gory details of the attack on the convoy, right down to the bodies being blown apart and the callous way in which the three remaining soldiers were dispatched with cold efficiency.

"Do we have anything that can fly and fight like that, sir?" Pryde asked once the video had finished.

"From what I understand, there is a new class of fighter jet that is nearing the testing phase—the new Raptor F95. From what I gather it has similar flight capabilities to what we just witnessed, but they told me it would be months away from testing. They have a prototype built but that's as far as the project has gone, or so we were informed."

"Are you thinking they already sold the design to someone else, or maybe it was stolen?"

"That is a possibility I suppose. We need to find out the truth and see who has this design before anything else happens. They already stole those experimental missiles; what else will they go after, and what use do they have planned for the missiles?"

"I take it that's where I come in?" Pryde said.

"Yes, I want you to find out about those plans from the company that are developing the aircraft and see what you can learn from them. If there was a theft, we need to know about it."

"Copy that sir, I'll leave right away."

"You have the details on your PIN."

Pryde took out the small device, the Personalised Information Network, or PIN, which acted as a personal internet link. It also was the comm link terminal which connected to every communication network available which he could communicate through via his ear implant.

On the small screen, no larger than the palm of his hand, he saw the name of the company, the address and who to contact.

"I'll contact you as soon as I have something, sir," he said as he left.

Chapter 3

Triganus II

The Haynes Corporation was one the largest tech giants in the entire sector. Jeremy Haynes was the CEO of the mega corp and was the person who Pryde had arranged to meet.

It was early in the morning when he arrived at the Central Office of Haynes Corp. A towering edifice to capitalism, over one hundred and fifty floors of Plascrete and glass. The lobby on the ground floor was watched over by a receptionist desk that was manned by a young woman flanked by two security guards, who all sat behind a circular desk in the centre of the large area.

The young woman, the face of the company, the first point of contact when anyone entered the building, looked up when he entered.

"Good morning sir, how can I help you?" she asked, giving him a warm smile.

"Yes, I'm here to see Mister Haynes please," Pryde replied, returning her smile.

"Who shall I say wants him, sir?"

"My name Pryde and I'm from the Ministry of Intelligence."

The smile faded just for a second, but was back in place in an instant. To the casual observer it would have been missed, but Pryde was a trained observer and the momentary slip did not go unnoticed, which told him they were afraid of scrutiny. Something was not quite right here.

She checked the screen in front of her and typed something onto a hidden keypad and read the reply. Looking up, her smile firmly back in place, she said, "Mister Haynes will see you in his office. He's on the Penthouse floor; the elevator is behind us. William will escort you."

William, the security guard in question, stood up from his seat next to her.

"Come this way please," he said, ushering him in front of him.

Pryde walked in front of him, knowing William was keeping him in front so he could keep an eye on him, a security measure and standing operating procedure.

Inside the elevator William placed his wrist against the sensor in the control panel, which gave them access to the floors above a certain level. The top five floors were inaccessible except to certain personnel in the building, the top echelon in the business.

The ride to the top was fast and smooth. When it ended, the doors opened and William led the way out into a well-lit corridor. There was just one door in this area and William pointed him in that direction.

"I'll wait out here for you, sir, and escort you back down when your meeting is through," the tall, craggy-looking security guard said.

Pryde entered through the door into a lush office that had a panoramic view of the city below through the wall to ceiling windows that ran around two of the walls. It was a corner office and the largest of those on this floor. The furniture was made from indigenous wood that resembled mahogany. Haynes stood up from behind the desk set in the corner to greet him.

The floor was carpeted with a thick pile wool covering that could have been Axminster. The walls had paintings on them and, from his brief knowledge of art, they looked to be classics.

The room was tasteful yet subtle, but still reeked of wealth.

"Welcome. Mister Pryde, is it? What has the Ministry sent you here for?" Haynes asked as he came around his desk to greet his visitor. Holding out a hand, he walked over to Pryde to get a better look.

Pryde took the offered hand in a firm grip then said, "We are interested in how the Raptor F 95 program is coming along?"

The shock of the sudden directness showed on Haynes' face. He wasn't expecting him to be this direct, perhaps to go around the bush a while before coming to the point, feeling him out before asking the real question. This caught him off guard, which was his intention.

"Down to business, I like that, not wasting any time," Haynes replied. Pryde recognised his answer for what it was.

"Unlike I, sir, you didn't answer my question, so I'll ask it again. How is the new Raptor F 95 program coming along, or more to the point, has it been hacked, stolen or did you sell it to someone else?" he said.

"I'm offended by your assumption and quite frankly I think this meeting is over. We're done here."

"So that's a yes then. In that case there will be repercussions, legal ones seeing as how the design you sold to a third party was used in a terrorist attack recently."

"Now wait just one minute. What happens when we sell anything is not our responsibility, it is down to the buyer to decide how it is to be used," Haynes floundered as he tried to regain some ground but instead dug himself even deeper into the hole he just fell into.

"So, you admit to selling the design to a third party," Pryde said, hoisting Haynes on his own verbal petard.

Haynes leaned against the desk—fell against it, really—as he realised the mistake he just made.

"You have to understand, we were falling behind on the testing. We were never going to meet the deadline we set, and then they came along with extra funding and said they would take the designs when we had fixed certain bugs in the design and that the building of the prototype would be done by them. It was a deal too good to pass up. We were back on track with the testing and we could fulfil our order to the Coalition, it was a win-win situation."

"Not really, a squad of soldiers were slaughtered by your design and a raft of experimental ordinance was stolen. I can only imagine that they plan to use what they stole and that more lives will be lost. I hope they paid enough to ease your conscience, Mister Haynes."

"I'm so sorry. What can I do to help put this right?"

"First off, you can give me all you have on the buyer, and secondly you can put all your resources into getting the Raptor F 95 ready for combat. We will be needing it sooner than you said," Pryde said.

"You'll have everything you need; you have my word."

"Thank you, sir, I'll be in touch," Pryde said, then turned to leave the office.

Outside he was escorted to the elevator once more by Williams, who held a finger to his ear as a call came through. It was from Haynes.

"Williams, the meeting is over, kill him," Haynes said.

"Copy that," Williams replied as he ushered Pryde into the elevator.

Chapter 4

As the two of them entered the elevator, Williams spoke to someone else through his comm link.

"We're on our way down," was all he said.

Pryde had a bad feeling about this; his instinct honed from his experience in the field told him something was wrong.

By the time they reached the ground floor he was on high alert.

Just as the elevator came to a stop, Williams took out his sidearm, already fitted with a suppressor, and turned to fire at Pryde. Seeing the move, Pryde deflected the arm as the gun was fired. The bullet hit the side of the elevator cubicle harmlessly. Pryde elbowed Williams in the side of the head, slamming his head into the wall. Turning to him, he grabbed the gun hand and held it against the wall as he used his other hand to grip Williams' throat. He used a pinch with his thumb and forefinger to pinch off Williams' oesophagus, causing him to choke as his air waves were cut off.

In desperation, the guard thrashed around trying to escape the grip on his hand so he could use his pistol. Pryde increased the pressure on the throat pinch, then when he saw Williams' eyes start to flutter, he released and hit him with a roundhouse elbow strike, snapping his head around. He fell to the floor, lights out.

Stabbing at the button to open the doors, which Williams had shielded, clearly thinking he had the situation under control, Pryde walked out from the cubicle. The other guard was still sitting behind the reception desk and, when he heard the doors open, turned to get up.

Pryde walked toward him; the surprise on the guard's face was evident by the startled expression.

"Thank you for your time, have a nice day," Pryde said as he walked toward the exit.

The guard was speaking, "Yes sir, he's leaving now," Pryde heard him say. He continued on to the doors to the street beyond.

"Excuse me sir," the guard said loud enough to be heard but not too strident to raise any alarms with anyone else in the lobby.

Pryde walked out the door, ignoring him, then turned up the street to where he would be able to get a ride to the space port.

There was an entrance to an underground car park he had just passed by when he heard the sound of engines approaching fast, and he turned to see three bikes emerge from the entrance.

As soon as they hit the street, they turned toward him. He saw pistols drawn and he moved just as bullets hit the ground where he was standing. Diving to the ground and rolling onto his knees, he had his own pistol drawn and returned fire.

Of the three bullets he fired back, one hit the nearest rider's shoulder, knocking him off the bike.

The bike skidded toward him on its side and Pryde was on his feet in seconds, reaching it. He grabbed the handlebar controls, hoisted it back onto the wheels, and threw a leg over to get on board.

Twisting the accelerator grip, he turned the bike away from the others. Hunkering down over the power cell, he leaned forward as he sped down the street away from the other two riders.

Keeping his head down and weaving to avoid the bullets fired at him by those chasing, he kept his attention on the road ahead.

Traffic from other vehicles was busy; this was a busy street in a busy city so Pryde had his work cut out avoiding hitting or getting hit by another vehicle. It was in his favour, the mode of transport he had chosen, or rather stolen, as he could dodge and weave through a lot of it unscathed. Unfortunately, that went the same for the two riders chasing after him.

More bullets chased after him as the riders fired with little regard for bystanders. He was travelling in the opposite direction of where he needed to go, but it was out of necessity rather than choice. As he weaved in and out of traffic choking the street, he desperately looked for somewhere to turn.

A turn was coming up controlled by a signal system. This was his chance. Accelerating to the junction, he turned left across traffic on that side, forcing them to stop. This caused a few minor fender benders as at least two vehicles collided in their haste to avoid hitting or getting hit by the rider.

The two chasing riders were forced to slow down to navigate through the blockage caused by Pryde's hasty turn. It took them several moments to get through and by that time they had lost considerable ground.

A glance over his shoulder and he knew how much ground he'd gained at the junction, but they were undeterred and still determined to catch him. Once they were through the blockade, they increased their speed in an effort to catch up.

Pryde knew this couldn't continue—he had to escape. It was obvious now that Haynes either had something to do with the attack on the convoy with his design or that he knew who was. Pryde had to get that information to the right people.

As he turned down another side street, he saw the end of this road end in a 'T' junction. By his reasoning, if he kept left he would eventually be heading in his original direction, toward the space port.

Coming to the junction, he didn't slow, instead throwing the bike into a tight left, skidding turn. The chasing riders opened fire as he turned. As Pryde keeled the bike over to make the turn, bullets struck the ground in front of him, stitching a path toward him. The last two bullets struck the bike's side, and sparks from the impacts ignited the fuel cell. As the bike tipped over, Pryde rolled free just as his transport blew up.

The shockwave from the blast sent him rolling farther along the pavement as burning debris from the explosion rained down on the immediate area.

Before he could get to his feet, the two riders were within range and were firing at him once more.

It was only due to the fact that they were speeding toward him on bikes that their aim was off. Bullets pinged off the pavement, forcing Pryde to duck and move away. Reaching for his Walther Q9, he held it in a double handed grip as he aimed at the riders. He fired a three-shot salvo at the first rider. One bullet shattered the windscreen and the next two slammed into his chest, knocking him sprawling from the bike.

The second biker was aiming over the handlebars of his ride to fire. The bike was bouncing, which put off his aim. The bullets he fired hit all around Pryde, who remained calm and returned fire with a carefully aimed, three-shot salvo. The first two bullets slammed into the upper torso, rocking him back on the seat, then the last shell hit him in his right eye and took off the top of his skull, killing him. Losing control of the bike, he fell backwards, sending his ride skidding across the ground.

Pryde was on his feet and he caught the bike as it slid closer. He righted it, then mounted it, powered the engine up to top revs, and took off away from the chaos he'd caused.

As he came to the end of this street, he saw a sign informing him where the space port was, so he headed in that direction.

Chapter 5

"What do you mean he's getting away? Stop him, whatever the cost!" Haynes screamed. He was in his office alone and had just been informed by his security who was monitoring the progress of the team sent after Pryde that they had failed.

"Copy that sir," Jarvis said; he was the security chief at the headquarters building, a military veteran of twelve years who left the service to join the private sector. The last ten years he'd been employed by the Haynes Corporation, working his way up through the ranks until he reached his present position.

He ended his conversation with his boss, then called in reinforcements. They had a fleet of aircraft available at all times to protect the building, he now called them into action.

Giving them the location of their target, he said, "Under no circumstances is he to get away. I don't care what you have to do, just stop him."

"Copy that," replied all three pilots in unison and Jarvis sat back to watch the fun on the screen before him. They had satellites orbiting the planet that could be tasked to watch anything, and right now they were all on this guy. There was nothing he could do to escape. It was just like sitting down to watch your favourite movie. All he needed now was some popcorn and he would be sorted.

Pryde rounded another corner with the space port getting closer with every second.

Overhead he heard the sound of an aircraft approaching.

Surely that was illegal to fly this close to the ground inside a city as populous as this one was? He glanced over his shoulder and his fear was realised. Coming in fast on an attack vector were three Raider Jet copters. He could clearly see the weapons pods in attack formation. The sleek craft had the main double rotors above the pilot's cabin rotating in opposite directions and the tail rotor encased to help with stability. It had a crew of two in the pilot's cabin, seated one behind the other; the rear co-pilot would handle the weapons while the man in front flew the aircraft.

He had seconds to evade being shot by the fifty cal shells that could be fired from the front mounted gatling gun.

Twisting the bike through a series of tight turns, he headed down an alley between two tall buildings, hoping to throw off the chopper but it chased them anyway. Keeping above the buildings the first jet copter kept watch on the fleeing bike while the other two went different ways. Pryde knew they were trying to box him in somehow and he became almost desperate.

Dialling down any anxiety he may have felt, he concentrated on the job at hand. His entire focus now was on escaping. If he had to kill anyone to save himself, so be it.

As he burst free of the alley, he turned left onto another street narrowly missing traffic going either way. Riding down the middle of the street in between vehicles going in both ways he kept the bike in a straight line. Peering overhead he saw the jet copter follow his direction. With nowhere to go he knew he was basically trapped.

The jet copter opened fire with the fifty cal Gatling gun strafing the vehicles either side of Pryde. The large calibre shells destroyed cars on both sides causing untold damage. Explosions erupted as cars erupted showering bystanders with flaming debris forcing them to seek shelter.

Increasing his speed Pryde barely managed to keep ahead of the trail of destruction following hard on his heels. Seeing a gap in the traffic he swerved across both lanes into another street.

This put him directly in the path of another of the jet copters. As he rode forward, he looked up to see the rocket pods on either side of the aircraft fire. Several rockets streaked toward him, giving him little time or chance of escape.

With nowhere to go on either side of him—he was hemmed in on each side with buildings or parked vehicles—he had no choice but to increase his speed. His hope was that they would pass overhead and miss him. Rockets generally were line of sight weapons, effectively a fire, once and done weapon.

Pryde cranked the bike up to maximum revs, reaching speeds of close to two hundred kph in seconds. Leaning forward over the handlebar controls, he urged the bike forward in a race literally against time. The two came close, and the jet copter had rushed past overhead after firing the rockets to get clear of the explosions they all knew would come. Pryde passed the deadly rockets so close he could feel the heat from the fuel powering them onward.

With his speed still increasing, the rockets hit the ground and exploded in a huge fireball. The ensuing destruction sent cars on either side of the road hurtling into buildings on either side of the street. Some were sent into the air, riding on a shockwave of immense power. Flaming detritus rained down on the immediate area, sparking small fires where they touched anything combustible.

Pryde felt the power of the shockwave hit him in his back like a sledgehammer. The force of the blast sent him wobbling down the road, almost knocking him off his ride.

He knew he could never outrun three jet copters; eventually they would corner him and it would be all over. He had to come up with an alternative.

Then he saw it.

Chapter 6

On his left he recognised something that told him where he was and a plan began to form in his mind.

There was an entrance to a ramp that led to a rooftop car park. He knew the jet copters would follow him wherever he went and were watching his every move, so he took the ramp.

It spiralled around the outside of the forty-story building with hardly any cover except for the side of the ramp, which was a safety precaution to prevent vehicles from driving off and crashing to the floor. This was the second most hazardous part of his insane plan, proven when the jet copters positioned themselves on three sides of the building and opened fire with their Gatling guns. They followed him around the building, covering two sides each, overlapping and taking over from each other, so that they covered all four sides. This gave him no respite from the devastating firepower of the Gatling guns.

The Plascrete side of the ramp was systematically destroyed as he rode as fast as he could to the top of the parking structure.

He knew the moment he reached the top he would face all three of the aircraft. This was the end of his plan and therefore the most dangerous. If he got this part wrong, he would die.

Not allowing emotion to cloud his judgement, he emerged onto the roof of the building.

The jet copters were all positioned to face him as he appeared on the roof at the top of the ramp ready to open fire. There was a row of other vehicles parked facing him. Pulling the bike up on its rear wheel, he increased speed to maximum and headed for the nearest car. It had a sloping front end so when he hit it he dropped the front wheel onto the bonnet and rode up the car, effectively turning it into a ramp.

Once he rode on top of the car, he continued into the air, heading for the nearest chopper. As he sailed through the air he saw the pilot of the chopper realise what was about to happen. His expression altered from that of 'I've got you now' to one of disbelief. His eyes went wide as his jaw opened and he mouthed the words, "Holy fucking shit," before Pryde slammed into the cockpit canopy.

The chopper dipped its nose as the added weight of someone landing on the front end and sliding toward open space changed its attitude.

Pryde knew what would happen and waited as he slid toward the nose, then, as there was nothing to hold onto, slid off into space.

His hands landed on the barrel of the Gatling gun as he fell and he used his momentum to swing beneath the craft, where he caught hold of the weapons pods with his legs. Swinging up, he tightened his stomach to bring himself up to where he was finally facing the right way. He quickly accessed the door on the side of the craft before the pilot retrieved the pods back into the hull, giving him nothing to hold onto.

The door opened and he pulled himself inside. Closing the door after him, he lay there for a second as he regained his breath.

Moving quickly, he opened the door to the cabin positioned behind the rear seat and grabbed the second pilot around the neck in a choke hold. Hands grabbed at him as he desperately tried to break Pryde's death grip on him until Pryde swiftly snapped his neck by twisting his head savagely. Unclipping the harness, Pryde pulled the second pilot into the passenger section and took over his station.

The pilot in front was in control of the craft but from his position could not do anything about what was happening behind him. Pryde took out his Walther Q9 and calmly shot him in the back of his head, killing him instantly. He reconfigured the controls so that he controlled everything from where he sat and then went after the other two jet copters.

Before they could react, he fired rockets at the aircraft to his left. After a quick study of the weapons controls, the rockets could be configured for heat seeking, which he selected before firing. The rockets left the pods, travelling in a straight line until the onboard controls latched onto the jet copters heat signature, then turned, arcing back toward his neighbour.

Pryde moved away in a tight turn, taking his craft away from what was about to happen.

Seeing the rockets turn toward him, the pilot reacted too late and took evasive action. As he turned the chopper, the rockets slammed into the side of the craft, blowing it apart in a fireball that showered the roof below in burning debris.

The other chopper reacted faster and gave chase to Pryde. Tucking in behind the escaping chopper, he fired the Gatling gun, hoping to damage the tail rotor. Pryde swerved to the left, allowing the shells to fly past harmlessly. He still had the rockets configured for heat seeking so he fired the remaining few. He watched as they streaked ahead, then turned up and went over the top of his craft, heading for the craft behind him.

The pilot saw the rockets, turned to the left and took his chopper into a dive. Unfortunately, his manoeuvre took time off his escape, which meant the rockets caught up to him. The rear end of the craft was blown apart when the rockets slammed into it. The explosion destroyed the craft's ability to remain airborne and it went into a tight spin heading for the ground.

Pryde watched as it crashed in a huge explosion that destroyed the roof it had crashed into.

Thinking nothing more of it, he turned his chopper and headed for the space port.

C would be interested in this new development when he reported in.

Chapter 7

Haynes Corp HQ

"With all the firepower at your disposal and you still let him escape, how is that even possible? Are you that incompetent? Why am I even employing you?" Haynes ranted when Jarvis told him of the outcome of the chase.

"This was no normal operative sir. He had a certain set of skills that you only see in a very select few people," Jarvis argued.

"So, your argument isn't that you are incompetent, it's that this guy was simply better than you. Is that what you're saying, because that's what it sounds like to me."

"Yes sir," Jarvis agreed, falling right into the trap.

"Why am I employing you then? If you can't do your job I might as well fire you."

"If you fire me sir, who will you get to go after this guy?" Jarvis said, stumbling over the words, hoping to save his job.

"Someone better than you. You're fired, clear out your office, I want you gone, you have fifteen minutes."

Haynes ended the call and called someone else immediately. This was a situation he had to get under control and fast. When the call was answered he said, "I have a job for you. I'll pay double your normal fee, but it has to be done today."

"I'm listening," said the voice on the other end.

MI7 Substation Triganus VIII

MI7 had Substations dotted around the galaxy which ensured agents had a port of call should they need one when on a mission, rather like Embassy's did back on Earth. Each station was manned by a skeleton crew, usually just one or two people depending on what was needed in that area.

Triganus VIII was the small planetoid orbiting around that sun and it dealt with the star systems in that sector.

Pryde landed his starship on the landing pad near the station, which immediately connected to it via the docking tube. The planetoid was a barren rock with no atmosphere and therefore no vegetation nor indigenous life. It was ideal for a Substation as no one would think of visiting it unless they were particularly looking for it.

Leaving his ship on standby, Pryde entered the station through the docking tube. Inside was small, with only the crew quarters, a rec area, which included a kitchen, and the control room, where he found the commander hard at work.

"Nice to see a fresh face, Commander Pryde. You're new to this sector; what can I do for you?" Leonard Martin said, turning in his seat to greet him.

The control room was like the rest of the station, small and compact with room for maybe two, or three at the most, operatives working together. An array of monitor screens was aligned on the wall at the end of the room and there were three desks placed in a triangular formation, two side by side nearest the monitor wall and one other behind them with a desk that could control everything from it.

Martin was a slim man with wispy hair but fierce eyes the colour of a summer sky. Pryde had the impression those eyes missed nothing. When Martin spoke, he smiled with genuine warmth—he was clearly pleased to see another face after a long tour of duty in this remote station.

"I'm in a bit of a rush here so can we get down to business?" he said. He was still acting in mission mode so had no time for pleasantries.

"Certainly, Commander; what is it you need?"

"The Haynes Corporation had a new concept aircraft under wraps, but the design was either sold to a third party or was stolen. Now there is a working prototype out there somewhere which has been used in an attack to hijack a batch of experimental missiles. When I asked about it to Haynes himself, he said he knew nothing about it, but when I was leaving his building his security guards attacked and tried to kill me. What I need is for you to do a deep dive into their finances. See if they sold the design to someone. The way they came after me makes me think the design wasn't stolen but they had a hand in it being used."

Turning back to his desk he said, "I'll see what I can do for you."

Asteroid Belt in the Titanus system

The Titanus system was a star system with eleven planets orbiting a star similar in size to Sol. Three planets in the system were habitable. Titanus IV was a goldilocks planet which meant it was an E Class planet, Earth-like. Titanus III and V were made habitable by terraforming.

There was an asteroid belt between planets V and VI which acted as a barrier between the inner planets and those beyond the belt. Several asteroids within this belt were large enough and stable enough to house bases or stations such as Acheron.

A small planetoid Acheron was one of the largest bodies inside the asteroid belt and was the communications hub to a group that had hijacked the experimental missiles.

Nathan Jericho was a committed individual. Ex-Special Forces, he was now the leader of his own paramilitary criminal organisation called ICE, or Independent Criminal Executive. At a little over six feet tall, he still had the same physique he had when he was a top tier operator. His hair was still the same colour–as black as night–as were his eyes. Some had remarked upon seeing them that they reminded them of those of a shark–dead and emotionless.

"I'm listening," he said when the call came through from Haynes.

"The Ministry of Intelligence knows about the Raptor. They just sent someone to investigate but he got away."

"So, I'm guessing you told him enough to incriminate yourself, and then, to make matters worse, you tried to eliminate him. Now you want me to clean up your mess. How am I doing so far?" Jericho replied.

The line was quiet for a second which told him everything he needed to know.

"I told you to remain calm and to wait. I'll have to move the time table up now before they trace anything back to me," he said.

"What about this Pryde guy; what are you going to do about him?" Haynes blurted out, fear making his voice quaver.

"Well considering you tried to kill him and failed, it seems obvious he'll be coming back for you. I would suggest you find somewhere to hide, and fast," Jericho said and broke the connection.

He was furious. He knew Haynes would cave in at the first opportunity but he had needed him to pull off this mission. He had learned of the revolutionary aircraft he had been developing through a contact within Haynes' own corporation. Through the same contact he had learned of the experimental missiles they were about to present to the Coalition for testing. This contact had told him about the financial difficulties Haynes was facing. Haynes was about to go bankrupt after all the money he had lavished on the testing and development of the Raptor. It had gone massively over budget but, having invested everything he had in the project, he couldn't just ditch it. Haynes was hoping that the contract from the Coalition for this new missile would render enough for him to keep his head above water and continue with the Raptor program.

He had presented him with a solution. The Raptor was almost ready for testing; they had a prototype almost built but had no funds to finish it. Jericho had told him he would supply the funds to finish off the prototype whereby Haynes would gift it to him and they would use it to hijack the missile convoy when they left for the Coalition base for testing. Once the missiles were in his possession, he would auction them off to the highest bidder and share the funds with Haynes. Haynes had jumped at the chance of putting his corporation back in the black so things had gone ahead.

Jericho had never planned on auctioning off the missiles. He had a far more devious plan in mind which didn't include Haynes' involvement any longer. He had always intended on severing all ties with him as soon as he had what he wanted; he just never expected it to be this soon.

He accessed an encrypted comm channel and called his man inside the corporation.

"Trask, it's time. Do it now and leave no trace; a suicide would be good," he said, then closed the call.

Chapter 8

Haynes Corporation Building

Milton Trask was a member of ICE and the primary problem solver for them. If a problem arose, Trask made it go away.

Haynes was now such a problem.

Trask had been working for Haynes in a minor capacity for a few weeks, since the deal had been struck between Jericho and himself. Jericho had placed him there to ensure Haynes did nothing stupid or contrary to their contract. His end game had always been to eliminate the potential threat he posed and now it seemed that the time had arrived.

Trask was around six feet four inches tall with a muscular torso, so getting a position on the security staff hadn't posed much of a problem. Just one look into his emotionless slate grey eyes was enough to put most people off any thoughts of doing ill towards Haynes.

Trask knew Haynes' location—he rarely strayed far from his penthouse office suite, so he used his access to go up in the elevator.

"Trask, what is it? Has something else happened?" Haynes asked as Trask entered the office unannounced.

"I have a message from Nathan Mister Haynes," he replied, his voice deep and sombre.

"Why did he send you, he could have called?"

"It's not that kind of message."

Trask saw the fear bloom in Haynes' eyes then as he knew his end had come.

Before the smaller man could react, Trask had covered the distance between them impossibly fast. How could a big man like him move so gracefully, so fast? He didn't have time to ponder that fact as Trask grabbed him by the collar and dragged him effortlessly to the door. He had it open in seconds, dragging Haynes through into the corridor beyond. At the end of this short hallway was another door that led to a staircase. As Trask opened it and pushed Haynes through, the latter knew how this was going to end.

"You're going to throw me off the roof, aren't you?" he stammered, his voice breaking under the fear of his impending doom.

Trask remained silent, he simply pushed Haynes up the staircase to the door at the top.

"Whatever Jericho is paying you, I'll double it," Haynes said.

"With what? You're broke," Trask replied. He knew the financial trouble Haynes was in was the cause behind him working with Jericho. It didn't matter either way though; he would have done him for free anyway. Entitled morons like Haynes had always bothered Trask; he hated them and the way they had things in life just laid at their feet just because they had wealth.

The cold air from the roof hit them both like a dip in a freezing river. Trask smiled because, to him, this was invigorating. His smile was more than just that though; he was amused at the discomfort Haynes was feeling from the brisk temperature drop and high winds from the altitude.

Another shove and Haynes went sprawling towards the edge of the building.

"You don't have to do this, you know," Haynes pleaded.

"You've got it all wrong. I'm not doing this because I have to. I'm doing this because I want to," Trask countered with a cruel smile.

He lifted Haynes off the floor by grabbing him by the collar with his right hand and one of Haynes' ankles with his left hand, then hoisted him above his head like a rag doll. With one swift motion he hurled Haynes over the edge of the roof into the void beyond.

He saw the terror in his eyes as he was sent flying over the edge of the roof. He opened his mouth to scream as his arms and legs cartwheeled, trying to grab something, anything to prevent the inevitable plunge to his death. Eyes wide in shock as he realised there was nothing he could do, he screamed his terror as he disappeared over the edge.

Haynes' screams were heard all the way to the ground until the wet squelch of his soft body hitting the immovable ground cut it off.

"It's done," Trask said through the same encrypted comm channel to Jericho, "it seems Haynes couldn't take it anymore and threw himself off the roof of his building," he added as he headed for the door, leading back inside.

His job was done here; time to move on.

MI7 Sub Station

Pryde was sitting calmly waiting for the results of the search into Haynes' financials when he was contacted by C on an encrypted comm channel.

"Pryde, there has been a development."

"What is it sir?"

"Why didn't you inform me of the attack on you by Haynes' men?" C began.

"I didn't think it was relevant, sir; I got away cleanly. I am now looking into his finances to see who he had dealings with. I suspect he may be involved with the theft of the missiles as well sir."

"And you didn't think to report that Haynes attacked you? I could have had him brought in for questioning; instead now he is being scraped up off the floor outside his office building after leaping to his death."

Pryde paused for just a second, "Was there any indication that he was feeling guilty over his involvement in this?"

"Well clearly that is how it is meant to look, but we'll never know now, will we, because he's dead and dead men don't answer questions."

"I know that sir, but it also looks like he's been silenced so he can't reveal any details about his dealings with whoever he gave the Raptor design to," Pryde continued, unperturbed. He was running on mission mode so his empathy was turned off in favour of pure logic. He was focussed solely on finding and retrieving those missiles before they had a chance to be used. All other considerations were secondary.

"Have you any idea who might want him silenced?" C asked, calming down a little.

"If we can find out who he was in contact with over the sale or gifting of the Raptor designs, we might just find the other party sir."

"Carry on, and this time keep me informed," C said, then hung up the call.

Chapter 9

Cronus III

The hijacking of the missiles was completed efficiently and swiftly. Once it had been completed all traces of them disappeared.

All eyes shifted to other planets they could have been transported to instead of focussing on the obvious.

The missiles never left Cronus III.

They had been built at an installation owned by the Haynes Corporation and were hijacked en route to testing at a military base nearby. They were transported to a different location where they had been stored ever since along with the Raptor F95.

Jericho arrived at the base and entered via the roof top entrance. The area chosen was that of a secluded section outside any of the cities on the planet. It had rolling grassy hills and lakes that were used as camping sites for vacationers. The base ICE was using was underground built inside a section of natural caves that were interconnected. An entrance was built in the side of one of the hills above the caves. The hill had grass and shrubs growing naturally on the side and a large section was cut away and placed on runners so that it could open up allowing small craft to enter and leave. This opening dropped down into the largest of the caves which had been made safe by adding reinforced sections to the walls and sections of the roof to ensure no cave ins occurred.

As Jericho landed the small shuttle he looked around as he exited the craft. The missiles were on pallets on the floor over by the side at the cavern. Near them was the Raptor F95.

The Control Room for the entire operations of ICE was close by, adjacent to the main cavern. A set of steps ran up the wall, carved out of the very wall themselves which led to the glass walled control room.

Jericho walked up followed by Lucius Black his second in command. The two of them served together in the Special Forces regiment of the Coalition, the Recon Ranger Division.

The Control Room was square with wall mounted monitors on the far wall opposite the entrance. There were three rows of desks all with computer access which could be displayed on the huge monitors. All of them were manned with operatives working.

"Okay contact the Council, use all necessary precautions," he said as the two of them entered the room.

He walked over to the side where a small camera was set up on a tripod in front of a blank sheet to be used as a backdrop. A chair was placed in front of the camera in which he sat down in.

"Ready when you are sir," Black said from the side of the camera.

Jericho looked into the camera and began to speak.

***

SecOps HQ, Terra II.

Pryde walked into C's office and stood in front of the desk.

"What have you found?" C asked.

Pryde's expression was neutral which at times like this infuriating for those he worked with.

"Nothing sir, Haynes' financials were routed through so many different accounts on different worlds it was hard to keep track of them. I was told eventually they might find something but it would take more time than we have."

The intercom on the desk buzzed and Goodchild's voice came through.

"Sir, turn on your monitor. President Harada is on an encrypted channel for you," she said.

C turned around to face the monitor behind. A panel in the unit on the wall slid open to reveal the monitor which came alive showing the face of the Coalition President.

"Good afternoon Mister President, what do I owe the honour of this call?" C asked.

"I see you have your man present, that'll save time. I recently received a call from an unknown source. I will forward the actual call to you and then we can talk," Harada said and the image changed to the call the President had received.

A dark background was backlit showing the outline of a figure sitting on a chair, and nothing more. It was impossible to see who it was through the several other layers of encryption the caller used even down to the alteration of the voice.

"A shipment of missiles was recently hijacked and are now in my possession, verification will follow shortly. My demands for the return of said missiles are simple yet none negotiable. I want Five Billion Coalition credits deposited in an account of my choosing. When I have verification of the transfer, I will give you details of where the missiles will be. Failure to comply will result in punishment. You have twelve hours to obtain the funds ready for the transfer and then I will contact you. Before I leave, I did say that verification that I hold the missiles would be forthcoming. In one hour, you will have all the proof you need to help you make your decision easier."

"Wow!" Pryde said allowing emotion to creep through his block.

The President came back, "What do you think?" he asked.

"How long do we have left before they offer up their so-called proof sir?"

"Less than fifty minutes."

"What do we know about the missiles sir?"

"According to the specs from the military they are a new form of cluster missile. They can be configured to carry mini nuclear warheads. When launched the twenty mini warheads are released when the main missile reaches a certain distance from the target. They separate and spread out to cover a wider area. As they detonate, they combine to form a massive shockwave that spreads out to cover at least five times the initial blast area. The devastation caused by just one of these missiles would be too hard to contemplate, especially if they are configured for nuclear payloads, and there were twenty missiles in the convoy."

"We will get right on it, sir," C said.

"I don't have to reiterate just how important this is do I C? You have less than forty-five minutes to come up with something."

"I'll do my best sir."

"Keep me informed," Harada said then the screen went blank as the call was ended.

"Strictly speaking sir, we have less than twelve hours. I doubt there is anything we can do about the first deadline but from that we might learn something that could lead us to whoever is behind this," Pryde said calmly.

"Are you saying we should just allow them to kill potentially thousands of innocent people just so we can learn more about them?" C asked angrily as he speared him with an intense gaze.

"Not at all sir. What I said was I doubt we'd be able to do anything about stopping them in less than an hour. It is virtually impossible to prevent an event from happening if we don't know where it'll take place, it's just not possible sir."

"Point taken, but I don't have to like it."

"I'll have someone go over the call records of Haynes to see who he was communicating with prior to the missiles being hijacked. It might turn something up we can use."

"Keep me informed, and Pryde, hurry. I don't like the thought of consigning those people to death, not if there's the slightest chance, we can prevent it, understood?"

"Completely sir, I'll do my best."

"Keep me informed," C said.

Pryde gave him a nod and headed for the door.

Chapter 10

P ryde left the office and was going to call the substation when another thought hit him.

All munitions during transport were fitted with trackers that only certain personnel knew the codes for. In this case, the codes would be given to the person sending the delivery and the person receiving, and that was it. This was standard procedure, required by law, and was supposed to prevent this very thing from happening. The codes cannot be turned off until they reach the final destination because they are linked and have to be inputted at the same time to complete the entire code.

No sign of the trackers had been located, which means both parties were in on the hijacking.

As he neared Goodchild's desk, he said to her, "I think I may be on to something. Let C know I'm heading back to Cronus III and I'll contact him when I know more."

"I'll let him know right away, and good luck," she replied. Her well wishes were lost on him as he was back on full mission mode, all emotions completely under control. He had less than forty minutes to avert a disaster, and failure was not something he was comfortable with.

Cronus III

Pryde arrived at the Cronus III space port. It was situated in the largest city on the planet and dealt with eighty-five per cent of all interstellar traffic to and from the planet.

Inside his ship was a road car that he used to get to his next location. The car was an All-Terrain Vehicle built around the design of the Challenger military jeep. This version was built for normal traffic conditions with the ability to go off road should the need arise. It could seat five people comfortably and an extra two by dropping the rear divider. Large, self-inflating tyres were attached to a suspension that could handle the roughest of terrains. Inside the cabin the driver had a control panel that incorporated a defence system that protected the passengers from almost any attack and the shell could withstand most things up to a direct hit from a missile.

Pryde steered the vehicle towards the military base outside of the city. He had contacted the commander of the base before leaving Terra II, a General Grant. He was a twenty-year veteran of the Coalition Defence Force, which incorporated all the military into one cohesive unit. Fleet Arm was the space navy and air force, and then there was the Infantry, which was the entire ground forces. Grant was in command of the base which had Infantry and air strike capabilities and room for shuttles to travel to and from any starships that arrived and took up a parking orbit.

He was shown through the perimeter gates and allocated a parking space near the base commander's office.

The base was like all the other bases he had visited on many other worlds—a selection of low buildings which acted as barracks for the troops and larger buildings that were the administration offices. Hangars for all the aircraft and shuttles were at the far end near the runways and landing pads.

Officer's quarters were closer to the admin buildings and had more amenities than the normal troop barracks, as befitted their station on the base.

Grant's office was located in the same sector as the admin buildings near the main office block but separate from it. Pryde left his ATV there while he entered Grant's office building. His adjutant, Lieutenant Wilkins, was waiting for him in the outer office.

As with all officers, Wilkins was wearing his normal uniform: light blue shirt, dark blue trousers, and black shoes. His badge of rank was on his shoulder flashes and the insignia of the CDF was on his patch pocket over his heart.

"Welcome to Base Latimer. General Grant is expecting you, sir," the young officer said as he entered the small uncluttered office.

Pryde gave him a quick nod, then entered through the door to the inner office.

A sight similar to C's office greeted him. The room was squared away with everything in its place. The general sat behind a desk devoid of paperwork—the only item adorning it was a computer monitor which he seemed to be working on using the keyboard interface. The walls were bare and a thick pile carpet on the floor was the only addition to comfort.

A window opposite gave a brief view out onto the road beyond.

Grant was in his late fifties with hair the colour of sand. As he looked up from his work, he speared him with an intense gaze.

"Why has the Ministry sent one of their men to see us, Mister Pryde?" he asked without preamble.

Pryde's expression remained neutral, giving nothing away. When he spoke, it was in a calm, measured voice that showed no stress.

"I'm here to investigate the hijacking of a convoy containing a set of experimental missiles," he said.

"What do you expect to find here?"

"How it happened and why the missiles haven't been located via their trackers since."

"I'm not sure what you mean."

"As you well know, General, every missile has a location tracker which is deactivated by a code, which is in two parts upon arrival at the final delivery destination. The person sending the missiles has one part and the person receiving has the other part."

"You don't have to lecture me on military protocol Pryde, I'm well aware of this protocol and we followed it to the letter."

"And yet the missiles were hijacked."

"That was out of our control."

"You must have been involved in this General, because we lost track of the missiles shortly after they were hijacked, even though you never received them. Can you see where I'm going with this?"

"Are you suggesting I had something to do with this?"

"You're not as dumb as you look, are you, General?"

"You insist on trying to insult me, Mister Pryde? Is that wise if, as you suspect, I am to blame for this?"

"Can you explain why we lost all trace of the missiles even though the tracking codes were not deactivated then, General?"

"But the trackers are still active."

Pryde was genuinely surprised; he took a step back as he thought about it. What did that mean and why wasn't he told of this? This could have all ended hours ago. No, there had to be more.

"Excuse me General, but did you just say the trackers are still active?" he said.

"I did."

"So where are they?" he asked.

When the general paused, Pryde said, "You have no idea do you?"

"We have been working around the clock trying to locate them but the signal keeps getting masked or rerouted around several servers. Every minute we get a new signal from a different location. We haven't been able to narrow it down yet, but we're working on it."

"Why didn't you inform the Ministry of this?"

"I wanted to handle this in house, as it were."

"Well, it's too late for that now General; we have been contacted by the hijackers who demand a ransom. More than that, they are threatening to use one in less than an hour to prove their determination to use them. I think you'll agree that handling this in house is now not an option."

"I'll have everything we have forwarded to you. It'll be on your PIN before you leave," Grant said.

"Thank you General, I appreciate it. Let's just hope the delay in locating the missiles hasn't damaged the investigation," Pryde said as he turned to leave.

Chapter 11

Damian Richards was watching the ATV leave the base. His work as a consultant from the Haynes Corporation had him helping them try and locate the missiles.

Not a soldier by any means, he was small, no taller than five feet eight inches with a thin weedy body that most described as wiry. His hair had retreated from a forehead lined with worry, which since he'd been there had only gotten worse.

As he watched the ATV leave through the gates, he felt his pulse rate quicken. He knew the driver of the vehicle was from the Ministry of Intelligence. News and rumours raced through the base almost like that of a wildfire through decades old brush.

He made sure he was alone and couldn't be overheard, then he called an encrypted number.

"We just had a visit from someone from the Ministry. They're looking for the missiles; if they find out I've been helping you then I'm a dead man."

"Keep your head, is he still there?" Jericho replied.

"No, he just left, I'll send you the code for the tracking chip I placed on his ride," Richards said.

"Good; don't worry, it'll get taken care of," Jericho said and ended the call.

Richards tried to relax a little but he still felt anxiety churning his stomach into knots. This was not what he signed up for.

***

Pryde left the base and headed back toward the city. The roads he travelled on were empty of traffic and wound their way through open grasslands.

As he drove, he heard the sound of approaching engines, one from above and the others from behind. A glance in the mirror told him all he needed to know. A jet copter was coming in fast from behind and above. Chasing and gaining ground were three vehicles, all small and fast.

Bullets slammed into the back of his vehicle as the smaller cars opened fire. Passengers leaned out of the windows holding automatic weapons which spat bullets at an alarming rate.

Activating the SUV's defences on the armrest between the front two seats, Pryde selected the rear guns. Small machine guns protruded out from a hidden recess in the bodywork near the rear lights. Targeting sensors on the dash showed where the sights of the guns were aimed and, once they were on target, he returned fire.

He saw his first salvo strike the front of the leading vehicle, which looked to be a small two-seater roadster with twin guns mounted on the front wheel arches just above the headlights. The bullets hit the front grille, sending a series of sparks flying up. Flames started to spread from inside the engine, cowling behind the grille, which sent smoke up to obscure the driver's view.

Large calibre shells strafed both sides of the SUV from above as the jet copter opened fire on him. Pryde kept the SUV in a straight line to avoid getting hit.

The flames from the chasing vehicle now engulfed the entire engine and the driver panicked and steered the dying car into a tight turn, which sent it into a barrel roll. It spun, turning sideways, jumping, and bouncing down the dirt track road, which the other two vehicles had to avoid to prevent crashing into it.

The engine exploded, sending burning debris out, showering the ground, setting smaller fires in the grass on the roadside.

Speeding up, Pryde tried to widen the gap between him and the other two cars behind. He knew he wouldn't be able to outrun the chopper, so something had to be done about that.

The SUV's defences included small rocket pods that could rotate to face either front or back. They were set just behind the front wheels inside the bodywork. Using the same targeting sensors, he targeted the chopper, then fired.

Chaff was spat out from the body of the chopper as soon as the rockets were launched. The rockets detonated before they reached the chopper in a huge fireball.

Pryde turned his attention back to the two following vehicles. Larger than the one he had destroyed, their passengers were hanging out of the side windows, firing automatic weapons at him.

A burst from his rear tail guns struck the leading vehicle, shredding the front offside tire. This wheel was pushed out from the vehicle, then ejected as another took its place from inside on the same axle.

"Interesting," mused Pryde as he saw no slowing down of the vehicle.

Accessing the rockets, he aimed at the vehicle and fired a single rocket at it.

"See how you handle that," he said to himself.

The rocket slammed into the front grille of the chasing vehicle before the driver could react. The ensuing explosion destroyed the entire front end of the vehicle in a blast that threw the rest of it back into the last vehicle. Flaming debris from the explosion was scattered over the ground, hitting the other vehicle as it collided with its team mate. Both vehicles were sent into a tumbling mess with parts sent flying in various directions. Small fires ignited on the road side as brush caught alight.

Pryde said, "Just you and me now," as he turned his attention back to the chopper.

Chapter 12

Pryde's AI controlling the vehicle suddenly chimed a collision warning as another vehicle suddenly appeared in front of him, barrelling down the narrow road toward him.

It was a sleek roadster in bright red and he noticed mini gatling guns pop up from hidden recesses in the bodywork just behind the front lights.

Aimed above him, the guns spat out a barrage of shells at the oncoming chopper.

Pryde swerved around this new addition and spun his car around to face the chopper, which was now hovering as it had to deal with two targets.

Accessing his rockets, he fired a salvo at it as the other car continued to fire the mini gatling guns.

He had no idea who this was who had decided to join in this fight on his side, but he was grateful for the help.

The mini gatling guns battered the front of the chopper, which distracted the pilot long enough that, when the rockets were fired, he didn't have time to take evasive action. The rockets slammed into the front of the chopper right where the pilot sat. The explosion blew apart the entire front section in a blast that threw parts of the aircraft in all directions, scattering fiery debris over the ground in front of the two vehicles.

The pilot died instantly in the explosion, torn apart by the immense power from the blast.

The rotors were sent spinning in every direction; one of them narrowly missed Pryde's vehicle before spearing into the ground just feet from him. The rest of the chopper fell to the ground in a shower of sparks reminiscent of a firework display.

The threat of attack finally gone, Pryde turned his attention to his guardian angel. Training his weapons systems on the new arrival, he used the speaker on his audio unit to say, "Thanks for the assist; now identify yourself or I open fire."

The driver's side door opened slowly and a figure emerged, holding their hands in the air to show they were unarmed and posed no threat.

"Is this the thanks I get for saving your ass?" she said. She was tall and athletically built with hair the colour of the rising sun. Dressed in a stylish dark blue coverall that gave her freedom of movement, she exuded confidence.

"Who are you and why were you following me?" Pryde asked.

"Who said I was following you?" she evaded.

"This road joins the city to the base; where else would you be going?"

"I could have business at the base, or I could just be lost," she countered.

"Which is it then?" Pryde pushed. By this time, he too had got out of his vehicle and was facing her, holding his Walther Q9 at her.

She was about to give some other explanation further confusing the issue or simply evading the truth when he held up his hand to halt her.

"It doesn't matter what you say, I don't have time for this shit. Either tell me who you are or simply get the fuck out of my way," he snapped. He was calm but he wanted to give the impression he was losing his temper.

Nodding her head, she finally gave in and said, "Okay, you got me, I was following you. I was ordered to see what your investigation unearthed."

"Let me guess, you work for the Coalition Intelligence Agency."

Another nod of affirmation.

"What's the CIA's intention here?" he wanted to know.

"When we heard of the missiles being hijacked and the threat they posed, we instigated an investigation into it. We came to the same conclusions you did. My boss has never liked the fact that the Ministry responds to the President directly—he's always felt the relationship between the Ministry and the President was dangerous, so he felt we should look into this as well, just in case."

"Just in case, what, in case we screwed up? Or got all the glory?" he said, watching her reaction. It was there, extremely slight, just a flicker really, but he spotted it.

"I get it, he sent you to watch so if we screwed up then we get the blame and, if by some miracle you were able to swoop in at the last second to save the day, the Agency would claim all the glory and show the President he didn't need to trust us any longer. For you, it's a win-win situation and, for us, an almost certain path to being disbanded, that is if we screw up."

"Plausible deniability—if things go sideways, he can always state he knew nothing of it," she added.

"Not if this is all on record. By the way, this conversation is being recorded by the security unit in my ride," he said, "I'll soon have your ID once I run your face through records, so you have a nice day, agent whoever you are," he finished as he got back into his car.

Whoever attacked him knew exactly where he was and where he was going. Someone on the base gave them his whereabouts.

Spinning the car around, he headed back to the base.

Chances were that if they were working with his attackers, they knew where they had come from. He was hoping that it was somewhere nearby and they still had the missiles there.

If his luck held, he might have a chance at stopping this before they used the missiles to make their point known.

As he drove, he called HQ to inform them of his theory and, as he finished, he noticed the car was following him once more.

Accessing another comm channel, he called General Grant on the base.

"General, I was just attacked after leaving your base, which can only lead me to the conclusion you have a traitor on your base," he said urgently.

"That is impossible; I can vouch for all of my men," Grant replied angrily.

"Nevertheless, I want you to check all outgoing communications from your base upon my leaving it. Whoever that is, my guess is they're working with the hijackers."

"I'll do it, but just to prove it was none of my men responsible. It could have come from your department—they knew you were coming here as well," argued Grant.

"But the timing is crucial here; I was only attacked after I left the base. They didn't want me to report anything I found here. If the leak was at my end, they would've prevented me from arriving here."

"I'll get on it, then report my findings," Grant said.

"You can give them to me personally—I'm on my way back."

Chapter 13

G rant issued the order to check all outgoing comms chatter and it brought up one anomaly.

"Sir, Damian Richards made a call through an encrypted channel just as Pryde was leaving the base. I can't locate where it went, but it's within a few miles sir," the comms officer said.

"Who is this Richards?" Grant asked as the name wasn't ringing any bells.

"He's from the Haynes Corp, sir; he was sent to help locate the missiles."

"Oh, him," Grant said, then his eyes opened wider as realisation dawned on him. He relaxed at once knowing the fault wasn't with any of his men, as he knew it couldn't be.

He turned from the seated officer and called Pryde to tell him the good news.

"Detain him immediately, and don't allow him to talk to anyone," Pryde said, "I'm at the gates now, I'll be with you in seconds," he added.

Grant turned to the room and said, "Damian Richards, I want him located and detained immediately."

Richards was gathering his things together in a hurry. After relaying the news about the agent from the Ministry calling at the base, he became scared.

The men he worked for didn't take failure kindly and he had a feeling he could be next on their hit list.

He was just coming from his quarters when he saw the agent return through the gates. He had to leave and right now. If he was back, it could only mean that whatever steps Jericho had taken to handle him had not worked.

He called Jericho using the same encrypted comm channel. "Whatever you did to handle the agent hasn't worked. He's here now," he said, his voice low but almost breaking with fear.

"Keep calm Richards, everything will work out fine," Jericho replied.

"I'm not so sure about this. You said you'd look after me; you promised and now what?"

"I always keep my promises Richards, you will be taken care of. That you can be sure of."

Damian Richards, stay where you are and show me your hands," a voice shouted from his left. He glanced that way and saw a group of Marines heading his way. The speaker was pointing his left hand in his direction while his right hand was on the butt of his sidearm holstered at his hip.

"Shit!" he said. "Jericho, I've gotta go, they've come for me. If I go down for this, I'm taking you with me," he said, then closed the call. He dropped his bag and held up both hands. Panic spread through him, then his breathing increased as he realised there was no way out for him now.

"Fuck this," he said under his breath, then turned and sprinted for his life. He ran for the group of buildings that were the contractors' quarters while working on the base and dodged down an alley between two low squat buildings.

Secret ICE HQ

Jericho had heard the fear in Richards' voice. If they were on to him, then it was just a matter of time before he gave them something that could lead them to him.

Checking the time, he realised he could literally kill two birds with one stone.

His second in command was at his side and had heard some of the conversation.

"Trouble?" he asked when he saw the frown on Jericho's face.

"No, more like an opportunity actually. Change the target to the military base, Latimer. We can take out their ability to respond to us here and also deal with an annoying little problem that's just cropped up," he replied.

"Copy that," Black said and he turned to leave.

"When you've reset the target's location, fire the missile, let's not waste any more time on this."

<hr>

Base Latimer

Pryde had pulled up as soon as he entered the base. He'd seen Marines chasing a figure down an alley and knew it was Richards.

Somehow, they must have spooked him and now he was on the run. There was nowhere for him to run to, but chasing him was time they didn't have.

ICE had already warned of an incident that would prove their validity and time was running out to stop them from firing one of the missiles. Richards was the key and he knew it; that's why he ran.

The other vehicle pulled up alongside his car and she got out.

"What have we got?" she asked. Pryde gave her nothing in return, just a blank stare of distrust.

"Look I get it, you don't trust me, why should you? If the roles were reversed, I wouldn't trust me either. My name is Jasmine Fields, does that help?"

"Really, is that a real name or a cover name?" he asked with a raised eyebrow. Not waiting for a reply, he just turned and ran after the Marines. Fields kept with him, following a few paces behind muttering, "Of course it's my real name, why do people always ask that?"

"Where're we going?" she shouted after his fleeing form.

"Our one chance of stopping thousands of lives being murdered," he gave in and replied as he ran.

The Marines had almost caught up with the fleeing Richards. They chased him in between two barrack buildings. He came to the end and two armed Marines stepped out to block his path, their rifles up and aimed right at him.

"Freeze, do not move!" they both shouted.

Pryde almost ran into the backs of them as he skidded to a stop.

"Richards, where are they going to fire the missile from? We don't have time for your bullshit, either tell me now or I start shooting," he shouted as he pushed his way through the Marines. He stood a few feet away from his target, his Walther levelled at the man who was staring at him in fear.

He saw Richards relax just a little.

"You won't kill me, you need what I know," he said, dropping his hands confidently.

Pryde said, "Who said anything about killing you?" then shot him in the leg. The bullet hit Richards' knee, blowing out the back of the joint, collapsing the leg.

Pryde walked slowly up to the screaming man as he desperately tried to stem the flow of blood from his leg.

"You bastard, you shot me!" he screamed, pain distorting his face.

"And I'll shoot you some more if you don't answer my question. It's quite remarkable how much punishment the human body can take before blood loss shuts the brain down and death follows. We are not there yet, by any means, and this could take a while," Pryde said calmly in measured tones that he could tell sent another shiver of fear through his target.

Aiming his pistol at Richards' arm he said, "Here, let me show you," and he fired another bullet. This time it hit Richards' right elbow, shattering the joint and rendering that arm useless.

More screaming followed and Pryde became aware of Fields standing at his shoulder watching the whole thing. The Marines were quiet behind them but, from their utterings, it was obvious they weren't happy with what was happening.

Fields turned to them, "If you have a problem with this then I suggest you go someplace else. We're trying to prevent a mass murder here and we're running out of time," she said.

"No ma'am," they replied.

Pryde saw Richards didn't do any of this to continue as he held up his left hand to halt him.

"Okay, don't shoot me again. They have a base, not far from here, it's concealed underground. They have the missiles there. You have to believe me, I never knew they were going to use them, honest," he pleaded.

"Right, we need to move and fast," Pryde said. As he turned to Fields, he saw the Marines look up in the sky as warning alarms sounded around the base.

He followed their gaze up into the sky and saw a missile in the air headed right for them.

"We're too late," he said.

Chapter 14

S houts of "Incoming," galvanised the personnel of the base into action.

Some headed for the gates, running for their lives, others headed for aircraft to escape the destruction heading their way as others manned the defences, hoping to shoot down the missile.

"We have to go, now," urged Pryde. He knew what was coming having learned of the missile's specs and suspected that they couldn't stop or shoot it down.

"What about me?" Richards screamed.

Pryde turned around and shot him in the head.

"Consider that mercy," he said, then grabbed a startled Fields by the arm and pulled her after him.

"Wait, we can get to the shelters surely," she said as they ran.

"Won't help against this."

The bases defences began firing at the missile that was getting nearer with each passing second. Thousands of rounds poured out of the perimeter gatling guns, a veritable wall of steel which had no effect as it had reached its separation point.

Twenty smaller warheads ejected from the main body, all flying in different directions, separating along a line towards the target.

Pryde saw their only way out just ahead. A shuttle was being prepped for take off and had been left when the alarm sounded.

Increasing his speed, he said, "There, it's our only chance to escape this thing."

Reaching the shuttle, they jumped aboard, closing the door after them. Pryde sat in the pilot's seat and ignited the engines. Lifting off on thrusters only, he fired the main engine, boosting their speed to full in a few seconds even though they were only feet off the ground. He angled their take off upwards as steep as possible. The 'g' forces pushed them back into their seats as he desperately tried to increase their speed and rate of incline to give them their best chance of surviving what was about to happen.

Through their rear monitors they could see the missiles separating and heading out in a widening pattern before dropping in a wide arc toward the base.

Pryde checked their speed and did a quick calculation of distance covered and time they had left. It was going to be close.

The smaller missiles hit the base and detonated almost as one. Each blast took out an area large enough to destroy a city block, as the others detonated in sync, the blast covered a much wider area almost a mile wide. The explosions caused a shockwave that combined into one that spread out over a five-mile-wide area, destroying everything in its path at the speed of sound.

"Hang on, this is going to be tight," Pryde said as he saw the cloud expanding towards them, forced outwards by the shockwave behind.

When it hit, they felt the shuttle being shoved, like the very air was trying to throw them like a bucking bronco would its rider. Pryde hung onto the controls compensating for the turbulence and soon had it under control. The shockwave had dissipated and they were safe.

As he levelled the shuttle off into a more controlled flight, they both looked down at what was left of the base. It was just a hole in the ground, or several smaller holes forming one large crater. No buildings were left standing and all the vehicles and aircraft left on the ground were just wreckage. Any other aircraft that hadn't made it clear of the blast area were lying on the ground in pieces where they had dropped from the sky after being torn apart by the explosions.

Pryde was hard at work calculating the angle of trajectory of where the missile had been launched from using the onboard nav-comp.

"All those people are dead," he heard Fields say at his side. He had too been busy trying to locate the base to concern himself with the ramifications of the attack, one being the enormous loss of life.

"Yes, and if we don't find their base and fast, more people will die," he said coldly.

"Are you even human?" she asked, looking at him with disgust in her eyes.

From her expression, Pryde could tell she was wondering what kind of person could dismiss all those lives being lost in such a cold-hearted way. Sometimes he wondered the same thing himself. Was he human, or had he pushed his emotions so far down inside that he was becoming an actual sociopath? Having this ability to shut off his emotions certainly made him ideal for this job. He never hesitated to make harsh decisions in the field, never allowed emotions to cloud his judgement, but by doing that had he lost his humanity?

"Yes, I'm human. Right at this moment though, I choose not to allow my feelings to get in the way of my job. Right now, that job is to find whoever has those missiles and prevent them from using them to kill more innocent lives. When I've done that, I'll grieve for those people who died, but until then, I have work to do," he said.

Out of the corner of his eye he saw her turn to look out the side window. Any other thoughts dissipated when the computer brought up a possible location for the base the missile was fired from.

"We have them," he said.

Chapter 15

Secret ICE HQ

Jericho watched the destruction of the base on monitors that had tapped into satellite feeds.

"That was impressive," he said with a slight smile.

"We are going to be inundated with offers to buy these things when this hits the media feeds," he added.

"What's that?" Black said, pointing to something at the edge of the blast going up into the air at a steep angle.

"Shit, someone is getting away," he added when he recognised what it was.

"Good, word of mouth will help validate this incident," Jericho said, then thought better of it. "Bring whoever that is here to me. I have a suspicion it's the mysterious thorn in our side. I would like to meet him before he dies."

"What if it's just some lucky bastard who got away in time?"

"Then he can die as well; either way I want whoever is in that shuttle brought here, now."

"Copy that," Black said, and he went off to organise it, leaving Jericho staring at the monitor watching evidence of his actions play out for all to see.

"We have incoming," Fields said as the sensors warned them of two aircraft chasing them.

"Where did they come from?" Pryde said; he'd been too focussed on sending a sit-rep out to C that he hadn't noticed them.

"Probably that hidden base you were on about to your boss," she commented.

Pryde increased speed to the maximum thrust on the main engines. If they could gain escape velocity then maybe they could reach one of the starships parked in orbit and safety.

Something slammed into the rear quarter of the shuttle, rocking the two of them in their seats.

"We've been hit," Fields said, "Are they trying to shoot us down?"

"No, they fired grapplers at us. They're trying to take us in."

"At least they're not trying to kill us then."

"Not yet at least; that could come later. They probably want to know what we know."

"That's not very reassuring."

"Like I said, they'll keep us alive until they learn everything they want from us. Our job is to stay alive and delay giving them what they want for as long as we can to give the CDF time to find the base and the missiles."

Their forward momentum slowed dramatically as the grapplers were reeled in. Pryde shut down their forward drive and just kept the thrusters active to prevent the shuttle from falling. The grapplers did their job and dragged them back toward the forward section of the ship chasing them.

"Can we escape, pull free?" Fields asked.

"Not in this bucket, she doesn't have the power."

"What about severing the grapplers, does she have anything that can do that?"

"This is just a military shuttle, for transport only. I doubt she even has shields."

"We're screwed then, is that what you're saying?"

"For the time being, maybe. Don't give up hope though, we're not dead yet," Pryde replied, but as he glanced her way he knew his words gave her little comfort.

MI7 HQ, Terra II

C checked through the sit-rep from Pryde one more time.

"And you lost contact with them shortly after this transmission reached us," he said. He was standing in the Situation Room after being told of the communication from Pryde.

"Do you have the coordinates mentioned in the report?" he asked.

"Yes sir, they're on screen right now."

"Have you scanned the area for any other craft going down past the blast site?"

"Yes sir, there is no sign of any other aircraft going down past that area."

"So, it's unlikely that his shuttle was damaged in the escape from the explosion and went down somewhere outside that area," C said to reiterate.

"No sir, extremely unlikely."

"The alternative is what then, that he was snatched in mid-air?" C said, and even as he said it he knew how preposterous he sounded.

"That seems to be the case sir, yes."

C looked at the man, his eyes narrowing in disbelief.

"Are you serious?"

"Sir, it's quite possible for a larger aircraft to fire grapplers at another aircraft and drag them aboard. It's dangerous and the risk of collision is, well, huge, but it can be done sir. It's much easier in a zero g environment and I wouldn't advise it in the atmosphere of a planet, but I've run the numbers sir, and it is possible."

"Well, that would make sense; if they wanted to know what they knew it would make better sense to capture them than simply blasting them out of the sky. In that way they could find out where we are in our investigation and act accordingly. Okay then, pass on the coordinates of the base to the commander of the CDF on Cronus III and inform him that we suspect that is where the missiles are being stored. Give him all the information we have, including that one of our operatives is inside the base being held captive."

"On it, sir."

"Keep me informed of what his response is and what action he intends to take. Make it known in the strongest terms possible that I want to be kept in the loop over this. I'll be in my office, I need to let the President know of our progress," C said, then without waiting for a reply turned and left the room.

Chapter 16

Secret ICE HQ

The aircraft carrying the shuttle with Pryde and Fields on board entered the base through the rooftop access point.

A group of armed men surrounded the front section of the larger aircraft aiming their weapons at the cargo hold where the shuttle was stored.

Pryde opened the shuttle door and walked down the ramp that led from the cargo bay to the ground inside the base.

"Hi guys, you looking for us?" he said as he and Fields exited from the cargo bay.

"Nice, I never took you for a funny guy," a voice said from behind the armed group forming a barrier.

"And you are?" Pryde said looking right at the man who spoke.

"Well, I guess if you're the hero, that must make me the bad guy," Jericho replied with a confident smirk.

"Do you have a name?" Pryde asked.

"Don't you already know?"

Pryde returned the slight smile, from the smile on his captor's face he knew he was being tested to see how much the authorities knew about him and therefore how close they were to capturing him.

"Oh, we don't need to know who you are, we know where you live," he said.

"Well, if that's all you know then we can dispense with keeping you around."

"That would be unwise," Fields said.

"And you are?" Jericho asked looking at her.

"Someone you need to keep around. Like I said, it would be unwise to kill me at least, I can't vouch for him," she said indicating Pryde at her side with a tilt of her head. "If I go missing then you can guarantee that the full force of the CDF down on your location with enough firepower to level this entire area. If you want to survive your next few hours then I would seriously rethink your next move."

"So, you know where we live and there are forces bearing down on us as we speak. Thanks for the sit-rep," Jericho said then turned to his men, "Put them somewhere secure, I've not done with them yet, oh and search them thoroughly," he said and walked off.

A guard came forward and began to frisk Pryde first, removing his Walther, then moved on to Fields where he removed her pistol, Pryde noted that it was a Sig PX336.

When he was finished, another tall man stepped forward holding a pistol and said, "Come on, follow me, I'll show you to your rooms."

"I like that, you must be the bad guy's sidekick," Pryde said with a deadpan expression.

"Yes dear, let's go see our rooms," Fields said.

"You know, you two make a cute couple," Black said as he ushered them through the group and across the floor.

Several of the armed guards followed them across the open space giving the two agents time and opportunity to view everything there. As they reached the far end their escort stopped at a row of iron doors that had a single window in each. Locking pads set in the wall in between each door gave access.

Black opened the door they had stopped in front of by placing his palm against the pad. A strip of blue light passed up then down as it scanned the palm print and the door unlocked.

"In you go," Black said as he pushed the door wide open.

Pryde stepped inside after Fields then turned around to face the door, Nice room, we'll take it. What time is dinner served?" he said.

Black smiled, "Like I said, cute couple. Don't get too comfortable though, you won't be staying long," he said then closed the door and locked it.

"Well, at least they didn't kill us," Fields observed.

"Not yet," Pryde said.

CDF HQ, Terra II

General Aslam was a thirty-year veteran of the CDF and in command of operations in this sector. He was just short of six feet tall and still in good shape for his advanced years.

Resplendent in his uniform he contacted the Council HQ to speak with President Harada through an encrypted comm channel.

"Mister President, we have just learned of the location of ICE. I have sent a starship to deal with the problem sir and will keep you updated on our progress," he said.

"I have recently been informed of the location by C of the Ministry. Do you think we can clear this up before the final deadline?" Harada asked.

"We're working toward that end sir. Does this mean the Ministry has someone in or near the base sir?"

"I'm afraid I can't answer that question General, all I can say is that you as well as anyone know the risks involved in this line of work and sometimes difficult decisions have to be made. Do what you must to bring this to an end."

"Copy that Mister President and I will keep you informed as soon as I have any news."

"Please do General. All our hopes go with your men, and we're all hoping for a speedy end to all of this," the President said then ended the contact.

As he sat there thinking about what his men were about to face off against, and the fact that a friendly operative could be in the crosshairs, he said to himself, "As do we all, as do we all."

Chapter 17

Secret ICE HQ

"Did you notice those missiles they have where we were brought in here?" Fields asked.

"Of course, they are a bit hard to miss," Pryde answered.

With a nod Fields admitted, "Okay, I know it was a bit of a dumb question."

"Then why ask it?" Pryde said, not looking at her. He was busy scanning the room for anything they could use to escape, any gaps or loose sections of wall or even something they could loosen to get out of the room. So far though he had come up with nothing useful.

"Found a way out of here yet?" she asked.

"You're not that dumb then," he said.

"Is that a 'yes' or a 'no' then?"

"It's 'not yet' but I'm working on a plan."

"Then you better work fast. If your sit-rep got through and the CDF are sending troops, they won't be coming on a rescue mission. They'll be coming to bomb the crap out of this place and I don't know about you, but I'd rather not be here when that happens."

"You have a point. In that case, let's expedite matters, shall we?" he replied.

From the buckle of his belt, he took out a sliver of thread hidden inside the stitching.

"What's that?" Fields asked, leaning forward a little to get a better look.

"Thermex thread," he replied as he began to place strips of the hair thin thread on the hinges of the door. "Cover your eyes," he warned as he placed an arm over his own after turning his back on the door. On his PIN he activated the thread which began burning with an intense bright white-hot heat right through the hinges holding the door in place.

The thread burned fast and without any sound and, once it was done, the hinges were melted away completely. The light instantly faded, returning the room to its former dull state.

Looking at Fields he asked, "Are you ready?" which she answered simply with a nod.

Pryde kicked the door and it fell outwards from the cell, narrowly missing the guard placed outside. Moving before he had time to react, Pryde was on the guard, rendering him unconscious from a blow to the face. In seconds he had disarmed the unconscious man and was distributing his armament between himself and his partner.

They were free, which was just the first step. The rest would be much more difficult.

An alarm sounded the instant the door to the cell was opened. The computer installed in the base that oversaw all the security noticed the moment the door was opened by an unauthorised method.

Jericho was in the Command-and-Control room so he was alerted the moment the alarm sounded. It took but a glance at the security screen to see where the breach occurred.

Black was at his side seeing the same thing. "Find them, and kill them," he said to his First Officer.

Black moved off to carry out his orders. He contacted the guards through the closed circuit comm channel they used saying, "Spread out, the intruders are somewhere loose in the base. I want them found and killed on sight. Check every level, leave nothing to chance—go."

Jericho heard what had been said and looked at Black, who saw the fury behind his eyes.

"They won't last long sir," he said.

Once Pryde and Fields were out of the cell they turned and ran deeper into the base.

"We need to find somewhere deep inside this place where we can contact my boss," Pryde said.

The cave tunnels went deep into the hills above them. Twisting and turning, the tunnels formed a maze. The same reinforcement that shored up the main cavern was evident in the tunnels here as well.

A row of doors lined one tunnel as they ran past, all with the same locking panels at the side of each door. The tunnel was devoid of life though, and there were no signs of any of the guards here.

A grille covering ventilation shafts that ran through the caves to the power plant helped to purify the air inside the base and Pryde noticed one above the door of one of the rooms.

"Are you considering climbing through those things?" Fields asked as she saw where he was looking.

"It might be our only option," Pryde replied as he looked around. It wouldn't be long before the troops arrived and they had to try and prevent these terrorists from firing off any more of these missiles. They couldn't do that if they were in the spotlight.

"What about that there?" she suggested as she pointed to another door.

Pryde looked where she was pointing and walked over to it. It opened and he peered through the gap.

"This could work, it leads down to a lower level," he said.

"Let's go take a look, we might find something we can use," she said.

Holding the ARX F5 assault rifle up at his shoulder, Pryde led the way into the stairwell. They went down to the next level and cracked the door open to look through. It was another large room, with a high roof supported by concrete support columns that ran across the ceiling. On the floor were large vehicles built for construction work, earth movers and diggers.

Seeing no one around, Pryde opened the door wider and entered the area. Fields followed, holding the Heckler and Koch VPX pistol in front of her in the standard grip in line with her shoulder to sight down the length of the gun.

"This must be what they used to dig this place out from the natural caves," she said as she looked around. Her eyes went wide as she couldn't help but marvel at the engineering feat that produced these stunning results.

Pryde moved ahead not seeming to notice much about the place, but in fact noticing everything and storing it all up in a memory vault for later use.

"Let's see what else there is down here and where it leads to," he said, walking past the mechanical behemoths without a second glance.

Around the room were other doors that led off to who knew where and Pryde knew they were in a vulnerable position here, out in the open.

"Come on, we need to get out of here," he said just as his concerns proved to be true when a door to their left opened and several armed men came out. They saw the two of them and, without warning, opened fire on them.

Chapter 18

Pryde moved the instant he saw the wide staring look of fear and anger in the eyes of the men. He knew before they even acted that they weren't here to capture but to kill.

Ducking to his right, he ran between the two nearest diggers. Fields followed suit, narrowly evading getting shot as a hail of bullets slammed into the huge machines.

"How the hell did you know that was going to happen?" she asked breathlessly as adrenaline pumped through her system.

"The moment that alarm sounded I knew they would send out troops to kill us," he replied as he moved behind their cover.

"Why not try to recapture us?" she asked as she followed him, keeping close.

"He learned everything he needed from us in our first conversation. He kept us around to play with at some later date. He had no intention of keeping us alive, and our escape just moved up his timeline for us."

"Makes sense, I suppose. Okay, so what's your plan for getting us out of this?"

"Simple, we kill them before they kill us."

Black led one team on the same floor as the cells were located, searching for any sign of the missing intruders.

The comm link he shared with all the troops inside the base alerted him to the action taking place on the floor below.

"Follow me," he said to his team, then through the comm link said, "All troops converge on level Three."

Bullets struck the massive digger, ricocheting off the metal framework.

Pryde and Fields cowered behind, keeping their heads down to prevent themselves getting hit by a stray bullet.

"How's your plan going so far?" Fields asked through gritted teeth as anger flared in her.

"I've got them exactly where I want them," he replied.

The men who had burst through the door to this floor had remained in one group. Pryde signalled for Fields to go one way and he would go the opposite direction. As they came to the edge of the machine, they had a better view of the group attacking them. Pryde saw all the group's focus on the spot where the two of them had disappeared. If they moved fast, they could catch them off guard.

Pryde moved first, Fields waited for his signal. He fired a fast double tap at the lead man, dropping him, then moved on to those around him. Fields fired from her position, killing another member of the team.

Confusion ravaged the teams' confidence, replacing it with fear as they were picked off with nowhere to hide.

Pryde finished off the last attacker and emerged from his cover.

"Come on we have to move fast, there will be more coming," he said.

Looking around at all the options, Fields asked, "Which way? There's so many directions they can come at us."

Pryde turned his attention to other areas of the room. At the far end he noticed a large sliding door.

"Over there," he said, indicating what he'd spotted, "that must be how these diggers and earth movers were brought in here," he added.

Fields looked at him with a frown, "You're not suggesting we ride one of these monsters out of here are you?"

Pryde's expression never altered.

"You are suggesting that, holy fuck!" she said.

"Get aboard that one, it's nearest to the exit," he said and he ran on ahead.

The vehicle was massive at least, thirty feet high at the tallest point, which was the pilot's cab. To reach it the pilot had to climb several steps placed just aft of the front wheel arch. Pryde climbed up first, followed by Fields. He opened the door and pulled himself inside just as they both heard another door open behind them.

Gunfire made them look behind just as bullets struck near the door of the cab.

"Holy crap!" Fields shouted as Pryde pulled her through the door into the cab.

He had the engine started and accessed the remote control that operated the massive doors in a second or two. More bullets hit the vehicle as the new team rushed them, firing as they came. The sound of bullets striking the vehicle sounded like a swarm of angry bees attacking them as they sat in the cabin, protected.

The gigantic doors at the far end separated in the middle and he moved the vehicle forward into the next room. Slowly they gathered momentum, picking up speed, but Pryde knew they were never going to win any races in this thing. Having a top speed of around six miles per hour didn't lend itself to any kind of a sprint.

The dashboard in front of him showed there might be a way of delaying, or, at the very least, discouraging those chasing them.

The first men to reach the side of the vehicle were killed by Fields, who shot them from her vantage point up above. Having rolled the side window down, she had time to take careful aim at them before firing.

"I'm running out of ammo—whatever you're planning, better make it quick," she said over her shoulder.

The digger was fitted with a rotating tool at the front and thermal lances down each side so that the vehicle could bore into the ground. Pryde activated the thermal lances and had them target the group attempting to get aboard by running up alongside.

The lances projected a heat beam of intense white-hot plasma that melted bedrock and enabled the vehicle to form a tunnel when boring into the ground.

The heat beams cut through the first three men who tried to climb on board before they even got close. They were sliced through the middle with unerring accuracy. They died screaming from the shock and pain of literally being cut in half.

"That'll work," she said as she saw the effect that much direct heat had on human flesh and bone.

Glancing through the rear window to the cab she could see what was happening behind them.

"They stopped following," she said.

Pryde noticed a hint of worry in her voice. "That's good, right?" he said, keeping his attention on getting the digger through the doors—their pace, agonizingly slow, was getting them nearer every second.

"Not really," she admitted, adding, "not when they have a rocket launcher."

"Shit!" he exclaimed, an uncharacteristic slip of his emotion barrier. Things were indeed getting interesting.

"This thing is tough, reinforced, built for hard work and for going places other machines cannot," he said, not sure if he was trying to reassure his partner or himself.

"Can it withstand a direct hit from a rocket though?" she said.

"I guess we'll find out pretty soon," he said as a glance in the rear-view mirror showed him their time had run out as a rocket streaked toward them.

Chapter 19

The CDF starship Devlin dropped out of hyperspace near the planet and took up station ready to deploy the troops.

On the bridge Captain Agatha Maynard sat in her command chair, staring at the main viewer at the planet below them. Her hazel eyes narrowed as she took in every detail displayed at the side of the screen as sensors swept the coordinates they had been given for the location of the ICE base.

"According to sensors, sir, the base must be deep underground on at least three levels," said Commander Abraham Rahim, her First Officer.

"Okay, let's hail them and let them know of our presence here," she said.

"Channel open, sir," said ops.

"This is Captain Agatha Maynard of the Combined Defence Force starship Devlin. If you do not surrender the missiles and yourselves, I will be forced to open fire on your location," she said as she relaxed into her chair. She knew it would be best to appear confident when dealing with this sort of situation.

"They're replying sir," ops said.

"On screen," Maynard said.

The forward viewer's image changed from the planet below to that of a large room with Jericho standing centre stage. In the background could be seen, quite clearly, the stack of stolen missiles. When Jericho spoke his voice was calm, relaxed, and confident.

"Captain Maynard, what a lovely surprise. It's good to see that the CDF is taking this threat seriously. Now we both know that you won't open fire first for fear of retaliation. These missiles you see behind me are not all of them. I have one targeted at a civilian site, ready to be let loose, and while I won't bore you with the details, just be sure that millions will die. I'm sure you've been made aware of the devastating effects these things have when they detonate, so I'm pretty sure you won't want that on your conscience," he said.

"Okay so you tell me what you expect to get from this. You know I can't just turn around and leave," Maynard said, stalling for time.

"I suppose not, the CDF will not want to lose face here," he said, glancing down as if trying to come up with a compromise, then returning his eyes to hers, said, "but the thing is, I don't give a fuck about any of that. You have my demands; I expect them to be met. It's as simple as that."

"Okay, let's just say for a second that they give you your money. What happens then? You know I'm not going anywhere."

"Oh, I'm pretty damn sure I can incentivise you to leave."

Maynard's eyes opened wide at the audacity, "Are you threatening me?" she asked, keeping her voice under control despite her bewilderment at his claim.

"I never make threats my dear; it's a statement of fact, nothing more."

"At least we have that in common," she said. She turned her head to speak to her First Officer, ensuring her words would be heard by the man on the viewer, "Target that base with the ship's main weapon."

"Copy that sir," he said from out of sight of the viewer. Maynard turned to face the viewer once more, her lips pressed together in determination, "I don't make threats either. Surrender now or face the consequences, you have ten seconds to comply," she demanded.

She signalled for the viewer to be cut off with a thumb drawn across her throat, a sign everyone understood.

"Main gun targeted sir," the weapons controller said.

"Fire on my mark," Maynard said, watching the time count down.

Tension on the bridge spiked at the potential of hostilities beginning. It had been a while since they had experienced actual combat. Drills gave them something, but it was nothing like the horror of the real thing and Maynard hoped those down on the planet had the same feeling as she did about it and would see sense. She hoped they didn't want to engage in battle either, but she was about to be proven wrong on so many levels.

Jericho saw the communication go offline and knew what the play was.

He could see behind the confident glow in the eyes of the captain that there was a hint of fear there. She didn't really want to go to battle with them, and she was hoping he would back down due to the overwhelming firepower the starship had over them, or so she thought.

He had taken every precaution when building this base. He knew that at some point there was every possibility he would have to defend it, so he made sure it was well armed.

"Okay people, let's show these idiots we're not to be fucked with. Target that ship with the plasma railgun and open fire," he said.

Jericho quickly went to the War Room, which was just off the main section where he had taken the call from the Devlin. He had wanted them to see he had the missiles present to give credence to his claims. The War Room was where all defences for the base would be controlled from.

A bank of monitors took up one complete wall, showing all the defences from the massive plasma railgun to the close quarter defence gatling guns. On the main screen they saw the ground above them open up and the railgun appear.

The instant it appeared the plasma railgun fired, sending a plasma round up through the atmosphere aimed directly at the starship in geo-synchronous orbit above their position.

The plasma round travelled at Mach 9, giving the starship no time to evade what was coming their way.

"Incoming!" shouted ops as the ship's sensors picked up the plasma round aimed right at them.

"Shields!" shouted Maynard as she gripped the arms of her command chair.

It was clear for all to see on the forward viewer as the plasma round grew closer.

"Where the fuck did they get a plasma railgun from?" she said and braced herself for the impact. Chiding herself for not taking this threat seriously enough and for severely underestimating the enemy, she vowed to not make that mistake again, if they survived the next few minutes that was.

Luckily the shields were erected in time to protect the ship. The plasma round smashed into the electromagnetic barrier where most of the energy was repulsed and what couldn't be repulsed was absorbed.

The impact pushed the ship back several hundred feet and it took the helm a few moments to regain control, a few moments when they were open to further attack.

Maynard felt her body pressed against the arm of her command chair as the entire ship was sent spinning. Her breath came in short gasps as she fought to control her fear. Through gritted teeth, she snarled, "Helm, get us back under control. Weapons, target that base and open fire."

The officers complied with their orders and in seconds they were able to get the ship back on an even keel and return fire with their own plasma railgun.

"Let them have another round, don't give them a chance to recover," she shouted. Anger distorted her features as a fury fuelled by the adrenaline coursing through her took hold. As she watched the plasma rounds fired at their target on the viewer, she regained some of her composure and her experience came into play.

"Tell the Captain his Marines have clearance to deploy," she said, "let him know we'll keep them off their backs for as long as we can," she added.

Chapter 20

Inside the War Room Jericho watched as the starship retaliated by firing its own plasma railgun.

The plasma rounds were large and on target, not to mention deadly. When they hit the ground above the energy was transferred directly into the ground. It destroyed the top layer of soil and whatever was covering the base in twin explosions from both rounds. Soil and debris were sent flying high into the air as the base's cover was chipped away. Soon Jericho knew that his base would be uncovered and vulnerable to attack.

On the screens showing the outside world he saw the ships leaving the starship heading right for them.

"Here come the troops, typical playbook," he said, "I could've written this attack myself."

There were a few of his men with him in the War Room while the rest hunted down the two intruders with Black. To those who remained he said, "Deploy the Close Quarter

Gatling guns. When those landing craft get near us, shoot them down. Keep targeting the ship with the Plasma railgun and get ready to repel boarders."

After issuing his orders he left the room to allow them to carry them out.

Guarding the missiles were two men looking around staring at the roof. Dirt and rubble had dropped down from the roof after each plasma railgun round had hit, shaking the room to its foundations. Their eyes were still wide as he walked over to them. He was going to give them something to do to take their minds off their fears.

"You two load the missiles into the Raptor—we're leaving as soon as you've got them on board," he told them. This brought a smile to their faces at the prospect of escaping this battle.

"Copy that sir," they both said, and they got to work immediately.

As the two men began loading the missiles, Jericho checked in with Black through their comm channel.

"Have you finished them off yet?" he said.

"We have them cornered sir, it's just a matter of time now," Black replied.

"Hurry up and get it done, we're leaving with the missiles. There is a CDF starship in orbit just chomping at the bit to pound us into dust. It's looking like they're not going to play ball over this so it's time to make them see the error of their ways. Kill those two bastards, then get back here pronto."

"Copy that sir," Black said.

Jericho returned his attention to the Raptor being loaded with the missiles. Everything there was going as planned, which just left one last thing to do before he vacated this base.

Leaving the men to finish, he left the chamber to complete his last task before he could say goodbye to this base.

The digger was lifted off its wheels when the rocket struck the rear section, exploding in a bright powerful fireball that lit up the entire room.

Pryde and Fields were thrown forward against the windscreen as the back of the vehicle was thrown several feet in the air. As it slammed back down on the ground, they bounced around in the pilot's cabin, falling into the footwell.

"Holy shit!" Fields screamed, gritting her teeth in fear. Sweat broke out along her forehead as adrenaline flooded her system once more.

"There's your answer, but I doubt we can survive another blast like that one," Pryde said. He saw through the rear-view mirror the damage done to the back of the digger. The entire rear quarter was bent and buckled out of shape and from his seat he could tell that a large portion of it had been destroyed —he could see pieces of twisted metal strewn over the ground behind them.

The engine was still running but the rear wheels had been bent, and he suspected the axles they rode on had been so bent they would never work. The vehicle had a severe lilt to one side and to the rear.

"We'd better get the fuck out of here then," she said.

She pushed the door open and peered out to see where the gunmen were. Having seen no sign of them, she climbed down from the cab. Pryde followed when he saw she had made it safely to the ground.

Tossing the ARX F5 down to her, she covered him as he too climbed down.

"Let's go," he said, retrieving his assault rifle and covering their rear as Fields went on before them toward the front of the vehicle.

When they reached the front of the digger Pryde saw their chance.

"Run for the door, I'll cover your back," he said and pulled the charging lever back to inject a round into the breach.

He stepped out and targeted the first man he saw and fired. His first salvo caught the man high on the chest, knocking him back off his feet. The second three shot burst blew the back of another man's head out while the rest ran for cover.

He was aware that Fields had taken off at a sprint the moment he began shooting and, seeing their attackers dive for cover, he took off after her.

Reaching the large doors a few steps behind Fields, he threw himself flat against the doors to slow his breathing down. No gunfire followed them, which was worrying.

What were they up to?

Peering around the edge of the door, he saw what was left of the group who attacked them retreating the way they had come.

"What the fuck?" Fields muttered as she too saw them disappear. "What the hell are they up to?" she asked.

"Whatever it is, it can't be good for us," Pryde said.

Chapter 21

J ericho found what he was looking for and quickly got to work.

He had gone to the lowest level in the base where the fusion generator was kept. This powered all the requirements the base had, including the automated weapons, life support and lighting. After working for several minutes at the control board inputting a new set of demands, he left for the main chamber.

Behind him the fusion generator would follow the new instructions and begin a series of protocols that would send it into a catastrophic overload that would result in its self-destruction and inevitable explosion that would not only destroy this entire base but would take out most of the landscape where it was located to within a two-mile radius.

No alarm would sound, no warning given, and they had ten minutes to evacuate and get clear or die in the resulting explosion. This would cause enough confusion for the CDF forces to deal with and give him and his men the cover they needed to make their escape with the missiles. By the time the wreckage had been sifted through and they had learned the truth of what had happened, Jericho and the missiles would be far enough away, planning their next step.

This had all been meticulously planned months ahead, and so far, everything was going according to plan.

Captain Tobias Greene felt the familiar rush of adrenaline that came from the thought of going into battle hit his system like a round from a railgun.

The shuttle he and his men were in came in to land just beyond the location of the enemy base. There would be four more shuttles, each carrying ten men like his had, giving them fifty troops on the ground ready to kick the enemy's ass.

He was young for a Captain, still in his early twenties, but his exemplary career had given him the right qualifications to earn the recent promotion. This would be his first away mission in command of a full team.

As he and the platoon formed up the last shuttle arrived with all the extra firepower they would need for their mission.

Three portable rocket launchers were brought out and set up. All aimed at the area where the plasma railgun had fired upon. The ground was battered with massive holes in the side of the hill displaying some of the base within.

"Target that base," Greene said.

Two Marines to each rocket launcher operated the controls and targeted the area they were about to open fire on.

"Weapons are hot and on target," they announced.

Pryde and Fields both reached the doors at the same time and investigated the room beyond.

"Where did they all go?" she said.

Pryde said, "But why did they disappear like that? In time we would've run out of ammo and they would've overrun us. Why did they turn tail and run?"

"Let's go find out," she said.

They set off across the floor back the way they had come.

"What could possibly have gotten them to pull out like that?" Fields said. There was no one in sight. The entire area had been evacuated.

Pryde ran through all the scenarios he could think of in his mind. The only one that made sense was the threat of something happening to the base. True, there was a troop of Marines coming soon and a starship had attacked from orbit, but somehow he thought it must be something larger, more imminent than that. The only other thing that came to mind was if the base was in danger of destruction.

"They've set this base to self-destruct to cover their tracks. They're planning to escape with the missiles during all the confusion the explosion will cause," he said as it all finally made sense to him.

"Are you sure?"

"No, but it's the only thing that makes sense."

"Then we better get the hell outta here. We can't let them win; we have to stop them."

"I agree," he said, then the two of them ran back thee way they had come.

The rocket launchers opened fire at the base, targeting the defences first. The plasma railgun had been destroyed by the starship, which just left the close quarter gatling guns that had appeared to protect the base against the Marines, who were ready to invade.

The rockets blew apart the gun emplacements, leaving the base undefended. When the smoke had cleared from the multiple explosions, Green gave the command to move forward.

Chapter 22

Jericho returned to the main room where, by this time, the Raptor had been loaded with the missiles.

"Time to go guys," he said, and the men climbed aboard the new ship.

He had put the base's defences on automatic so it would appear the base was still occupied when the Marines began to break through and invade this area. All was in place for his escape.

As he sat in the pilot's seat, he called his First Officer.

"Black, where are you? It's time to go," he said, and then what was left of them came around a corner running toward the Raptor.

They quickly boarded the futuristic aircraft and the doors were secured. Jericho lifted the craft off using vertical thrusters only. The roof above them had been compromised and, for his scheme to succeed, he would need another exit. Having planned ahead, Jericho had an emergency exit already made, but it would be tight as it was nothing more than one of the caves that was part of this whole labyrinthine system, one that led away from the main area he had made the base for ICE. Hoping it hadn't been compromised in the attack from above, he pointed the nose of the Raptor in that direction.

Gripping the controls tightly, he set the aft thrusters to one third and set off.

Pryde and Fields made their way back to the main area where they had first entered the base. No one had hindered their feverish dash to escape the imminent destruction of this entire area.

To facilitate this, Pryde guessed the power needed would be enormous and probably whatever generator was used to power this base was set to cascade into critical overload. If that was the case, then this entire hillside and an area covering at least a few miles would be devastated.

There was no way of knowing how much time they had left and the only thing left to do was inform the Marines to back off and for them to get the hell away.

When they reached the area, they found it deserted. No sign of the missiles nor the Raptor was to be seen anywhere. That was how they had escaped, by loading the Raptor up and using it to make their escape. But which way had they gone? They certainly didn't go through the roof hatch—it had been destroyed.

"Where the fuck are they?" Fields asked, voicing the question racing through Pryde's own mind.

Looking around at all the tunnels and doors leading off from this space, he said, "There must be another way out of here, there has to be. He would've planned this and had an escape route already planned out, but where?"

"My guess is wherever the open doors lead to, that's the direction they would've gone."

What she said made sense. They wouldn't have had time to close any hatches or doors after they left so it made sense that any open doors were the way they had gone. They needed a way out and, after scanning where they were, he thought he had an idea.

"Over here, follow me," he said as he ran across the floor to a small shuttle left behind.

In seconds they had climbed aboard and got the engines started. Pryde activated the ship's AI and gave it instructions to find a route out of the base and a map appeared on the Heads Up Display in front of his eyes. On the map a route through the tunnels was clearly marked in red.

"Okay, there we have it, our way out of here," he said and the two of them strapped themselves in.

Setting the nav-comp to follow the route laid out on the HUD, he left it to the AI to fly them out of there.

The thrusters lifted them off the ground and then propelled them into the first of a series of tunnels that would take them away from the base.

Pryde used the comms in the shuttle to contact the starship in orbit.

"To the captain of the CDF starship above this planet, I have vital information about the base you are about to attack on the surface below. It is rigged to explode so if you have men ready to breach, I would suggest you pull them back immediately," he said urgently but as clearly and concisely as he could.

"How do I know you are not one of the terrorists?" the captain replied.

"Get in touch with C at MI7, he'll verify who I am, now move your men. There's no telling how long before this place goes up and we'll need you to be ready to search for the Raptor F95 leaving here with the missiles."

"Thank you for your input. I'll certainly verify it, now get off this channel."

"Do you think he'll listen to you?" Fields said.

"He has two choices."

"Is that the best you can do? If those Marines breach the base, they'll all get killed when it detonates. Don't you think we should try a bit harder to convince them?" she asked. She was getting fed up with his seeming indifference.

"Knock yourself out," he said. His focus was on the HUD and if the AI was steering faithfully and following the route laid out. He didn't have time to waste on the Marines; he had to catch the escaping men and rescue the missiles.

"You really are a heartless bastard," she said, turning away from him.

Pryde honestly had no idea what she meant—when he dialled down his empathy and cut himself off from his emotions, he lost all ties with humanity.

On the HUD the AI showed a catastrophic build up in the fusion generator in the lowest level of the cave system. What he saw actually broke through his barriers. The countdown was down to five minutes.

"We may not make it," he said, which drew her eyes to the HUD.

She remained quiet; there wasn't an awful lot she could say but silently she said a prayer for them to reach safety.

Contacting the starship again, he said, "Captain, the fusion generator in the caves is set for a catastrophic overload. It's going to blow in less than five minutes, get your men to safety, please."

Chapter 23

Captain Maynard had to make a decision and fast. If the voice was being truthful with their warning, then the Marines she had ferried here were in danger. If not and she acted accordingly, then she would be responsible for the target getting away with the missiles.

Either way it seemed that her mission here was doomed to failure one way or the other. She chose the option where her men would be safe.

"Contact the Marines and order them to retreat. I want them to return here now. Tell them the base is about to blow, that should spur the ground pounders along a bit," she said.

"Copy that sir," ops replied.

"I want all sensors looking for that stolen ship. We know what her signature is, I don't want it getting away, is that clear?" she said, her jaw set firm in determination.

A thought occurred to her, "Scan the base for any build up of energy, if that fusion reactor is set to blow, there should be at least an increase in energy output as it builds up," she said.

Captain Greene and his men were about to breach the base when the call to pull back reached him.

Holding up a fist halted his men on the spot. He listened to all the information given to him. His eyes went wide from the shock as he looked around at his men.

"Pull back to the shuttles, now. This place is rigged to blow," he screamed at his men waving frantically for them to move. Urging them back to their transports, he waited behind to ensure they all got on board the shuttles before him. When he was certain no one had been left behind, he got on board the last shuttle and gave the order for it to take off.

Something had gone badly wrong here and he was just glad they had been warned of it in time.

Pryde watched through the front viewport of the shuttle as the walls of the tunnel flashed past them. The AI controlling the shuttle had chosen the top speed that was safe to navigate through the many twisting tunnels to get free before the base exploded.

"That was close," Fields commented as they nearly clipped a wall as they took a bend into another tunnel.

Pryde was quiet seeing there was no need to say anything. He was not in control of anything that was happening so he figured commenting was a waste of energy, another sign of how detached he was from his humanity.

Something Fields had said resonated with him though, as vague as it was now in his memory, he knew, in certain respects, she was right. She had said he was a cold-hearted bastard. It was a comment made purely to elicit a reaction, made all the more factual for her as he ignored it. It was proof that, in her eyes, she was right. Fact was she couldn't be farther from the truth. He chose to be this way so he could perform his job more efficiently. It wasn't that he couldn't feel any emotions, but that he chose not to feel them. Not many people had this ability and many misconstrued it as proof that he was a psychopath, or sociopath as the two were quite often confused as being the same.

That was a conversation for another time though. Right now, he had to concentrate on finding the Raptor with the missiles on board.

"Time is running out," Fields commented after a glance at the HUD showed the timer counting down to zero.

"Hold on tight, this last bit could get a bit rocky," Pryde said as he saw the route on the map. Sure enough, the shuttle ducked beneath an outcropping as large as a truck, almost taking the top off the shuttle as it barely scraped through, then had to rise above a solid wall that appeared from nowhere. The two of them were pushed back in their seats from the 'g' forces exerted on them from the sudden manoeuvre. As they reached the opening above them, they flew straight ahead, then turned to their right to finally emerge into the open.

"We made it," Fields said.

"Not yet," Pryde replied, flattening her new found relief in an instant.

As the shuttle went into a flat out horizontal sprint, keeping low above ground, they both stared at the timer which had almost reached its final destination of zero.

When it came, the explosion startled them even though they knew it was coming.

The intensity of it was breathtaking in its purity. The entire top of the hill the base was located beneath was thrown high into the air in a cascading eruption of immense force. Huge chunks of the hillside the size of houses were thrown hundreds of feet into the air where they broke up into smaller pieces as they fell to the ground. A bright flaming cloud of destruction followed from the bowels of the base, throwing up debris from within.

A shockwave of devastating proportions spread out, chasing the smaller shuttle in an attempt to destroy them as it destroyed everything in its path.

Through gritted teeth Pryde urged the craft on with words of encouragement, "Come on you bastard, move your arse."

The shuttle was pushing its engine beyond maximum as if it had heard him and was desperate to comply.

As they watched the shockwave gain on them through the rear viewpoint displayed on the viewscreen, Fields closed her eyes, unwilling to see her own death creep up on her, while Pryde stared it in the face. If it was to happen, he would see it coming and face whatever form it took.

Slowly the shockwave seemed to lose ground as the gap between them began to widen.

"We did it, we outran it," he said, which brought a sigh of immense relief from his partner.

The shuttle eased off on the acceleration and began to slow, then finally came in to land at an open space.

"I'm not, you know," he said softly.

"Not what?" she replied. The way her brow creased was testament to how confused she was by this sudden change in him.

"A cold-hearted bastard."

"Really?" she said.

"Really. I have the ability to close off sections of my emotions when necessary so I can perform more efficiently. I feel as deeply about things as anyone, but when I'm working, I choose not to allow those feelings to affect my performance. However that sounds, it doesn't make me a cold-hearted bastard. It just means I will feel everything you feel now, but at a time when the danger has passed and people are safe."

Fields' eyes narrowed as she listened to him. She had a different appreciation of him after hearing his explanation, especially as he had made the effort to explain. Clearly her comment had touched a nerve.

"And you do this by choice?" she asked, still not fully understanding the method or the reasoning behind it.

"Yes."

"Does feeling disconnected from the rest of humanity really help you manage more efficiently?"

"Without the worry or concern for consequences I am able to make decisions faster by taking out the human element.

Take a hostage situation for example. If I am faced with a terrorist holding a hostage in front as a shield, I won't hesitate to take the shot if I have it. My reactions won't be hindered by doubt in my ability, I won't have to worry that I might hit the hostage if I take the shot, I'll simply act without self-doubt or without remorse. Those few seconds wasted by all of that save lives."

"Have you ever been in that kind of situation?"

"Yes."

"Did it always play out like you described?"

"No."

"So, you're not infallible then."

"No one is, we're all human. I've always known I was different; I could compartmentalise my feelings better than most and the more I practised the better I got. When I first came to this line of work, I kept my ability under wraps for the most part. The first time I was met with the situation I described I allowed my emotions to creep under my barrier and I hesitated. I was met with a feeling of self-doubt, only for a brief moment, but it was enough for the hostage to act. He saw my hesitation and killed the hostage in order to make me vulnerable, hoping that he could shoot me in that instant of remorse. I was faster than him though, but barely. We both fired, I killed him, he wounded me. I spent a month in rehab after a week in hospital. That was the last time I ever allowed my emotions to affect my work," he explained.

"You do realise that while you were explaining all this to me, the perp has gotten clean away," Fields said.

"Not really, I programmed the AI to recognise the Raptor's engine signature. It tracked it but it was lost when it went into hyperspace. You see, having control of my emotions like that helps me to multitask much easier," he said with a hint of a smile.

"Don't let it go to your head Mister, it's big enough already," she replied, hiding her smile as she looked the other way.

"Come on, this is far from over. We have work to do to stop them from deploying those missiles," he said.

Chapter 24

Captain Greene returned to the Devlin and went straight to the bridge, where Captain Maynard was waiting for his report.

"What happened down there, Captain?" he ranted as he stormed through the doors.

"We had information that proved to be accurate so I decided to follow it and pull you out before you were all killed," she replied.

That rocked the young captain back on his heels. "We saw the explosion as we were leaving the atmosphere but I never connected it to our away mission," he said.

"That explosion was the base being destroyed. The blast radius was over a mile wide. If you had remained down there a few minutes longer you would have been caught up in it."

Greene nodded his head and a little shamefacedly said, "In that case then, sir, we owe you our lives."

"Don't thank me, thank the man who gave us the heads up."

"I will, where is he?"

"I'm afraid he's not here. We have no idea who he is or where he is now. He disappeared after giving us the information. We noticed a shuttle leaving the base somewhere, we suppose was at the very edge of the base. He must have escaped through another exit someplace, possibly the same way that the leader of that group did. We lost sight of it when it entered hyperspace."

"Good Samaritan, 'eh?"

"It certainly seems that way. More likely an operative who wants to remain anonymous though."

"That makes sense. What's our next play then sir?"

"I'm awaiting orders from Fleet Command. If the base has been destroyed, they'll probably want us to investigate the site."

"Me and my Marines can secure it if you need us to."

"That would be my guess, Captain. I would suggest you go take some time with your men while you can. I'll give a sit-rep to Fleet and see what they say. I'll let you know what they decide as soon as I get word."

"Copy that sir," Greene said and left the bridge.

Pryde said, "Okay ship, take us to Terra II."

The shuttle took off and went up into the air.

Pretty soon they were through the upper atmosphere and entering a hyperspace window heading back to Terra II.

"I'm sure your bosses will want an update on this so I'll drop you off at the CIA HQ on Terra II; that's where you're based, I presume," Pryde said as the darkness of hyperspace surrounded them.

"It'll do, for now," Fields replied.

"This is unusual. We are connected by our profession and yet we can't talk freely because of it," he observed.

"We won't always be on the clock though," she said.

"Are you suggesting we get together once this is over?"

"Why not?"

He thought about that for a second. His emotion barrier was still in place so he couldn't understand why she would even think of making a suggestion like that. He also recognised that she was reaching out to him to connect on a more personal level; having shared experiences would help form a bond between them, however short their connection lasted.

"Let's get this finished first, then maybe we can make plans. Work comes first," he said finally.

"I'll drink to that," she agreed and then they were through the hyperspace window close to Terra II.

* * *

Deep Space, near the Natara Nebula

The Natara Nebula was a cloud of ionised gases that stretched for several thousand kilometres. Smaller than some nebulae, this one was ideal for Jericho. It was small enough to not be seen from any nearby planet by the naked eye and large enough to hide using the gases that formed it to refract any sensor signals.

As Jericho steered the Raptor closer to the cloud, he was hailed.

"Glad to see you're okay boss," the voice said, coming through the speakers as clear as if the person talking was standing next to him.

"Is everything ready?" Jericho replied, ignoring any pleasantries. He was still pissed that he'd had to give up his headquarters so soon. He'd expected to have to fight at some point but they had caught up to him earlier than expected. It seemed that they were going to be unwilling to pay his ransom after all so more encouragement was obviously required.

"Everything is in place sir; we are good to go."

The hail had come from the flagship of his organisation, the Phobos, a gigantic battle cruiser that had been decommissioned and taken over by ICE, then refit to Jericho's specifications.

Over fifteen hundred metres long, it had twenty-seven decks with a cargo area spacious enough to house over fifty small one man fighter craft. It had plasma railguns, fore and aft, with missile tubes also fore and aft. For close quarter protection, Gatling guns were placed down each side of the battleship.

As Jericho closed on his flagship it emerged from the cloud and he smiled as he always did when he saw this magnificent beast.

"Permission to come aboard?" he said.

"Permission granted," the voice said, and Jericho allowed the automatic pilot to take the minute craft by comparison into one of the docking bays amidships of the Phobos.

Chapter 25

MI7 SecOps HQ

Pryde and Fields landed at the spaceport and made their way to the HQ.

C was in the Situation Room when he reported in.

"I have to apologise sir. I lost the Raptor with the missiles," he said as he walked up to him. He was confident as he approached simply because his barrier was still up.

C turned around to look at him and his eyes fell upon Fields.

"Agent Fields, welcome to our little boathouse," he said.

"Thank you, sir, I'm so pleased to be here," she replied.

Pryde looked from C to Fields with his eyes narrowing in confusion at their byplay.

"Is there any news on the Raptor, sir?" he asked, trying to bring the conversation back on topic.

"We were able to obtain visuals from your sensor logs from the AI on your shuttle and ran facial recognition on the leader. We now finally have a name. Nathan Jericho."

"What do we know about him?" Pryde asked.

"He was a member of the Special Forces, Recon Rangers for several years, but when he left he went off the grid."

"Why did he leave?"

"He voiced several unpopular opinions at the latter stages of his career, mainly about him being passed over for promotion and the way the Rangers were being used, and so it was decided that he would resign his commission, with his career intact, before he was forced to retire."

"And now what, he's running his own paramilitary unit for hire?" Fields asked.

"It seems that way, yes."

"And I'm guessing that's all we know at this point," Pryde said.

"Correct. We know his background and his career in the Rangers, but after that there's been literally nothing. It's as if he dropped off the grid completely, until recently when he surfaced as the culprit of the hijacking of those missiles. We still don't know if he has another agenda or if it was as it seemed when he first made contact, a simple extortion racket. It's clear now though that since we attacked his base of operations he will seek to regain the advantage, and part of that will be to punish us for our actions against him."

"I agree, sir," Pryde said calmly.

C knew how he worked, so he recognised that his seeming indifference to the potential loss of life was not intentional.

The stifling of the emotional context was intentional so he could focus on the job; he was certainly not indifferent to the pain and suffering it would cause, and he would deal with that later when all this was over. Still, C found it slightly disconcerting how he was able to do it and he had to constantly remind himself he wasn't some kind of monster.

Fields, on the other hand, was clearly still trying to understand it and was frustrated, angry and couldn't quite comprehend how anyone could be so cold. Throwing her hands in the air, she grunted her frustration at him as she turned away finding it difficult to voice her feelings.

Ignoring the outburst, Pryde said, "What do we have to go on sir? Millions of lives are at stake here and we have to do something to stop Jericho."

"Not much, I'm afraid," C replied.

Turning back to the two men, Fields said, "What do we know about the missiles?"

"They are a new type of cluster missile with a greater payload and wider spread. Once deployed, twenty smaller missiles split out from the main body and spread out to cover a much wider area. Each smaller individual missile is controlled by the computer onboard the main body. Once programmed for a target, they seek out a wide range of signals, including heat and electronic signatures, to deliver the payload to the intended target," C explained.

"What about the payload, sir—can they be configured for variable warheads? Is a nuclear payload an option?" Fields asked almost breathlessly as she was rapidly coming to her point.

"Yes, it is, why?" C asked.

"Then they'll need the nuclear material for the payload and, as we know, there are only a few places where that kind of material is available. They'll have to go to them if they want to maximise their point."

"Excellent work Fields. I'll get the word out to every planet where nuclear material is stored to inform us immediately of any unusual activity or interest," C said. His whole face softened with relief as they finally had something to work with. He left the two of them as he went about his work.

"What now?" Fields said, nervously moving from one foot to the other.

"Now we wait. Look, I know you want to get back out there and do something, I get that. Until we have a target though, we might as well relax a little to conserve our energy. Trust me, when things start to heat up, you'll need all the energy you can muster," Pryde told her.

"That's easy for Mister Calm and Collected over here to say. We don't all have your ability to close off our emotions, you know."

Pryde wasn't hurt by her comments, even though he saw by the way she avoided his eyes that she regretted saying them. Instead, he said, "Let me buy you a cup of coffee and we can sit and relax, even if it's just for a moment or two."

Looking into his eyes, she saw no pain from her comments, only understanding, so she said, "I'd like that, thanks."

—————————————————

Chapter 26

—————————————————

Natara Nebula

The bridge of the Phobos was on the top deck near the middle of the gigantic vessel. Surrounded by triple hull plating, it was also protected by primary and secondary shields, all of which was due to the extensive refit the starship had undergone.

This ship was the mobile headquarters for ICE and could be relocated at a moment's notice. Their present position though, near the nebula, gave them all the protection against detection they needed for the moment, at least.

"Get me Trask on an encrypted channel," Jericho said after he had arrived on the bridge to ensure things were running as expected. "I'll take the call in my quarters," he added once he was confident everything was secure and going as planned.

Jericho had a cabin near the bridge so he could get there should the need arise. Not having spent too much time on the ship meant that his quarters were Spartan in the decoration department. There was little of himself in this room, just a desk to work at, a bathroom for ablutions and a bedroom–nothing too grand, with just enough to accommodate his daily needs.

He sat at the desk and activated the small monitor as the call was routed through to him.

Trask's face appeared on the screen with no indication of where he was.

"You have something for me to do?" he said.

"I want you to source nuclear material for the missiles. When you have it in sufficient quantity, call me back and I'll give you further instructions," Jericho said.

"Copy that," Trask replied and cut the transmission. There was no need for lengthy conversations, especially over an encrypted channel. No matter the level of encryption, there was always a chance that it could be hacked or broken, and he was not about to allow that to happen this close to the end—Trask understood that.

As he stared at the blank screen, Jericho's thoughts turned to those who had opposed him. What had begun as a simple extortion job had now turned to something quite different. Now he wanted them to suffer. They had sought to deny him what he demanded and that could not go unpunished. He had been forced to resign his commission from the Rangers because of his opinions and views, and now they sought to deny him of what he wanted. They were wrong about his viewpoint that the Rangers should be used to weed out the bad seeds in society, removing them as a surgeon removes malignant tissue. They are wrong now to deny him his compensation. He had considered the money he demanded as what was rightfully his for him being forced out from the only job he had ever loved, the only thing he was ever good at, compensation for all the years he had donated to the CDF when he had followed all of their orders which he knew were insufficient to get the job done. They would never allow him to go that extra step which would have eradicated the problem for good. Instead, they insisted on only killing when absolutely necessary, as a last resort.

They were about to learn that he had been correct in his world view all along, and they would pay dearly for dismissing his opinion. Now they would also suffer for denying him what was rightfully his, too.

He was doing this not just because of the principle of the thing but now out of revenge. He would prove to them all that, if he had been able to eradicate the problem at the source, then what he was going to do to them would not have been possible.

It would be a harsh lesson for them to learn and he was going to enjoy every last second of it.

Akora IV

Situated at the hind end of the galaxy, Akora IV was a haven for refuse. This far from the highly populated systems closer to the core, it was ideal for storage of nuclear material until it decayed.

The planet was a barren world with a small colony of a few thousand people living and working at the plants above ground. The nuclear material was stored in waste disposal dumps deep underground where it was kept in lead storage units, miles from the population. All the workers wore protective suits that prevented radiation from seeping through and harming them.

The space port was near the colony and was covered with a shielded area powered by some of the waste stored at the site. They siphoned off radiation to power their own plant, which made it self-sufficient.

Trask landed at the space port and entered the domed colony. This far from civilisation, most security concerns were much laxer than the core systems. Not many people visited this planet except those on business, legitimate or otherwise. It was in everyone's best interests to not keep too many records and in that way money could be made for everyone.

Knowing who the best person to see was, Trask went straight to where he knew he'd find them.

"Benny, good to see you," he said as he walked into the bar. The Cosmo was one of the bars that served the colony and was Benny's local. Benny was a grizzled fifty-year-old administrator of the colony's mining and storage operation and the man to go to if you wanted things done.

"Trask, to what do I owe the pleasure of this visit?" he replied, turning on his bar stool to look at the visitor.

The bar was dimly lit and filled with dark wood furniture. A long mahogany bar ran almost the entire width of the room. Backed with mirrors, the bar had an array of bottles and optics across it for the customers to choose from.

Benny was not your usual administrator; he was overweight and wore crumpled suits that had seen better days. His hair was the colour of mud and he had bags under his dull eyes that could be used on a weekend getaway.

"I'm here on business Benny. Let's go somewhere a bit more private, shall we?"

"Sure, my office is just behind the bar here," Benny said and got off his stool.

The two of them left the bar and entered a smaller office that was even more depressing.

"What can I do you for Trask?" Benny said, walking around the desk to sit down behind it.

"The people I represent need some nuclear waste that can be weaponised. Need I remind you that this has to be kept quiet."

"You know me better than that Trask. In fact, I'm really offended you'd even consider I would do anything like that."

"Well Benny, let me put it this way. I know you'd sell your own Grandmother for a pay day so let's be clear about this. If I find out you blabbed to anyone about our upcoming transaction, I will hurt you, bad."

"I hear you and let me just say, I would never, not to you at least."

Trask's eyes narrowed as he looked at him for any signs of subterfuge. He knew Benny better than most, and he also knew he couldn't be trusted except to procure things for a paying client. It was rare for him to be unable to deliver on a contract, which was why he came here first.

"So, can you get what I need, or not?" he said finally.

"Do bears shit in the woods?"

"How soon? This is time sensitive, so I need it right away."

"That'll cost extra."

"Why am I not surprised about that?"

"Give me a few to make some calls. Go grab a drink at the bar, on me, and when I have something, I'll let you know."

"Don't be too long Benny, the clock is ticking."

"Trask, if you can get it any faster elsewhere then go ahead, be my guest," Benny said.

Trask placed his hands on the desk and leaned forward to stare at the chubby administrator. "Don't get cute with me, Benny; you know better than that. Just get me the material. I'll be outside waiting," he said, then slowly pushed off from the desk and left the room.

Chapter 27

The redistribution of nuclear waste had gone as usual, without a hitch. This wasn't the first time a customer wanted a shipment of waste siphoned off for their personal use. There was a market out there that dealt with the recycling of waste material for nuclear generators. Since the use of nuclear power had been abolished, fusion reactors had taken over. In some cases, the waste was used in an abandoned technology that attempted to marry the two together by stripping the heavier isotopes from the waste material and using it as fuel for the fusion reactors. This had proven to be too dangerous due to the inherent dangers of using the waste. Although it had been officially abandoned, there were still some who used the technology as a way of cutting costs.

It was rare though for someone to want the waste for aggressive purposes, as nuclear missiles using radioactive material had long since been outlawed and the only reason he agreed to supplying Trask was because in the past he had been a good customer and could be relied upon to remain quiet about where he purchased the goods from. There was also the fear factor involved in any deal made with him. Trask was one hell of a scary dude and it wasn't wise to cross him.

Having completed the task of supplying the material, he was about to leave his office and return to the bar with the good news when a call was routed through to him, which made him stop and stare at the caller ID.

What the fuck did the Ministry of Intelligence want to talk to him about?

Sitting back down, he operated the monitor on his desk, opening the call. The image cleared, having travelled through subspace boosted by the subspace relays to reach him in real-time.

"Benjamin Rodriguez, what can I do for you?" he said.

"I am making enquiries about your supply of nuclear waste material. Has anyone made any requests of you that could be considered, out of the ordinary?" the face asked.

"To whom am I speaking with?" Benny asked, stalling.

"My name is James Holden, sir. I am an officer with the Ministry of Intelligence and we are looking into the misuse of nuclear waste materials. We believe that a certain individual is looking to procure an amount of the material for illegal purposes. Has anyone made any such enquiries to you?" Holden said.

Benny kept a calm demeanour as he listened. Keeping his face relaxed, he tried not to give anything away.

"I'm sorry Mister Holden, but I can't help you. I run a legitimate business here and enquiries of that nature are illegal," he said.

"Mister Rodriguez, that didn't answer my question."

Taking a calming, slow breath, Benny replied, "No, Mister Holden, no one has made any such enquiries. Does that answer your question, sir?"

"Thank you for your time sir, you've been extremely helpful," Holden said and ended the call.

Benny sat back, staring at the blank screen. Sweat beaded his forehead as fear gripped him like a wild animal tearing at his insides.

What the fuck had Trask involved him in?

Standing up so fast his chair fell over backwards, he stormed out of the office, re-entering the bar. He slowed his approach as he saw the big man turn to look at him, his eyes searching for any sign of subterfuge or betrayal.

When he reached Trask, he softly said, "Whatever you're into, I don't want any part of. Take your shipment and get the fuck away from me and never come back. Am I making myself perfectly clear?"

"Benny, my friend, what's got you so rattled?" Trask asked, keeping his voice conversational so as not to draw any unwanted attention.

"I've just had the Ministry of Intelligence asking if anyone has approached me for any nuclear material. They're onto you Trask, so I want you gone as soon as your shipment is loaded."

"That was fast," he observed, "you were happy to take my money, Benny, so don't play the wounded victim here. You didn't bat an eye when I told you we were going to weaponise the stuff so it's too late to play the innocent card now."

"What do I tell them if they come sniffing around here?"

"You tell them whatever the fuck you want; by that time it won't matter anyway."

"I won't cover for you, Trask."

"I never expected you to, Benny."

The two of them stared at each other, each one knowing this would be the last.

"I'll wait in my ship. You take care Benny," Trask said, then walked away.

Benny watched him leave and breathed easier for a second. His reaction was not what he'd expected. Trask was not the kind of man to be crossed—he had survived by covering his tracks and instilling fear of retribution in those he came in contact with. For him to simply walk off after their exchange was completely out of character.

Turning to the bar he said, "Scotch, make it a double."

As soon as Trask got back to his ship, he checked the hold and, sure enough, the material had been deposited inside the shielded containers.

Setting course for the Phobos, he lifted off from the space port. With one last detail to take care of before going to hyperspace, he targeted the section of the colony where the bar was located with his weapons. When he had a good lock, he fired several missiles, watching them hit the dome and destroy the entire area, including the bar where Benny would be.

The explosions blew out the dome, allowing the vacuum of space to suck all the atmosphere contained in that area of the colony. Those who weren't killed in the explosions would die a slow, agonising death in the vacuum. The other sections of the colony would be sealed the instant a breach was detected, rendering the rest of it safe, but anyone caught outside those seals would be left to die.

His work here done, Trask gave a sigh followed by a sad smile. "Goodbye Benny," he said, then entered the hyperspace window, leaving it all behind him.

Chapter 28

SecOps HQ, Terra II

As soon as Holden finished his call with Rodriguez he went straight to C's office.

"Sir, I think I may have something," he blurted out breathlessly. He was a young officer, keen to impress, but not at the detriment of his work. His blue eyes sparkled with energy as he danced from one foot to the other in his haste to impart his findings.

"Okay Holden, calm down; take a breath and tell me," C said, stifling a smile. He remembered being that enthusiastic when he was starting out. Now was not the time for reminiscence though.

"I was just speaking with Rodriguez on Akora IV sir and he was extremely evasive when I asked him if anyone had approached him for nuclear material."

"Define evasive son," C asked, wanting a little more clarity.

"I asked him if anyone had approached him about nuclear waste and his reply was that he was running a legitimate business. When I told him he hadn't answered my question he got more defensive, stating that to sell such items was illegal. When I probed further, he was very clear in his reply saying that no one had approached him, but it was the manner in which he answered me sir. It was very deliberate, as if he was holding something in and was being extremely careful not to let it slip."

C placed his fingertips together to form a steeple and placed his chin on top, his eyes narrowing in thought.

"And what did you deduce from your conversation?" he asked finally.

"He is definitely holding something back from us sir, and, considering the location of Akora IV being so far from the core systems, it isn't hard to think that would be where you'd go to make a deal off the beaten tracks. I think we should look into it, sir."

"You do know that if I send anyone out there to investigate, and it turns out to be a false lead, we will have wasted valuable resources and, more importantly, time we do not have," C pointed out, staring the young man in the eye. To his credit, Holden didn't falter; he remained true to his convictions and replied with, "I take full responsibility sir."

With a smile C said, "There won't be any need for that son."

His brow crinkled as he said, "I don't understand, sir."

"In this department, the buck stops here. I like your commitment though, it shows you have the courage to stand by your decisions and convictions. Good work, Holden."

"Thank you, sir," Holden said before leaving the room.

Pryde was in the small canteen where operatives could take a break grabbing a coffee with Fields when he was summoned to C's office.

"We've had word that someone could be buying nuclear material from the mining facility on Akora IV. There's no definitive proof as yet, but I think it's worth a look," C said as the two operatives arrived.

"If you're right, sir, then our worst fears could be realised if we don't stop them," Pryde said. "Is there anyone that far out who can take a quick look? By the time we get out there, whoever it is will be long gone. If we have someone nearby, they can see who comes and goes and tracks them."

"You do realise that if they do spot someone, there's no way to track them once they enter hyperspace," Fields said.

"I understand that, but if they can grab an ID off the ship being used, we can look to see when it turns up elsewhere. I know it's a long shot, but at the moment it's all we have."

"Do you think Jericho will have the means to weaponise those missiles with the nuclear material, or will he need a facility to perform that task for him?" Fields asked.

"Depends on where he is, I suppose. The process to weaponise nuclear waste is pretty specialised, so I would assume he'd need somewhere dedicated to this type of operation, or at the very least somewhere that could be adapted for it," Pryde said.

"Good idea. We can certainly look into facilities that cater to those processes and see what we come up with," C said.

He operated the intercom on his desk and said, "Goodchild, send Holden in here please."

He looked at the two of them, "I have just the man to look into this, he's the one who found the link with Akora IV," he said.

The door opened and Holden entered looking at the other two present as he quickly stood to the side, his hands clasped tightly in front of him.

"No need to be nervous Holden, they won't bite. I need you to do something for me. These two will fill you in with what they need," C said.

"Certainly sir," he said, smiling. "If you'd like to follow me, I'll see what I can do to help," he said to Pryde and Fields.

As they arrived at the desk which was Holden's workstation a notification popped up on his monitor.

"That's interesting," he said as he took his seat and read the report.

"What is it, anything we should know about?" Pryde asked.

"Well sir, it seems the facility on Akora IV has just been attacked. They are sending out Mayday signals as a large portion of their colony has been destroyed. There is no number of fatalities as yet but it seems that the colony and mining administrator could be among those who died."

"Well, if there was any doubt before, there certainly isn't any now. That place was where Jericho got his nuclear waste from," Fields observed, to which Pryde gave a nod of agreement.

Chapter 29

Coalition Council HQ, Terra II

President Takashi Harada was still in the Situation Room waiting with all the others in the Council. Those present were the heads of the CDF, the Chief of Staff and various other advisors.

Since the first message had come in, they had been waiting to see what else would happen. Harada knew whoever had the missiles would be calling again soon after what had happened to their secret base.

He was crippled with doubt. Had he made the wrong decision when he sanctioned the attack on the base? How many more would die because of his failure?

To his right and down the table sat Ibrahim Yusef, Director of the Coalition Intelligence Agency.

"Okay Ibrahim, tell me you have something for me, anything," he said, his eyes boring into the man down the table.

Yusef was in his sixties and had worked his way up through the ranks in the Agency from an analyst through field agent to management. He had worked hard to attain his present position and he was vocal about his dislike of the President's association with the Ministry of Intelligence's SecOps Division. On many occasions, both publicly and privately he had stated his opinion of the close connection of the two, calling the latter the President's personal hit squad.

"I have an agent working closely with MI7 who seemed to have taken point on this investigation, sir. She has relayed to me details of an operation that is ongoing and assures me of a result soon," he replied.

"Is that the best you've got Ibrahim? That seems extremely vague to me, and at this point in time we don't have the time to be vague," Harada said, turning to look at the man to his right, Chief of Staff Donald Warburton.

"Okay Donald, what do you suggest we do?" he asked.

A hand went up from the man on Warburton's right, catching Harada's attention.

"What is it, Walter, do you need permission to leave the room?" he said. Walter Wallace was actually General Wallace, overall commander of the CDF. Wallace's lips pursed at the contempt shown of him by the President's comment, but regardless he ignored it and said, "With respect sir, shouldn't the CDF be handling this?"

Harada stared at him before speaking, "General, who was it who gained you the intel to perform the attack on Cronus III? Furthermore, who was it who informed your men of the danger they were running into, thus saving all those lives?" he turned to Yusef at this when he added, "It wasn't your agent in place, was it Ibrahim? Now can we put this infantile jurisdictional argument to bed and move on to find a solution to this problem before any more lives are lost?"

Warburton glanced down at the table so no one saw his pleasure at the roasting the two political adversaries had just received. When he brought his eyes back up, his usual stoic expression was firmly back in place.

"Mister President, I would advise that we allow the agents investigating this situation the time to do their jobs but at the same time have the CDF put on a standby for such a time as when their services are required," he said calmly so as not to escalate the tension already present in the room.

"Your best advice is we sit and wait, is that it?" Harada said, sitting back in his chair, looking around the table.

"I'm afraid it is sir, yes. We let those in play do their jobs, have trust in their abilities and be ready to move decisively when the time comes," Warburton said.

Pausing as he took in, what had been said his mind whirled as he tried to come up with a more proactive solution, one that meant they weren't sitting here with their thumbs up their asses and where millions of lives weren't lost. When sanity prevailed and he found the advice was sound, he leaned forward, once more resting his elbows on the table top.

"I agree. As much as it pains me to say this, you're right; doing nothing at this time is the best option. We allow the experts to do their jobs and hope the faith we have in them is not unfounded. I believe we all have work to do gentlemen. I won't detain you all any longer," he said and moved to stand up.

The meeting was at an end.

When everyone had left, Harada made an encrypted call to C. His face was dark when he saw the image open up on the small desk mounted monitor. He saw the lines of stress stretching across C's normal stoic expression and the tiredness around the eyes which told him that he wasn't the only one feeling the pressure.

"Tell me you have some good news, William, we are in dire need of it here," he said.

"I wish I could, Mister President. Unfortunately, we still don't have anything concrete to go on, but we do have some leads we are looking into which we hope will give us something to take action on," Chambers replied. His shoulders sagged when he spoke, another clear indication he was as frustrated at having only this news to depart to his boss.

"I have faith, William, you know that, but there are those who would relish seeing you and your department fail in this. I'm certain they have a whole list of 'I told you so's' already rehearsed and ready to be delivered."

"With respect, sir, let them play their silly political games. I have more important things to deal with here, such as trying to save millions of peoples lives. If these people weren't so invested in trying to bring my department down, then maybe they would have come up with something they could have used against Jericho and his group."

Remembering something said recently, Harada said, "On that very subject, watch your back William, you may have a cuckoo in the nest. I know you have vital work to attend to, so I won't keep you any longer, just keep me informed of any progress you make," and then he closed the call.

Chambers was right; if the CIA Director wasn't so keen on getting rid of MI7, he could have come up with something they could all use. If Jericho does indeed take action, and more lives are lost, then a serious look into the conduct of the CIA in this would seem to be warranted. At the very least their inaction, or focussing on the wrong subject, would seem to prove dereliction of duty, and for that he would ensure heads would roll.

This was the very thing about politics that he hated with every fibre of his being. People go into this career not to help or represent the people they work for but to further their own needs, their own agendas, which is the exact opposite of what the job was about. Weeding these people out was difficult though. By their very need to look after number one, they ensure they have their backs covered every step of the way and they make sure they are accountable for nothing.

Well, enough was enough. This was where he was about to take a stand, and if more lives are lost in this then he would make it his purpose in life to bring those responsible to account.

For the moment, he would allow this to play out, however ruthless that seemed; he needed to give these people enough rope to hang themselves with so that he could tighten that knot around their neck. This time they would pay for their part in all of this. This time, there was no hiding behind plausible deniability.

Chapter 30

MI7 SecOps HQ

After the call ended, C sat thinking about the cryptic message the president had given him.

Without saying the words, he had as much as told him they had a traitor in their midst. It didn't take a genius to figure out who he meant.

Fields was a CIA agent, so it was obviously her he was talking about. Pryde was focused on the mission so chances were that he wouldn't even consider looking at her for anything duplicitous, and therefore he was easy prey to be fooled by her. If she was working some angle to get into his head to see if she could grab the glory for herself and the CIA, he probably wouldn't see it coming.

What made him the best agent he'd ever had working for him, in this case, also made him the most vulnerable.

He had to get out in front of this;, and he definitely couldn't afford politics getting in the way of them doing their job.

Using the intercom on his desk, he called Goodchild, "Can you ask Pryde and agent Fields to come to my office immediately please," he said.

"I'll get right on it, sir," she replied.

Chambers sat back and within a few moments the two of them entered his office.

"You wanted to see us, sir?" Pryde said, his brow creased slightly as he wondered what was behind the sudden summon.

"It's just come to my attention that agent Fields here may have another agenda behind her working this case," C said, looking straight at her to gauge her reaction.

"You mean beyond wanting to find the people who are behind this? Is it possible that the CIA planted her here to learn what we know so they can steal it and claim success for themselves, or to gain some sort of proof as to why we failed, should that happen. I know that the director has long held a belief that we have too much influence with the President and has attempted on several occasions to sever those ties," Pryde said matter-of-factly.

Fields turned to look at him, her mouth slightly agape as she blurted out, "Why would you even think that?"

"Let me see," Pryde said, and then after a brief pause and without looking at her, said, "Your sudden appearance to help me out during the attack after I left Latimer base was a little too convenient for comfort, and your eagerness to remain by my side and work with me even though you are trained and expected to work alone also seemed a little suspicious. If you put all of that together with the fact that your boss hates this department and would do anything to end it, even going as far as allowing millions to perish rather than actually doing his job, then I think it would be hard to refute the evidence."

"None of that is evidence; it's nothing more than conjecture, you can't prove any of it," she argued.

"I don't hear anything to argue against it either. Simply denying it does not prove it isn't true," Pryde said.

Chambers interrupted with, "Either way, I think it best you go back to your boss and do some actual work and leave us to ours. Agent Fields, we don't need your help from now on."

"Is that absolutely necessary, sir? I mean, an extra pair of eyes can be a valuable asset in this case," she said looking at him, her pain of disappointment turning her mouth down at the corners.

"Agent Fields, you can't be trusted to be truthful in this. How do we know you aren't relaying everything you learn here to your boss back at the Agency Headquarters? We don't have time to play these sorts of games. We need to find those missiles before Jericho fires another off, this time at a more populated area. No, I think it best you leave."

Pryde held a hand up, "Sir, what if we could use her?"

"Excuse me, what? Use me? What the fuck is that supposed to mean?" she said, her teeth clamped firmly together in a grimace of anger.

"Yes Pryde, what exactly do you mean?" C asked, wondering the same thing.

"If she is working for the Agency in an attempt to learn something with which they can destroy us and not, as she claims, with us to bring Jericho to justice, why not feed them a little disinformation to keep them occupied and off our back so we can perform without us having to check if they're watching all the time."

"Wow, you said all that without pausing for a single breath," Fields observed.

Turning to look at her, his mouth creased up on one side as he wondered how that was even relevant.

"It would give us a certain leeway, a modicum of wriggle room," C agreed.

"Exactly sir," Pryde said, turning back to face him.

"So, we're not even going to discuss that what you propose would place me in violation of my orders?" she offered.

"Which are?" C said, giving her every chance to come clean or continue with her charade.

"Never mind, if it means I get to stay and help out I'll do it," she said.

"Now that we have that cleared up, where are we on finding where the labs are that are capable of weaponizing the waste material for missile warheads?" C said, drawing a line through that aspect of the conversation.

"We have drawn up a short list of contenders, sir, and now Holden is working through which one is the most likely to be called upon to do the actual work," Pryde informed him.

Before Chambers could say anything further, the man in question burst into the office again.

"Sir, we have just picked up activity at one of the sites we were looking into," Holden blurted out, his eyes wide with excitement.

All eyes turned to him as C asked, "Where?"

"The Mistral Labs on Galapharm V sir."

"Are you sure about this Holden?"

"Positive sir, the Raptor just landed there."

C looked at Pryde and Fields, "You two get moving, I'll inform the local tac-team to be on standby for your arrival," he said.

Both agents moved fast, leaving the office in a run, leaving Holden at the doorway with his excited smile still plastered across his face.

"And Holden, we really must discuss this annoying habit you seem to have of barging in my office," C said, shaking his head slowly.

The smile on Holden's face dissipated rapidly as he looked at him. His head dropped to his chest as he said, "I'm so sorry, sir, it won't happen again."

He was about to leave when C halted him with, "On the contrary, both times you interrupted us you brought valuable information to us that was vital to this investigation. In the future, if you have information such as that, feel free to bring it to me, but knock first. At least that way you are showing the others that you are acting in a professional manner and not receiving preferential treatment."

This brightened Holden up again. His smile returned as he said, "Yes sir, thank you sir."

"Okay, you can go back to work now. And Holden?" C said.

"Yes, sir?"

"Excellent work," C said and returned his attention to his monitor; he had calls to make as this meeting was clearly over.

Chapter 31

Mistral Labs, Galapharm V.

The Raptor touched down in front of the building that was located in the Central Desert plains, just east of the main city on the planet.

Much like the Mojave Desert on Earth, the Central Desert was not purely sand dunes but had vegetation and a landscape similar to that of the Southwestern United States.

The Mistral labs were located there for security and safety reasons—much of the work done there was classified and highly dangerous, so both secrecy and safety were priorities when the facility was first planned.

The location itself was deemed to give it enough security so that only a token security force was employed there, numbering less than ten.

Three of them greeted the craft as it landed at the front entrance not knowing who, or what, they were about to face.

Jericho led the way out of the Raptor in front of his team of four.

"Excuse me sir, can we help you?" one of the guards asked as the two of them stood at the entrance.

With a wave of his hand, Jericho gave the signal and his men drew weapons and opened fire. A savage salvo of bullets cut down the guards, leaving the entrance clear.

"Bring the missiles out," he ordered when the way was clear, and he continued into the building first, followed by Black and the other two members of his squad.

The labs were inside a three-story sprawling complex that covered almost a mile. It also reached deep into the ground beneath for two miles where the most dangerous work was completed.

Once Jericho was through the front entrance, the area opened out into a spacious lobby that was controlled by a single guard operating a bank of monitors that gave him a view that covered not only the exterior but everything that occurred inside the facility as well.

Getting to his feet to respond to what he'd seen outside, he was quickly dispatched with a bullet to the brain from Jericho the instant he came through the door.

The bank of monitors was left free and clear, and the operation of manning them was taken over by one of Jericho's team.

"We're in control," he said after sitting behind the desk.

"Let's get these missiles down to the labs, now," Jericho said, waving a hand to urge his men on. He knew the authorities including both the Ministry and the CIA would be on the lookout for them. He'd already guessed that they might consider him wanting to configure the missiles into nuclear warheads and would be looking into any and all labs that could do the work. In that respect, they probably had this place under surveillance and would have someone on standby to act.

Time was definitely going to be tight on this one. As he saw the last of the missiles brought through the entrance toward the elevators that led down into the bowels of the facility, he turned to the last of his men and said, "You remain up here and keep an eye out for anyone coming. The instant you pick up anything on your sensors, inform me; is that clear? Your job is to hold them off and keep our path clear to the Raptor. Everything relies on us being able to get out of here with the missiles."

Nods all around and the fire in their eyes told him they understood the importance of their part in all of this.

Leaving them to it, he made his way back inside and got into the elevator with the missiles.

When they reached the laboratory level they exited and were confronted by two guards who had no idea what was happening. Two bullets, one to each head, took care of their interest, leaving their way open to the lab itself.

"What is the meaning of this?" a man in a white coat asked, his eyes blazing in fury and indignation at the interruption. When he saw the two dead guards, he realised this was more than he had signed on for.

Waving his hands in front he stammered, "Whatever it is you need, I'm sure we can accommodate you."

His eyes darted from Jericho to the others and the missiles that appeared behind them and his mouth dropped open.

Jericho looked around the spacious room filled with equipment and apparatus he had no knowledge of. Seven people were present in the lab, all wearing the ubiquitous white lab coat. The man who had challenged them on their arrival seemed to be in charge and it was to him he spoke next.

"I have some nuclear material which I want weaponised for these missiles. I want it done now and I want it done fast. If you comply with my demands, then I'll allow you all to live. If you refuse, then you will die, slowly and agonizingly," he said calmly. Looking around, he picked his target and brought up his pistol and fired. The bullet hit the man standing next to the man in charge in the throat, smashing through in a bloody stream of gore.

Blood splashed the side of his face and shock opened his eyes wide as he stepped away from the dead man. Struck dumb by the sudden death, he just looked at the shooter.

"Just in case you are not convinced of my intentions here, I think that should bring you all some clarity. If you don't want to be next, then you need to get to work," he said.

The sudden shooting of one of their colleagues did the trick and galvanised the rest of them into action.

Jericho stood back and watched things take place with one eye on the time. He knew that he had a limited slot where they could get this done before things got interesting.

Chapter 32

Pryde and Fields arrived at Galapharm V in his starship and immediately went towards the Central Desert plains.

The starship was large enough to carry all the equipment Pryde needed for his missions, which included jet packs, bikes and ground vehicles. It also had an impressive armoury, which held everything from pistols to rocket launchers and anything in between.

Fields had shown respect for it all when she had boarded her before they took off for the present location saying that she wished she had something similar herself.

"Okay ship, take us in. Put us down somewhere close to the Mistral Labs, but keep the chameleon cloak active so we're not picked up on any of their sensors," Pryde said as they entered the planet's atmosphere. He was in full mission mode and all emotional responses were dialled down to a minimum. He would act without emotion, remaining calm and clear headed throughout the time this operation lasted.

"Copy that, sir," the AI replied.

The chameleon cloak was a program that operated to bend light around the ship, making it appear to be part of the background. Other cloaking devices had been tried but they had never seemed to work—distortions around the cloaked vessel were too easy to detect, which made the cloak useless. The chameleon cloak was different in that it made the vessel appear as if it was part of the background like the chameleon of Earth did, changing the skin tones and textures to appear like the branch it was sitting upon or the leaves it was surrounded by.

There was still a little distortion around the craft, especially when it was moving at higher speeds, but on the whole it had been proven to be quite effective.

As they came in to land, they could see the Mistral Labs on their viewer and the Raptor quite clearly parked near the entrance.

"Okay big boy, what's the plan here?" Fields asked.

Ignoring the comment, Pryde said, "We try to get inside that place without being seen, then relay our findings to the tac-team who are standing by."

"Standing by where? Do you see them anywhere? Are they even here yet?" she replied, indicating the open landscape with a motion with her hand.

"Now that you mention it, they should be here by now," he agreed. "Ship, scan for any signs of the tac-team being nearby and contact them to let us know their location," he said.

"Copy that. Hailing them now, sir," the AI replied.

"Captain Hale here, commanding the Galapharm Security Service. We've been alerted to your situation and are en route now to your location; eta, three minutes," a voice replied through the speakers in Pryde's ship.

"Captain Hale, be advised, come in quiet; we are trying to use the element of surprise here," Pryde said.

"And you are?" Hale asked.

"The man in charge," Pryde said emphatically, which did not go down well with Hale. He responded with, "Be advised, 'man in charge', this situation is under the jurisdiction of the GSS, and you have no authority here. We are well versed and extremely well trained in how to handle situations like this, so again, be advised to stay out of our way. You have been granted the temporary status of consultant, nothing more. Take no action or you will be taken into custody," and then the comm channel went dead.

"Was that part of your plan big boy, to piss off the locals?" Fields asked with more than a hint of a smirk.

Shaking his head at the stupidity of the captain, he simply said, "Not really."

"This is going to go really bad, isn't it?" she asked.

"For Hale and his men, probably. For us, not so much," he said. Looking at her, he added, "I think we'd better get ready for the fireworks."

"Fireworks, what fireworks?" she said as he got out of his seat and went back into the rear section to prepare.

"What fireworks Pryde?" she asked again, this time more forcefully.

"You'd better come get ready, cause when things go south, and they will, it'll be our best chance to get inside that facility and try and stop Jericho," he said as he was taking a pistol from the rack on the bulkhead. He chose a Walther Q9 and placed it into his shoulder rig. Then he took three extra mags and slotted them into the loops in the rig. Around his waist he wrapped a belt that had several pouches, into which he placed several small, round objects–grenades. Finally, he took a rifle from the rack opposite–an ARX900–along with three extra clips, which he placed in slot loops on the belt. He had already dressed in the liquid body armour suit, which would protect him from almost everything except a direct hit from a rocket.

"Are we going to war?" Fields asked when she saw the amount of munitions he was packing to take with him.

"Better to have it and not need it rather than to need it and not have it," he said.

"I hear that," she said and hurried to follow suit. She quickly started to choose which weapons she wanted from the variety on offer and picked out a Heckler and Koch VPX, along with the same rifle as Pryde had picked. She grabbed extra mags for both, along with a handful of grenades as well just as her partner had done.

"Look big boy, what do I call you? I can't keep calling you big boy," she asked, "I mean, what's your name?"

"Does it matter?"

"It does, yes. If you get killed, I don't want to be that person who says 'I didn't even know his name'. If we are going to fight together and put our lives on the line, don't you think I at least deserve to know something about you, like your name for starters?"

"Not really, no. We're here to do a job; let's do that, shall we?"

"You really are a cold fish, aren't you," she said. It was a statement of fact rather than an insult and one Pryde recognised.

He glanced her way sheepishly, then softly said, "Duncan, my name is Duncan."

"There you go, big boy, that wasn't so hard was it now," she said with a huge smile across her face.

He looked at her with a slight head tilt, unsure if all of that was a ruse to break through his carefully built barrier or not, and he was still trying to decide when she said, "Okay Duncan, time to roll."

Chapter 33

Captain Hale was a six-year veteran of the GSS. A Special Forces soldier with an exemplary career, he had been in command of GSS Team Six for a year and was eager to prove his superior's faith in him.

Him and the entire Team Six were coming in hot aboard a VP22 Tilt Rotor combined attack and carrier chopper. It had the capability to attack ground targets with its array of gatling guns and rocket pods, as well as being able to transport up to thirty troops to a combat zone.

This particular VP22 carried the entire Team Six, all twenty men, to the Mistral Labs.

They would arrive in less than thirty seconds confident they had the situation well under control. They were about to be proven wrong.

"Sir, we have an incoming vehicle, looks to be a troop carrier," the man on guard duty at the entrance informed Jericho.

"Under no circumstances are they to be allowed to land and deploy. Take off in the Raptor and take care of them, and keep on lookout for reinforcements," Jericho replied. Turning to Black, he said, "We have company, see if you can't get them motivated a little more."

Black moved away to instill more fear into the technicians so they would finish work faster.

Outside the building the Raptor took off, almost leaping into the air on her vertical thrusters, then turned to face the incoming aircraft.

———

The pilot of the VP22 said, "Looks like we have company, sir."

Hale was sitting next to him and saw what he meant, "Whatever the fuck that is, blow it the fuck out of the sky," he ordered.

"With pleasure, sir."

Activating the weapon systems, the pilot chose the air-to-air missiles first, wanting to end this fast. He smiled as he heard the weapons lock chime and fired the two missiles at the target aircraft. His pleasure quickly turned to dismay as twin particle beams shot the missiles out of the sky, halfway to their target.

"What the fuck?!" the two men both said. The pilot fired all his rockets at once, his smile gone now and a grimace of fear firmly in place. The rockets fared no better as they too were blown away by the particle beam weapon.

Firing the gatling guns, the pilot thought he had them until the Raptor took a turn to starboard that no aircraft should be able to perform. It was almost a complete ninety degree turn to the side which should be impossible by any standards of aeronautical flight. The shells from the gatling guns passed by harmlessly which made the pilot fear the worst only to have those fears realised seconds later as the same particle beams that had shot down his missiles and rockets sliced through the middle of the VP22, cutting it in half.

With all power severed, the VP22 fell from the sky to smash into the ground, killing everyone on board in the explosion that followed.

"I see what you mean about fireworks," Fields said as they both saw the destruction of the tilt-rotor aircraft and all the troops on board.

"They never listen," Pryde said with a shake of his head, then added, "C'mon, time to go."

The hatch opened at the back of the ship and they exited down the ramp.

Pryde took the lead, keeping low to avoid any sensors sweeping the area outside the facility. A fast sprint across the area between them and the building was covered in moments and they were at the front entrance ready to breach.

"How much longer?" Jericho asked Black. Pressure was building inside the chamber as the lab technicians worked at a feverish pace to finish off weaponizing the warheads.

The pressure wasn't getting to him though, as he was used to working in high pressure environments; to Jericho, this was just another day at the office.

Black was overwatching everything and said, "Just finishing off the last warhead now. We'll be able to move in a few minutes," he said.

"Start loading the completed warheads onto the Raptor. This last one can be loaded last and made ready to fire when we're ready to leave."

Black leaned in closer to his friend, not wanting the others to hear what he was about to say. "Are you really going to do this then?" he asked.

Jericho leaned back to look at him in the eye, his lips curling down in disgust, "They have to pay, you know that. They failed to pay us the ransom we demanded; they even attacked our base. Now they have to see what their actions have caused. I warned them, but they wouldn't listen; well it's too late now," he said in an effort to keep his voice under control.

Black held up both hands in a submissive gesture, then said, "Okay boss. I'm with you all the way, you know that."

"Good. Then I suggest you carry out my orders," Jericho said with a definite sense of finality.

With a nod, Black departed to get the warheads loaded back onto the Raptor.

Chapter 34

Pryde and Fields were at either side of the door, ready to move.

Pryde gave the signal and they both moved in.

The only guard left was the operative manning the reception desk who brought up a weapon the instant he saw them appear.

Bullets peppered the door as they came through, narrowly missing them and forcing them back to reassess their situation.

"Now what?" Fields asked.

"I'll cover you as you try to flank him. Go right to see if you can get a clear shot, and I'll hold him off as long as I can," he replied.

"If I get shot and killed here, I'll come back to haunt you," she joked.

"No such thing as ghosts," he responded with a straight face.

"Humour's lost on you, isn't it?" she said.

Giving her a sharp look, he said, "Get ready to move."

He brought his rifle up to his shoulder, ready to fire, then came around the door jamb and started firing three shot bursts at the man behind the desk. The first three shells tore up the top of the desk, sending shattered slivers of wood and plastic into the air.

"Now!" said Pryde, and Fields ran through the open doorway to her right, dropping into a roll. She came up on her knee with her pistol extended and she fired. The bullet hit the man high on his left shoulder, spinning him up and around as his face contorted into a rictus of pain.

Pryde saw his opportunity and altered his aim. His next salvo hit the man's head, destroying it in a veritable explosion of blood and brain matter. He collapsed in a tangle of lifeless arms and legs, all life having been torn from him.

Pryde ran into the room, scanning the area with his rifle to ensure no more threats presented themselves.

Fields was at the desk. Ignoring the dead body, she accessed the data banks on the bank of monitors for a layout of the facility. Bringing up a schematic of the interior, she said, "They must be down in the lower levels; that's where all the work is done. Up here are just a bunch of administration offices," she said.

"There has to be a way down there then," Pryde observed, and his eyes landed on the elevator doors. Placing both hands on the joint where the two doors met in the middle, he forced them apart. The elevator opened up showing a shaft that ran deep into the bowels of the facility where an elevator car waited at the bottom to be loaded.

"Got you," he muttered as he took out several grenades, primed them then dropped them down the shaft.

"What are you doing?" screamed Fields when he dropped the grenades. "There's lab workers down there who will now either get killed or become hostages," she added as she watched him walk briskly toward her. He pulled her down behind the desk as the grenades exploded.

"Not for much longer," he said coldly as they cowered behind the desk.

The explosion destroyed the bottom of the shaft, sending a fireball up the walls to force its way out of the open doors at the top. They heard and felt the blast beneath their feet as the walls of the entire building shook as if some giant had just shaken it like a rag doll.

Windows shook, cracked and then shattered from the force demonstrated by the blast. The cables holding the elevator car snapped and snaked their way out into the room flapping like angry snakes having been disturbed from their slumber.

The sound of the explosion was so loud they felt it pounding in their chests, like a thing alive, angry as it tried to flatten them for even daring to be there. When the noise had abated and the dust was beginning to settle, Pryde stood up to view the damage. The entire ground floor was littered with debris and detritus from the blast.

"Well, they won't be coming back up that way anytime soon," he observed.

"You're right, they'll have to choose one of the emergency exits," Fields said.

"Emergency exits?" he said, turning to look at her, his brief satisfaction at trapping them fading rapidly. "What emergency exits?"

"I was trying to tell you about the layout here before you went all macho man and blew up the elevator shaft. There's a series of tunnels that lead out from the lower levels to a safer location away from the main building in case of a breach or fire or, I don't know, if some idiot blows up the elevator shaft."

Disregarding the rebuke, Pryde said, "Show me."

Black heard the grenades being dropped and knew exactly what they were the instant he heard them clatter against the roof of the elevator car.

Luckily for them, none of the warheads had been loaded inside yet but it meant they had to move, and fast.

"Get them away from there as fast as you can," he shouted.

Jericho heard the urgency in his friend's voice and knew something was wrong.

As the two men stared at each other, Black said, "Grenades."

That one word galvanised everyone into action. Immediately they grabbed the warheads closest to the elevator and carried them as far away as was viable. The others which were en route there were quickly turned around and taken away as well just as the grenades went off.

The ensuing explosions blew out the elevator cab, destroying it in a huge fireball that blew out the doors, sending them spinning deep into the room. The fireball that followed spread out reaching every available space it could find, its fiery fingers burning and destroying everything they touched. Smaller fires broke out from this fiery embrace threatening to engulf the entire room in a conflagration that would trap everyone inside before burning them alive.

Jericho was already working on a solution. He had studied the layout of the facility before choosing this as the place to weaponise the warheads. He knew that, if they were attacked, they could find an escape route from there quite easily.

"Okay guys, we trained for this, so let's make it work. You all know where to go, so let's get to it," he shouted, forcing his voice to be heard above the clamour of the blasts.

"Bring the Raptor around to the alternative exit; our primary egress is unavailable so we're coming out the other way," he said to the pilot through the shared comm link the team used.

To their credit, some of the men were already moving toward the emergency exits available, and Jericho's shouted commands broke through the others' stupor to also get them moving too. In short order they were all heading down one of the tunnels that would take them and the warheads far away from the building. By the time those who had attacked had realised what had happened down here, they would be long gone and moving on to their next objective.

Chapter 35

Seeing the warren of tunnels displayed on the monitor before them Pryde knew they had to whittle it down to the one they would use.

"Activate the interior sensors and see if you can pick up any life signs in any of these tunnels. Failing that, check for ambient radiation. Those warheads will give off increased levels that should show up on sensors," he suggested.

"Already on it," Fields replied as her fingers danced over the keyboard. "Got them," she said, pointing to the layout on the screen. A red dot signified the position of the targets.

"Right, let's go; we can intercept them as they come out," Pryde said.

As they went back through the front entrance Pryde saw the Raptor circling back over the building.

"That thing is going to pick them up," Fields observed.

"We have to get there first and stop them," Pryde said as he began to run.

"How the fuck are we supposed to do that?" she asked followed behind him.

"I'll let you know that when we get there."

"Holy shit, you have no idea do you, you're making this up as you go along, aren't you?"

"Save your breath, I get the idea you're going to need it."

"I knew you'd say that."

Jericho knew these tunnels well enough to navigate them blindfolded. His training helped him absorb details faster than most people with normal lives.

"We're almost there," he said, replaying the schematic in his mind.

A few more corners and they would be there. Light from the opening hit their eyes like a stab to the brain after being in dark tunnels.

"Where's our ride?" Black said as they reached the entrance. Before Jericho had time to reply the sound of the Raptor's engine filled the air nearby and they saw the sleek out of this world aircraft come in to hover near them.

"Get the warheads on board now," he shouted above the noise as the Raptor came in to land.

Standing to one side of the tunnel entrance, Jericho watched the technicians carry the warheads toward the aircraft being guarded by his men. Keeping his attention split between the convoy of men carrying the warheads and the surrounding area, he felt he had everything under control and that things were moving along as planned. Having to exit through the tunnel system wasn't how he'd foreseen this going, but it was something he had planned for in case anything arose that was not part of the original plan.

The best, most successful campaigns were those that took everything into consideration and had contingencies for every possible eventuality. This was what he had tried to do with this plan—so much was at stake that he had to plan ahead for even the most outlandish outcome and, in that way, have all of his bases covered.

At the moment he was watching to see if whoever had attacked them would follow them down the tunnel or find another way around to this exit. Whichever route they took, he knew they were coming, and he was ready.

Pryde saw the Raptor drop down to land up ahead.

"There they are," he said. Already with his ARX900 at his shoulder ready to fire, he increased his pace. When he got within sight of the entrance to the tunnel, they could see quite clearly the men ferrying the warheads into the Raptor from the tunnel.

Fields was about to rush forward to start firing when Pryde put a hand on her arm to halt her advance.

With a tilt of his chin to the side he said, "Over there."

Realising if she had taken a step further, she would have walked right into the man standing at the entrance's line of fire.

"Thanks," she whispered. "So, what do we do now?" she asked, regaining some of her composure.

"We need to stop them from leaving here with those missiles," he replied.

"Okay, Mister Obvious, I never would've even thought of that. I'm so glad you're here to impart your wisdom," she sniped back at him.

"You're welcome," he replied, ignoring the sarcasm.

"How dangerous are those warheads? I mean, will they explode if they get blown up or hit with a bullet?" she asked.

"No, they need specific arming and detonating protocols entered into the computer controlling them."

Pryde gave her a sideways glance with narrowed eyes as he wondered where she was going with those questions but then realised that too was obvious.

"That's okay then," she said, reaching for a grenade.

He placed a hand on hers stopping her.

"Look at those men carrying the warheads, they're the lab technicians. If you toss that into the mix all those men and women will die," he warned.

"I thought you were all about getting the job done, no matter the consequences," she said, looking up into his eyes, her brows pinching together in the middle as she tried to understand.

"I am, but not if innocent people will die. What you misconstrue in me as being cold blooded is nothing more than efficiency. Sometimes ruthless, yes, but I never place an innocent life in danger unless there is no other way."

"What do you suggest then?" she asked. She thought now she had a better understanding of how he was, which was progress and something she could work with.

"Okay, how about this. You take the guard at the entrance and then cover me; I'll handle the rest," he replied and moved forward, out from the cover they had been using.

"Oh shit!" she exclaimed as he moved, not giving her time to argue or even think.

Pryde moved forward, his attention entirely on his targets as he relied on his partner to have his back, and he started firing.

Behind him Fields came out into the open area where she turned her own ARX900 on the man standing guard at the tunnel entrance. The moment her target saw Pryde he brought his own weapon up to fire.

Fields fired rapidly at him, missing him barely as he saw her at the last moment and ducked inside the tunnel.

Pryde cut down one of the guards and turned his fire on the next nearest target.

The men and women carrying the warheads panicked at the sound of gunfire and were rooted to the spot in terror, not daring to move knowing they had nuclear warheads in their hands.

The guards moved behind some of the hostages, using them as a human shield, but Pryde didn't allow that to deter him or allow any doubt to cloud his judgement. If he had a clear shot at a target, he took it.

The first man hiding behind a technician showed a portion of his head as he aimed a rifle at Pryde, resting the barrel on the hostage's shoulder. Pryde took him out with a bullet through his left eye, which blasted through the brain exiting through the back of his skull. Quickly he adjusted his aim and dropped another guard, who was hiding behind another technician, a woman this time. He gave just a hint of the top of his head as a target and had it blown clean off by a high velocity bullet through his forehead.

Seeing the efficiency with which Pryde had dispatched two of their numbers, the rest of them ran for the more effective cover the Raptor afforded them.

Pryde dropped two more as they ran for cover.

Fields kept the last guy inside the tunnel entrance having no idea who he was or the significance he played in this whole scenario. Bullets pounded the wall of the tunnel from her rifle, sending chips of concrete into the air.

Their advantage of surprise was soon decimated when the guards reached the safety of the Raptor and the weapons systems on board came into play.

The gatling guns swivelled around, aiming at Pryde, then opened fire.

Pryde saw the motion and was running for cover before the guns started shooting.

At the sound of the rapid firing gatling guns, Fields turned and ran for cover following Pryde's lead. Using the landscape as cover, the two of them got behind an outcropping of rocks. The gatling guns began firing at it, chipping away their cover with each round.

"We could do with some backup right about now," Fields said.

"We're not done yet," Pryde said.

Chapter 36

Jericho saw the two operatives retreat to cover and saw his chance to move.

Making a dash for the Raptor, he shouted for the missiles to be gathered up from where the hostages had dropped them. He didn't want to leave a single warhead behind and, as long as the two attackers were being pinned down, he saw no reason why it couldn't be carried out.

The hostages had disappeared though, taking their chance to escape when the shooting started and their captors made a dash for the ship. This meant Jericho's men had to come back out and pick up the remaining warheads.

Jericho stood in the open, screaming at them to come out when he saw Black, his second in command, in the doorway of the Raptor looking at him. His expression changed, his eyes and mouth opened wide as he screamed something back at him.

Turning to look where he was pointing, his arms waving madly for Jericho to move when he saw something small and round arcing through the air to land close by him.

It registered in his mind then what Black had been screaming.

"Grenade."

"What do you have in mind?" Fields asked.

Pryde reached for a grenade from his belt, primed it, then tossed it into the air in the direction of the space between the tunnel entrance and the Raptor.

"This," he said, then ducked down as they both waited for the explosion.

Jericho saw the small object land nearby and ran for his life. He'd gone three steps toward the Raptor when the grenade went off.

The blast ripped through the air, smashing into his back, lifting him off his feet to toss him like a rag doll through the air. Landing in a heap closer to the Raptor, he was stunned by the noise and the power of the blast. The shockwave had hit him like an express train hurling him through the air. Shrapnel in the grenade tore his flesh as easily as a hot knife through butter.

Black was running to him the instant he saw him flying toward them. He gently picked up his battered and bloody body and ran for the Raptor, getting inside and shouting for the pilot to get them the hell away from there.

The strange looking craft lifted off into the air and quickly turned away from the area, firing its main engines to depart from the killing zone.

Inside the craft Jericho was barely conscious. His injuries were extensive, and his torso was ripped with gashes running down his back that blood ran freely from. His legs were mangled, torn and bloody with bone fragments sticking through the flesh. His breathing was laboured from the crushing impact on his internal organs from the blast and, as he looked at his friend, he realised, if he didn't receive medical treatment in the next few minutes, he would surely die.

Pryde and Fields watched the Raptor take off the moment the gatling guns ceased firing.

They were too late to stop them leaving but just had enough time to see Black rescue Jericho.

"Shit, fuck!" Fields shouted angrily at the sight of them escaping again.

Pryde glanced at her, unsure why she was so angry.

"Let's get back to the ship and report back to HQ," he said as he moved away to contact his ship.

"Aren't you the least bit pissed that they got away?" she asked, staring at him, open-mouthed.

"We made them leave behind three of their warheads, we killed a number of their crew, and we injured their leader. I regard that as a positive, don't you?" he replied calmly.

"No, quite frankly I do not. They got away with several warheads and we damaged their crew, which to me means they'll be more inclined to strike back at us. That means more innocent lives will be lost," she countered, her hands balled into fists at her sides as she tried to contain her anger, which now seemed to be directed at Pryde.

"We almost killed their leader Jericho. If he survives, then he'll need medical attention, which they are looking into right now; of that, I am sure. It means they will delay any plans of retribution for the time being at least. You see, those plans to strike back, which you so rightly put it, will only be considered once Jericho is well enough to witness them. We have time to locate them and stop them for good."

His explanation calmed her somewhat. It made sense they would want their leader to see his plan put into operation, but there was one snag to this theory which she mentioned.

"But if Jericho dies, then the whole thing will change. They'll strike straight away," she said.

"I know, that's why we need to get back to HQ right away. We need to locate them first," he agreed.

Chapter 37

Phobos, ICE HQ, Natara Nebula

The Raptor docked in the Phobos docking bay and Jericho's injured body was transported immediately to Med Lab where they began treating his injuries straight away.

First, they injected a serum of broad-spectrum antibiotics to fight off any possible infections, then a dose of nano-meds which would repair damage to internal organs and any internal bleeding that would be hard to reach via surgery. When all that had been done, they immersed him in a med-tank filled with healing fluids that would continue the process. Whilst he was in the tank, he wore a breathing mask even though he was placed into a medically induced coma.

Black stood by the side of the tank as the team of doctors finished their work and came to talk to him.

"We've done all we can at this stage, but I don't think we can save his legs," Laurence Koenig said. He was a soldier first who had been a field surgeon. When the Phobos had been refitted, Jericho had wanted the best medical equipment they could find for the Med Lab and Koenig had supervised what he needed and the installation. It was one of the best Med Labs on any starship in any fleet but still not as good as a full-sized hospital.

"What are you saying Doc, that he'll lose both legs, that he'll be in a wheelchair for the rest of his life?" Black said, turning on him, his fists ready to strike in his anger.

"I'm afraid so, yes, but not the last part. I can manufacture a pair of bionic legs for him that will work just as good as his real ones ever did, maybe even better, but you have to decide now or we could lose him."

"What is that supposed to mean Doc?"

"The trauma he went through from the blast has done severe damage to him. I can heal the internal organs, hopefully, and I can give him something to reduce the pain and help him fight off any infections caused by the shrapnel embedded in his body, but I cannot help with the legs. The infection and damage caused to his lower limbs will start to spread throughout his body, so we need to amputate now to prevent that from happening. What I need to know from you is, do you think he'd want to live out the rest of his life sitting down or have full mobility when he comes around?"

Black looked at him, feeling his anger slowly dissipating, "When you put it that way Doc, it's a no brainer. Give him the bionic legs," he said and turned to leave. Remembering something, he looked back over his shoulder, "Doc, keep me informed on yours and Nathan's progress, okay?" and then he was on his way to the bridge.

MI7 SecOps HQ

Pryde and Fields reported back to C in his office the moment they returned to Terra II.

"So they got away again I see," Chamber said when he saw them enter.

"I'm afraid so sir, but Jericho was severely wounded and they left behind three of the warheads which we brought back with us. It seems they've been configured to deliver a nuclear payload," Pryde replied.

"Where are they now?" C asked.

"The lab has them, sir; they're trying to learn everything they can about them to give us a better understanding, not only how they work but how we may be able to stop them if deployed."

"Don't you mean 'when'? I can't see how they won't use them now, especially after we attacked them twice. Jericho, if he lives, will want his revenge now, that's for sure, and if he dies, so will whoever takes over the organisation, so the outcome will be the same no matter what."

"At least we have a little time sir, while they repair Jericho. If we can locate their present base of operations, we can mount an attack on them and finally shut them down."

"Well, we don't seem to be doing too well on that front, do we Pryde?" C snapped back, his frustration evident from the way he stared back at the two of them.

A thought occurred to Pryde then, and his jaw almost dropped open in an uncharacteristic display of emotion. "Sir, what if we could track them using the trackers all warheads have implanted in them should any get stolen? We now have three of the warheads, so using their trackers we should be able to reconfigure long range sensors to look for identical tracking signals," he said more quickly than his usual careful delivery.

"Good work Pryde; get onto the lab techs and see what they can come up with," C replied, his eyes brightening at the prospect of this being the first break they've had in the case.

"I'll get right on it, sir," Pryde said as he went to leave.

"I'll come with you," Fields said, and the two of them left, this time with a more hopeful sense of urgency to their gait.

Chapter 38

Starship Phobos, Natara Nebula.

"How is he Doc?" Black asked.

Both him and Koenig stood outside the Med Lab looking in through the glass wall at the body of Jericho lying unconscious in the bio-bed. He had a breathing tube attached and various wires snaking from vital areas on his body to machines at the side of the bed that monitored his vital signs. The bed itself was a scanner which checked various bodily functions and alerted the medical team should the need arise.

"I managed to repair all the internal damage using the nano-meds. The broad-spectrum antibiotics have kept any infection at bay and I finally fitted the bionic limbs after amputating his legs," Koenig told him as he stared at the body through the glass wall.

"Will he be okay Doc?"

"If you mean, will he live, then the answer to that is yes. If you mean, will he be different when he wakes up, then the answer to that is also yes. Different how? Now that is the question. His body has undergone severe trauma, which we managed to repair, but what the experience that trauma had on his mind is anyone's guess. If you put that with the fact that he'll wake up to learn we took away his legs, then you have an altogether different problem. What I'm trying to say is, we have no idea how he'll react."

"How long before he wakes up then; can you at least answer that?"

"I want to give him at least another twelve hours for his body to heal and adjust to what has been done to it. There's only so much we can do to repair a human body; finally it comes down to what that body will accept. We've taken all the precautions to prevent his body rejecting the bionic limbs, we integrated all the connections to his nerves and muscles so they should work as normal, but after those meds wear off and his body's natural functions take over, he could face further trouble. These things take time. The longer we give him to rest and recuperate then the better chance he'll have of survival."

Black placed a hand on Koenig's arm. "Thanks Doc, for everything. I'd better get back to the bridge. When you're ready to bring him out of the coma, let me know; I want to be there," he said, then walked off back to the bridge.

MI7 SecOps HQ

"What have we learned so far about the tracking chips?" C asked as he entered the Situation Room for an update.

The man performing the sensor scans was an agent named Whittaker and he was in charge of the operation.

"I've managed to isolate the tracking signal of the missiles, sir, and I've reconfigured the long-range sensors to search for it. It'll take some time, as the area we are trying to cover is massive," he said.

"Do you have any idea how long it'll take before you have a location?" Chambers asked. "It could be hours yet, but it also could be within the next few minutes. It's hard to tell considering the area we're covering, but the most it will take is another twelve hours sir."

"Another twelve hours; they could be anywhere by then."

"I'm sorry, sir, that's the best I can do."

"Okay, keep me updated on your progress," C said, thrusting his hands in his pants pockets. He hated feeling powerless like this and when he realised it was showing he took his hands from his pockets and walked back to his office.

***

Pryde and Fields were in his office waiting for any word from the sensor tracking.

"I hate this waiting game. It's the worst part of this job, waiting around on intel so we can act," she said just to fill the quiet that permeated through the small office.

"Just relax; there's no point in worrying about things out of your control, it's just wasted energy," Pryde said. He sat in his chair, hands on his lap with a calm expression as he watched her pace the width of the small room.

"How do you do that, just switch off like that?"

"I've explained already."

She looked at him, staring deep into his calm eyes, "There are times when I wish I could do that. It would make times like this so much easier."

"It's a gift," he said with no trace of humour.

Shaking her head, she couldn't help but smile.

"Maybe we should get some rest—we'll need to be sharp when the word comes in. It'll be up to us to verify where they are before we call in the heavy mob," he said, changing the subject.

"No, it's alright, I doubt I could sleep anyway," she admitted.

"Okay, if that's how you feel, I'll keep you company."

"So what do you want to do, surely you don't want to sit here all this time?"

"You're right, let's go down to the firing range and practice. When the time comes, we'll need to be sharp," he suggested.

"Great. Come on, winner buys the drinks when this is all over," she said with a huge grin spreading across her face.

He looked up at her, his confusion pinching his eyebrows in the middle, "Drinks?" he asked.

"To celebrate, you do celebrate sometimes I take it?"

"Only if I must," he said, getting to his feet, "come on, let's see how good you are on the range."

Chapter 39

Phobos, Natara Nebula.

Light seeped through the edges of his consciousness followed quickly by pain and discomfort.

It was a struggle to open his eyes and, when he finally battled with the weight of his eyelids enough to force them open, he was able to look around. Moving just his eyes, he saw the ceiling, the lights and some of the equipment that was in the range of his restricted movement.

Med Lab. He was in the Med Lab, but why? Confusion closed his mind off to the reality of what had happened, wrapping it in a cloud his conscious mind could not penetrate.

Try as he may, he couldn't remember what had happened. He knew him and his men had escaped through the tunnel after the elevator had been closed off. They ran through the tunnel with the lab techs carrying the warheads, and then as they reached the end there was a fight.

What happened after that was a complete mystery.

"Ah good, you're awake," he heard a voice say. He hadn't even been aware that he wasn't alone. The voice was familiar but the confusion clouding his mind made it impossible for him to recognise who had spoken.

"You'll be experiencing some confusion no doubt; that's normal considering what you have just gone through," the voice explained, which was good. At least he wasn't losing his mind, but it didn't help him understand what it was exactly that he had gone through.

"What happened?" he forced out the words through chapped lips and a throat that felt as if it was lined with sand.

"You were injured, severely, but we managed to get you back here in time."

"In time for what?"

"To save your life."

"How badly was I injured?"

When he saw the man's eyes narrow and his lips press together, he knew it was bad news. He tried to look around more closely, focusing on himself this time. Angling his vision down his body he saw the shape of himself under the covering. His two arms lay at his side on top of the covering; his torso was there, as were his legs—he could see them quite clearly beneath the covering, like two tunnels burrowing beneath the soothing cloth. Nothing was missing and he breathed heavily as his worst fear seemed to be unwarranted.

Looking around at the man, recognition came to him; he was their chief medical officer, Laurence Koenig.

"Doc, why are you so worried? I'm fine. I'm all here and I'm alive so there's nothing to worry about," he said as his mind finally began to clear. Things started to return to him, about the last thing that happened before he blacked out. It was still a little hazy but things would return to him once the drugs they'd given him had fully worn off.

"How do you feel Nathan?" Koenig asked and the worry lines creasing his forehead began to concern him also and he told him so.

"I'm fine Doc, really, but the look on your face tells me there's something you're not telling me. Spit it out Doc, what is it?" he said.

Koenig cleared his throat before speaking. Glancing down at his hands clasped in front of him, he seemed to come to a decision, then looked up at the man lying on the bio-bed. He said, "When you arrived, you had extensive injuries, both internal and external. I treated the internal ones the best I could and repaired any damage caused in the blast, but the external ones caused a bit of a problem. I had to amputate both your legs and replace them with bionic limbs. We kept you in a medically induced coma to give you the best chance of survival and your body time to heal and adapt to the new limbs, which proved to be the right decision. I want to keep you here for a few more hours so I can go through a few more tests to ensure everything is working fine, then you can return to duty."

Through all of it Jericho remained silent as he listened. He stared at the doctor as he tried to take in what he was hearing, his mind seemed incapable at first of accepting what it was being told.

He'd seen soldiers who had similar injuries as the Koenig had described and they too had received bionic limbs to replace those they had lost. Some had coped with the loss and replacement better than others, but all of them had severe problems adapting to the changes to their bodies, at least at first. Some never adapted and feelings of inadequacy and of being less of a person had taken over so they had taken their own life because they could no longer cope with it.

Seeing what this had done to fellow soldiers, Jericho had often wondered how he would cope in a similar situation; how would he cope if he ever lost a limb? Now that stark reality was looking at him squarely in the face and he was about to find out what the answer to that question was.

Staring up at the ceiling he asked, "Will I be able to function normally Doc?"

"I think so, yes. That's why I want to run a few further tests to ensure the new limbs are working as they should; it will only take an hour or so," Koenig replied.

"Okay, then when can we start? I have work to do."

"I'll make the preparations right away. I'll be back in a few minutes, don't go anywhere," Koenig said.

"You're a real comedian Doc," Jericho replied, keeping his gaze on the ceiling. He heard the door close behind the doctor, leaving him alone. Slowly he dropped his gaze to his lower body. It looked perfectly normal beneath the covering, but he had to look deeper, beneath the covering; he had to see his legs.

He gripped the edge of the sheet and flung it off him, and there they were. They looked perfectly normal, the skin tone was the same as his own, the musculature seemed like a normal leg, and he couldn't tell where his torso ended and the leg began. To the untrained eye it looked like he still had his own legs still. The only people who could possibly tell the difference would be those who knew, and himself, obviously.

His fears alleviated somewhat, he covered them back up again and relaxed a little. The real adaptation would come when he tried to use them but that could wait a little longer. He still needed to rest.

Closing his eyes, he was soon asleep.

Chapter 40

MI7 SecOps HQ

The firing range was built beneath the headquarters, deep underground behind several layers of sound proofing where the sound of gunfire would go unnoticed.

Pryde and Fields stood side by side shooting down range using their weapons of choice, Pryde with his Walther and Fields still using her H and K.

The targets were shaped in the form of human figures with target zones circled on the head and torso. So far, having shot several targets Pryde had proven to be the more accurate shooter, whether it was down to his calm exterior or just an innate skill with firearms it was hard to say.

"It looks like I'll be buying the drinks then," Fields said after losing ten targets straight.

"In that case, I think I'll look forward to it," he replied as he ejected another empty clip from the butt of his pistol and replaced it with a fresh one.

"Are we continuing?" he asked, turning to look at her around the partition separating them, "or have you had enough?" he added with a raised eyebrow.

"If I didn't know better, Duncan, I would swear you enjoyed that," she said, returning his gaze with a narrowed eyed glare of her own.

He looked at her and was about to say something when his ear wig implant chimed alerting him to an incoming call.

"Go ahead," he said and turned away from Fields to listen better.

"Come to my office immediately and bring Agent Fields with you. We have a possible lead on where they are," Chamber said.

"We're on our way sir," he said. He replaced his Walther in his shoulder rig and turned to Fields, "C wants us in his office now, they might have a location on Jericho and the missiles," he said.

The two of them made their way back up to the ground floor and went straight to Chambers' office where they were ushered in by Goodchild.

"The sensor sweeps have turned up what could be a signal from the missile tracking chips," he said as they entered.

"Where sir?" Pryde asked.

"It seems to be emanating from somewhere close to the Natara Nebula. We think interference from the Nebula is causing the readings to fluctuate slightly and that's why we've been unable to pinpoint exactly where it is."

"Do you want us to go take a look?" Pryde asked, already knowing the answer.

"Yes, I'll have a strike team on standby ready to move the moment you give the go ahead that you have an affirmative ID on the target; the details have been sent to your PIN," Chamber said.

"Copy that sir," Pryde said.

The two of them left the office and went to where Pryde's starship was parked.

<hr>

Phobos, Natara Nebula

After receiving the all clear from Koenig, Jericho tentatively made his way to the bridge.

Unsure how his new legs would respond, he was amazed to find them working just fine. Apart from him having a slight phantom tingle from his toes, he felt nothing unusual from the new bionic limbs.

It also helped that his pants covered them so he didn't keep looking down at them. Although they looked just like any other legs he knew they weren't his, so his eyes naturally strayed down to them.

He'd expected it to be a struggle to master them, as if they were something attached rather than a part of him, but soon found that not to be the case. The wiring of them was so subtle that his brain couldn't differentiate between these and his old legs. The natural impulses from the brain that stimulated the muscles involved in controlling the legs were the same to activate the bionic ones.

His brain may not be able to differentiate between the two but his mind certainly could and that was the problem

Koenig wanted to overcome. It would take time but Koenig had reassured him that pretty soon he would think of them as his own.

Black looked up from his screen when he entered the bridge and smiled. It seemed he wasn't the only one pleased that he was alive. The way everyone looked at him, the pinched eyebrows of concern, the way they glanced, then looked away told him they too were unsure what his reaction would be.

"Good to see you up and about," Black said, relinquishing the command chair and coming to greet him.

"Good to be on my feet again," he replied, then realised he wasn't on 'his' feet again. An ironic smile briefly creased his lips. Disregarding it he said, "What's our status?"

"We're at station keeping at the moment."

"Why?"

Black took a step back as he looked at him, his brow creasing as he wondered what he meant.

"Not sure what you mean," he said.

"Are all the missiles on board?" Jericho asked.

"Most of them, yes."

Jericho felt a sinking feeling as he listened. "What the fuck do you mean, most of them?" he asked.

"We were attacked as we were transferring them on board the Raptor. When you got injured, my priority was to get you on board and back here to safety so you could get treated."

"Meaning what, exactly?" Jericho asked, but he had a feeling that he already knew the answer.

"In the rush to get you aboard, we had to leave three of the warheads behind."

"How long was I out?" he asked urgently. Looking around he could see no signs of alarm which meant there was still a chance they could salvage the situation.

"At least twelve hours; your injuries were extensive," Black replied, and by his pinched expression he could tell he had no idea of the damage he may have done to their mission.

"Get us moving, I don't care where, just get us moving now," Jericho shouted, his anger flaring up fuelled by the thought everything he had planned for could all come crashing down.

Black issued the command to move away from the nebula—they couldn't make the jump to hyperspace this close to it. The interference caused by the nebula, the same thing that helped hide them from sensor scans, also made it impossible to jump to hyperspace.

"What's going on Nathan?" Black asked as he stepped closer so the others wouldn't overhear. His concern wrinkled his brow.

"Every single missile has tracking chips placed inside them, so they can be tracked as well, you know. When we had them all there was no way they could be tracked because they didn't know what to look for, they didn't have the tracking signature. Now they have three of the warheads, so how long do you think it'll be before they find us? And we've been sitting here for over twelve hours just waiting for them to come knocking at our door," Jericho said through gritted teeth as he tried his best to keep his anger contained.

Black's brow smoothed out as his eyes and jaw opened up. Jericho saw the moment he realised how badly he'd screwed up displayed all over his face. His cheeks reddened and he turned to issue more orders to the crew, this time with a real sense of urgency.

"Get those engines powered up, move us to a safe distance fast, then make the jump to hyperspace," he shouted, the words tumbling out fast.

"Where to?" the helm asked.

"I don't give a fuck, just get us the fuck away from here," Black replied.

"Terra II," Jericho shouted from the back of the bridge, "take us to Terra II."

Black's head spun around to look at him so fast Jericho could have sworn he heard vertebrae in his neck snap.

"It's time to make them pay," he said when he saw him look at him.

Turning back to the bridge, Black said, "You heard him —Terra II."

Jericho watched through the viewscreen as the nebula receded into the distance as they moved away to make the jump.

The COP had played hardball with him, fighting him every step of the way. Now it was time to bring the fight to their very doorstep. It was easy to distance themselves from the fight when it was happening many light years away and happening to other people. It was easy to keep to your principles when no one you cared about was involved in the struggle. It would be a different thing altogether if it was their lives on the line, the lives of people they loved and cared about. It would be interesting to see how well those same principles held up under those circumstances.

With a cruel smile slowly spreading across his face Jericho saw the hyperspace window open before them. In a few moments he would have the answers to all those questions, and so much more.

Chapter 41

The starship emerged from the hyperspace window several thousand kilometres from the nebula.

"Okay ship, scan for the missiles," Pryde said. He was looking through the forward viewport at the nebula but from this distance all he could see was the nebula itself.

"There is no sign of the missiles here, sir," the ship's AI reported, which stopped him in his tracks. He looked harder at the image before him, going to the viewscreen and magnifying the image several times to bring it into sharper focus.

"Where can they have gone?" Fields asked the question already running through Pryde's mind.

"Scan again, but this time run a deeper scan; look for any trace whatsoever," he said.

"I have already run several scans, sir, and I can assure you there is no trace here or anywhere near."

"We're too late," Pryde said, which was the only possible conclusion to be drawn from this.

"Contact C, at HQ," he said.

"Sir, he is hailing us," the AI said.

"Put him through," Pryde said. The quicker he got this over with, the faster they could continue the search, although it would be more difficult this time as clearly they knew they were looking for them.

"I have some bad news, sir," he said once C appeared on the viewscreen.

"Never mind that now," C interrupted him with a wave of his hand, "we've just had word that a massive starship has emerged from hyperspace and gone straight into orbit around the planet."

"It's Jericho, sir," Pryde said. This was it, the endgame. Jericho had been denied his pay-out so it was time to make those who were behind it suffer.

"I would activate the planet's defences sir, immediately. If that ship is Jericho's, and I have no reason to suspect otherwise, it's there for only one reason, and it's not a social call."

"Already done. You need to get back here right away, it's all hands-on deck."

"We're on our way, sir," Pryde said.

After closing the connection, he said, "Ship, take us back to Terra II."

Terra II

On the bridge of the Phobos Jericho could tell by the feverish glances his way that the tension had spiked.

"Are we really going to attack the heart of the Coalition with just this one ship?" Black asked as he stood by the side of the command chair. He kept his voice low so as not to add to the already mounting tension.

"Not entirely, no. I intend to give them something to think about, then, if they don't see things my way, I'll leave them with a little present and move on to greener pastures," Jericho replied in the same lowered tone his friend had used.

Black's shoulders relaxed a little as Jericho had expected. He could almost see what he was thinking, that there was still time to salvage something from this after all.

How wrong he was.

There was no turning back now, not for Jericho. He intended on making them pay, even if it meant he would die in the attempt. His reputation had been destroyed with this mission. It had not gone as planned and, when news reached the rest of the criminal fraternity, he would be considered a laughing stock, persona non grata.

If this was to fail, then he would go out with a bang, literally.

"Whatever it is you're going to do, I suggest you make a start before they send ships to intercept us," Black said.

"Agreed. Load each missile onto a shuttle and send them down to the planet to these locations," Jericho said. The locations showed up on Black's PIN. They had already been picked by Jericho as plan B just in case his primary plan somehow failed. He'd never expected to have to resort to this but, like any war, the outcome was always fluid and to survive it you had to know how to adapt to changes in circumstances. No one ever knew what the other side would do in any conflict—it was almost impossible to predict with one hundred percent accuracy what the opposition would do, so it was always considered good practise to have an alternative, just in case.

Black left the bridge to organise the deployment of the missiles, leaving Jericho sitting in the command chair getting ready to issue his demands to the Coalition Council.

The starship that Pryde and Fields travelled in arrived back at Terra II shortly after the Phobos had deployed the shuttles carrying the missiles.

Pryde directed the AI to take the ship down for a landing immediately after entering normal space once more. The AI put the ship down at the space port near the SecOps HQ and the two of them went inside to report in with Chambers.

They found everyone in the Situation Room; the tension in the room had risen since the last time they were there.

Chambers turned when he heard them enter and they walked over to him.

"I take it that something has happened, sir," he said.

C indicated the main monitor where Jericho appeared sitting on the command chair on the Phobos. "Jericho is making contact with the Council as we speak," he said.

All attention turned to the monitor to hear what was being said.

"Now that I have your attention, I'll give you one last chance," Jericho said.

In the bottom corner of the screen was a small image of the Council chamber where the call was being received. MI7 had intercepted the call to listen in. The President was speaking, "What is it you want, Jericho?" he asked.

"I have six of the missiles already reconfigured with nuclear warheads. You've already seen the power these missiles have with standard warheads, just imagine how much more extensive the damage, the loss of life will be if just one of them detonates, and then multiply that by six. If you don't want any of that to happen, then I suggest you give me what I want."

"Refresh my memory, what is it you want?" Harada replied.

"Since last we spoke, my price has just doubled. Now I want ten billion Coalition Credits. You have one hour or I detonate the first missile. If you haven't given me the money an hour after that, another missile will be detonated. I have chosen areas that will cause the most chaos. Think of the panic that will arise if you allow one of these things to detonate, and then just wonder how it will escalate if another goes off?"

Pryde was watching the conversation, switching his attention onto whoever was speaking. When Jericho mentioned the potential chaos in the population if the missiles blew, he saw Harada's expression alter. From the way his eyes narrowed and his lips pursed he knew he was angry, but there was something else, something deeper. Harada wasn't angry because people would die, he was angry at how it would affect his administration. He was more concerned at how his public opinion would be impacted.

"It's not our policy to make deals with terrorists."

"I'm not a terrorist, I'm an extortionist working my way up to being a mass murderer. You have one hour to see which path my career takes. It's up to you, Mister President," Jericho said, then the screen went blank.

The small picture in the corner showing the President remained in place where everyone could see the reaction on his face. His eyes almost blazed with a fury he struggled to contain.

"Does anyone have any idea if we can prevent this monster from carrying out his threat?" Harada said, standing up. His fists were placed on the table as he leaned on them for support, keeping his eyes firmly placed on the table in front of him. Pryde knew he didn't want to look the others in the face for fear that they, too, would see the truth written across his face.

When nothing was forthcoming from the room, he said, "I thought not. Tell the depository to prepare for the transfer of funds. I want to be ready just in case we have to pay up and smile. The important thing here is, if we have to pay, then this transaction must never reach the media, and I mean ever. Is that clear? If this goes bad and we have to pay up and I hear even a whisper of it reaching the wrong ears, then I will do everything in my power to destroy that individual, whoever they are. Now I'm sure there are things you all need to attend to so I won't keep you any longer."

C motioned for the feed to be cut as he turned to Pryde.

"Well, have we any actionable intel?" he asked.

"He claims to have sent the missiles to the surface in preparation to fire should the Council refuse to pay him; we should be able to track them then, sir," Pryde said.

"I would start at all major cities; he mentioned he wanted the maximum chaos and death toll," Fields suggested.

Pryde held up a hand, "No need. These missiles can be fired from miles away. There's no need to place them within a city; besides, it would be too obvious. He could simply place them on a boat off shore and fire them into a city from a safe distance. Sir, I would look at sites around major cities such as coastal areas or locations a few miles outside a city, probably a deserted area such as a wasteland or desert," he said.

"I'll get right on it. Is there anything else?" C said.

"I would think he would have a central command post where all the firing would be coordinated from. If we can find that, we might be able to shut them all down in one fell swoop," Pryde said.

"Good idea; you two get ready to move. If we find this central command post I want you to go there and shut them down."

"Copy that sir," Pryde said. Turning to Fields, he said, "Come on, we can wait back on the ship."

Chapter 42

"Do you think they'll cave in this time Nathan?" Black asked. He had finished off the organising of the deployment of the shuttles carrying the missiles and had returned to the bridge.

"If they don't want millions of people to die, they have to," Jericho replied.

"When you put it that way, I suppose they have no choice."

"There's always a choice, I'm sure they'll leave it to the last minute before they make the right one."

"Let's hope not. I'll be glad to be done with this and be gone where we can enjoy the fruits of all this hard work," Black commented.

A thought occurred to Jericho then. His eyes widened as he turned to look at his friend, "Did you disengage the tracking chips in the missiles?" he asked.

"No, you know that can't be done until the two codes are entered, one at the destination and the other from the place where they were sent from."

Jericho nodded as he remembered the protocol involved when shipping any missiles from one point to another. It was a way to keep them safe and to be able to locate them if they ever went missing, for whatever reason. In this case, it was a detriment to their operation.

"Well, we'd better hope they pay up before they remember the same thing. If they go looking for them, it wouldn't take them too long before they found them. I want the command post guarded with our best men and I want it done now, and it has to be done without anyone finding out about it. The less the CDF knows about this, the more chance we have of pulling it off," Jericho said.

"I'll get on it right away," Black said, but before he had time to move away, Jericho grabbed his arm.

"Handle this personally," he said.

With a nod, Black left to organise the team.

Jericho sat in the command chair staring at the viewscreen, his feeling of elation at finally getting what he wanted slowly dissipating with the news that there was a possibility that the missiles could be traced. This would be a race against time and it would be interesting to see who would be the eventual winner.

The starship carrying Pryde and Fields was already moving into the air as Pryde said to the AI, "Okay ship, coordinate with all the sensor scans being done by MI7 in looking for those missiles. Correlate all their findings so far and see if you can come up with a possible site for the command post that would control all the missile launchings."

"What about searching through all the ships arriving at the planet? They would have to log in with planetary control surely," Fields said.

"It would take too long to search through those records. Thousands of ships come and go every day and besides, once they log in on arrival, there's nothing stopping them from altering their final destination. It would be a complete waste of time," Pryde countered coldly.

"Sir, according to satellite signals, I may have located several of the missile launching sites and a possible location for their command post," the ship said.

"Good, relay all of that to SecOps HQ and inform them we're on our way to take a look at the latter, then set course for the command post," Pryde said quickly.

"Copy that, sir; message sent and course set," replied the ship. "Sir, we are being hailed," it added.

"Put them through," Pryde said.

"Pryde, we came to the same conclusions here so I've dispatched a tac team to the command post's location as backup," C said, his face appearing on the communication screen.

"Tell them to stand off until I give the all-clear sir. There's no point in them attacking a place if it turns out to be the wrong one. Fields and I will check it out first, then give the signal when we're sure it's the right place," Pryde replied.

"Copy that, and don't be too long in verifying this Pryde, we don't have a lot of time here. The CDF is itching to attack that starship the moment we get word the missiles have been neutralised, so work fast," C said, then closed the connection. Clearly nothing more needed to be said.

He glanced across at his partner and, by how her brow was lowered and her jaw was set in determination, he knew she was aware of the stakes here.

"Okay ship, take us in," he said.

Chapter 43

New Central Park

In the centre of New Seattle, the capital city on the northern edge of the largest land mass on the planet, there was a park area for the inhabitants of the huge concrete jungle to enjoy a touch of nature.

Stretching almost a mile across, it was a wooded area with walkways, areas of woodland and picnic sites for anyone who wanted to spend some time in the sun.

Black rendezvoused with the initial group who had landed in the centre of this park to construct the command post. From this vantage point, all the missile launch sites could be reached. New Seattle would be exempt should they have to fire because, if they had to fire one, Jericho was sure that the Council would soon fold, but to be able to do that they have to be left alive.

"Jericho wants us to be ready in case they try to take this command post," he told the men manning the equipment.

They had installed the command module in a clear open space where they could see anyone approaching. It was a small box with a set of touch screens and a monitor that images of the missiles could be displayed upon. From this one vantage point they could not only control all the missiles being launched, changing their target en route if required, but watch it happen in real time on the monitor.

The team of armed men Black had brought with him surrounded the post, aiming their rifles in the opposite direction, ready to fire should anyone try to approach.

"Get to work, I want this ready to go should he give the command to fire," he said as he paced around them, watching with a disturbing intensity as they worked.

Black was beginning to feel like Jericho was losing faith in him. Having him take charge of this part of the operation felt more like a punishment than a reward, and his feelings showed by the way he glared at the men manning the module as he paced around them like a hungry tiger waiting to be fed.

The ship carrying Pryde and Fields flew close to the park area.

"Sir, I am picking up strong sensor readings from equipment in the middle of the park. It could be the command post you are looking for," the AI controlling the ship said.

"Okay ship, park us on the edge of the park and we'll go in to take a look from there," Pryde instructed.

"Copy that, sir," the AI replied and landed the ship on the outskirts of the massive park.

"How're we going to get from here to the command post?" Fields asked.

"We have options, but first we need to arm ourselves just in case we run into any trouble like last time."

The two of them grabbed a pistol and a rifle each with spare clips for both. Grabbing a few grenades like last time, they had enough fire power between them to start a small war.

In the rear cargo area of the ship, Pryde stored various items he had used on occasion. This time he chose a small jet pack that was strapped to the pilot's back and had control armatures that were connected to handgrips. These controlled power and direction. Seeing him strap one of these onto his back, Fields followed suit. Then he chose a bike, a Python land bike. It had large tyres front and back with a suspension that could handle almost any terrain. The seat was placed just aft of the power cell that was just to the rear of the handlebars, which controlled power and the brakes. The power unit was automatic so the gear shifts were smooth as silk. Making almost no sound, the motor was the ideal transport for this mission as it would take them as close as possible without fear of detection.

These were the military versions of the bikes, which also meant they had an offensive capability if such a need arose.

Throwing a leg over the nearest Python, Pryde said, "Have you ever ridden one of these?"

"Many times," Fields replied with a smile as she remembered the fun she had riding the beast of a bike.

"Good, try to keep up then," Pryde said, then gunned the engine and set off down the ramp at the rear of his ship.

Chapter 44

General Wallace was in the War Room at the Coalition Council Building. This was where any military mission could be viewed from in real time.

Hundreds of military strikes had been watched in this room, relayed from whichever area of space it was taking place through hyperspace relays that boosted communication signals to almost instantaneous levels. Never before though had the inhabitants of the room watched something happen so close to home.

"Mister President, we have three of our battle cruisers forming a barricade around the Phobos, the Appleton, the Washington and the Ark Royal. They can target and fire their plasma railguns the instant we get the word that the missiles have been neutralised," Wallace said as he stared at the main monitor screen at the far end of the room.

Harada wiped sweat from his forehead with the back of his right hand, "Let's hope that word comes through quickly," he said.

"Why don't we take the Phobos out anyway, sir? It'll send them a message that we are not going to back down," Wallace suggested, taking his eyes from the screen to look at the Commander in Chief of the Coalition.

"I'm not sure that's the right way to go, General. If we jump the gun, then they could say to hell with it and fire them anyway. No, for the time being we will wait for the operatives on the ground to do their job of neutralising the missiles before we do anything." Harada said.

"I just hope we still have time then," Wallace said.

Fields overtook Pryde as they entered the park area. Both of them were riding along, using the AI on the ship to guide them to their final destination.

"I thought you said keep up," she said, glancing over her shoulder at him just behind her.

Her bike slowed automatically as they neared the spot they had been heading for, the onboard computer controlling the power.

As Pryde pulled up alongside her, he said, "It must be just over there." He put his bike on its stand and withdrew his Walther Q9 pistol. Jacking the slide to inject a round into the breach, he started forward, keeping low to reduce his silhouette.

The path they had chosen took them through the park on pathways lined by hedgerows at least six feet high, which afforded them some cover. As Pryde left his bike he went forward using the same hedgerows to hide behind. He came to the end of the path and peered around the end of the hedge to look at the open space beyond.

There was a lawned area of at least fifty square feet, on which the command post had been erected. Several control stations were facing outward, forming a rough circle with the operators standing behind them also facing outward. The guards stood watching for any approaching threats, their weapons raised and ready to fire. One man stood in the middle supervising it all.

Leaning back he said, "It's not going to be easy to creep up on them; they have every angle covered from what I can see."

Fields said, "What's your plan then?"

"I'm working on it."

Stepping forward, he had his pistol aimed right at the man in the middle.

"Drop your weapons or he gets a bullet in the brain," he shouted.

"Thanks for letting me know what you're going to do," Fields said as she stepped forward at his side, bringing her own pistol up to bear.

He saw the man in the middle hold up a hand to halt the guards opening fire on them.

"You do realise you're out gunned here. If you shoot me, they will kill both of you and the missiles will still be fired should the Council refuse to pay up. You will have changed nothing except ensuring your own deaths," Black said calmly.

"I have a fleet surrounding your ship right now just waiting for the word to open fire. At the same time there is a fully armed troop of Special Forces waiting for the execution order to come down on you right now. This is not a chance encounter, this has been meticulously planned with every eventuality considered and planned for," Pryde countered.

"Let's just say, for the moment, that I believe anything you just said. What do you expect to happen in the next few moments?" Black said, then added, "You don't even know who you're dealing with, do you?"

"Nathan Jericho is in charge, but that's not you. He would never endanger himself in this ploy, no, he's probably up on the starship sitting comfortably in the command chair thinking all is going well and that he is untouchable as long as he has the finger on the trigger of those missiles. No, you're probably one of his lieutenants, and if pressed I would go as far as saying that you recently failed to do something that pissed him off, and that's why you're down here and he's up there, safe and sound."

Pryde saw how his words hit a nerve in the twitch at the side of the man's right eye and the way he pursed his lips together in anger. The micro expressions were minor and disappeared as fast as they had appeared, but they had not gone unnoticed.

Tension in the group was mounting though. The guards were beginning to get a little twitchy listening to what was being said. The notion that they were about to be run over by Special Forces instilled fear in them. Pryde saw all their eyes go wide and they glanced this way and that as they looked at each other for confidence and support from their brothers in arms.

"I suggest you put down your arms and allow us to shut down the missiles before you do something you'll regret," Pryde said.

"And if I refuse?" Black asked, calling his bluff.

"Yes, what happens then?" Fields whispered out of the side of her mouth. Before he could answer one of the guards took things into his own hands and opened fire on them.

Chapter 45

Fields dropped back behind the hedge as Pryde ran for cover across the path. As he ran, he fired off several rounds at the shooter. The third shell hit him high on his shoulder, knocking him back, spinning him around slightly. He continued to fire, but the bullets went wide and high as the impact on his shoulder altered his aim drastically.

Fields joined the fray, firing around the side of the hedge which didn't afford much cover.

Bullets from the other guards ripped through the hedge, forcing the female agent down into a prone position on the ground. Taking careful aim, she shot the nearest guard to her in the ankle; the bullet shattered the bone. The man's leg collapsed under him and as he landed, and she fired once more, blowing a hole in his head, splashing his brains behind him.

Other guards scrambled for cover behind the workstations as they were out in the open. Seeing one of their numbers felled before their eyes gave them cause to concern for their own lives. These weren't all trained soldiers, criminals mostly with a few mercenaries from Jericho's days in the Special Forces.

Pryde reached the cover of another hedgerow across the open space. As soon as he reached it he aimed and fired in quick succession, taking out three guards in as many shots.

Their numbers dwindling fast, Black came to a decision. Getting behind one of the control panels, he called Jericho on the Phobos.

"We're under fire down here from a pair of agents. You might have to rethink your timetable," he said urgently.

Pryde saw the man in charge frantically make a call and he guessed correctly it was to Jericho. He fired off a quick salvo aimed at the console he was using as cover. Sparks ignited from each impact of the steel jacketed shells, making him step up again.

Pryde saw his stand up and fired at him once more.

The bullet slammed into Black's forehead, snapping his head back as the shell smashed through the tough bone above his eyes, then travelled through into the brain, causing massive damage before exiting through the back of his skull. A jet of red brain matter suspended in a mixture of blood and bone fragments showed the bullet's trajectory.

The man working the console watched Black fall back, dead, then looked toward the shooter. Pryde shot him, then targeted some of the other operators manning the command post.

Two more dropped to his accuracy before the guards targeted his position. The hedge he was using as cover was soon torn apart by automatic rifle fire.

The guards seemed to panic a little as they had seen their leader drop. With no one to step up and take command, they were a little unsure of what to do next. This played into Pryde's hands because any thought of firing off the missiles was discarded for the moment.

They began firing at both agents in an attempt to destroy them.

Pryde saw his cover whittle down to almost nothing. Shards of wood and leaves flew into the air as bullets shredded the cover, forcing him closer to the ground. Remaining calm, he planned his next move. Through the disappearing cover he could see the legs of the guards behind the consoles. Aiming carefully, he fired at one leg and saw the bullet shatter the ankle. Firing three more times he dropped three of the guards, then delivered the coup de grace on all three.

Fields took care of the last two guards by getting to her knees, then shooting them as their attention was diverted by the three deaths.

As they dropped to the ground, all that was left were the operators at the controls.

Pryde and Fields rushed forward into the open space, guns aimed at them.

One of the operators leaned forward and pressed some of the controls, then stepped back, hands held high with a smile of success on his face.

"It's too late," he said, "all of that was for nothing," he added, glancing at the console. His smile faded fast as his eyes saw something.

"What did you do?" Pryde said, coming at him pointing his Walther at his face.

"I don't understand it," he said, staring at the control panel on his console, his brow furrowing.

"I fired a missile but the command never got through," he said.

Pryde looked at the console, then went to each one to check them all. When he got back to the first one, he had formed a hypothesis.

"This was all a misdirect. These consoles never had any control over the firing of those missiles. Jericho set us all up just to waste our time," he said.

"Why? What's his endgame here?" Fields asked, her eyes pinching together in confusion.

"I doubt he ever had any intention of not firing those missiles. At least not after our first attempt to stop him. I think he's already targeted those missiles and all this was just a time-wasting gambit to give him time."

"Time for what, to escape?"

"No, I think he'll hang around to see the results of his plan."

Fields looked up in the sky, then back at Pryde. "He's up there right now just waiting to see what kind of chaos he's about to cause, isn't he?" she said.

Pryde gave her a nod, "We have to get up there and stop him," he said.

Chapter 46

The two agents were on Pryde's ship as soon as he'd informed C of the new development and the command post site had been handed over to the local authorities, who were waiting on the results of the military strike.

The command post was soon dismantled, the operators taken into custody, and the Special Forces team deployed to a waiting ship to take them onto the Phobos as soon as they could gain access.

As the ship left the atmosphere, Pryde was in contact with C.

"The ship is surrounded by three battle cruisers. They are too close for it to make a jump to hyperspace, but we can't make a move in case he fires off those missiles," C said.

"We have to get aboard that ship and take that chance, sir. I don't think he's got any intention of not firing them; now it's just a matter of when," Pryde replied.

"What do you mean by that?"

"He's enjoying watching us all scramble about trying to find a way to prevent him from firing. The longer he waits, the more intense the pleasure. He's like a small child pulling legs off an insect, watching it try to escape, pulling one leg off at a time until it can't go anywhere and he finally crushes it. We're still in the leg pulling stage, but when all our legs are gone, then he'll lose interest and fire."

"And if we open fire on him, he'll fire anyway, is that what you're saying?"

"Exactly. I think the only way to stop this is for me to get aboard his ship and stop him from firing; then you can tell the ships to open fire on him."

"That won't give you much time to escape though."

"It's the only way, sir. If you can think of any other way, I'm all ears. Trust me, I don't relish the idea of going down with that ship, but as long as he doesn't get to fire off those missiles it has to be worth it."

There was a pause on the comm link which stretched so long Pryde was beginning to think it had been severed. When Chambers finally spoke, his voice was low and resigned.

"Unfortunately, I can't. I'm sorry. I'll try to give you as much time as I can before giving the order to fire, and I'll hold them off as long as I can to give you time to try and get off there," he said.

"No need, sir; you need to destroy that ship to prevent him from escaping and attempting something like this in the future. We have to send a message to any potential Jericho's out there that this kind of thing will not go unpunished."

"Copy that. And Pryde, good luck," Chambers said before signing off.

"Okay, so how are we going to do this?" Fields said.

Pryde looked at her, "We?" he asked.

"Although I don't relish the thought of dying on that ship either, I also know you can't do this on your own. The chances of this being a success double if I go along."

"I can't ask you to do this," Pryde said.

"You don't have to, I'm volunteering."

"The chances of this being a success will greatly improve if you tag along, I suppose."

"Tag along, I don't think so. I'm going so you don't grab all the glory. This is a career boost my man, do you realise the kudos I'll get for saving the entire planet? Man, this is my ticket to Agency super stardom," she said.

"Right," he said looking at her, trying to gauge if what she said was true or if she was simply downplaying her involvement. Either way, he decided it didn't matter as long as she pulled her weight and didn't slow him down.

"Okay, here's what we'll do..." he said.

"The command post has been shut down," Trask said. He had joined Jericho for the final part of the plan.

"I expected as much. Don't worry though, everything is in hand," Jericho replied. He was sitting in the command chair on the bridge calmly watching everything unfold on the viewscreen that had linked to the sensor array and the communication satellites in orbit around the planet.

"Are you sure about that? Because to me it just looks like you're sitting on your ass waiting for something to happen," Trask argued.

Jericho snapped a look his way, his lips forming a tight seal as he contained his anger.

"Don't confuse my calm demeanour with unpreparedness. I have everything under control. The mark of true genius is being able to adapt to anything and everything that comes in your path," he said.

"And conversely, continuing doing the same thing time and again but expecting a different outcome every time is the mark of insanity," Trask countered.

Jericho stared at him, his eyes narrowing as he considered how much of his plan to reveal. A glance around the bridge told him all he needed to know. From the furtive glances his way from the crew he gathered, it was clear that they shared Trask's concern that things may be spiralling out of their control.

"You haven't even targeted those battle cruisers, nor raised any shields. We're sitting ducks here man and I didn't sign on for no suicide mission. We all expected to get paid here, and so far they have denied you every step of the way," Trask pointed out.

"I haven't raised shields yet because I want them to think they still have a chance of success. I want to see them scramble for any plan they might think will work and then I will close them all down. I am going to fire those missiles soon because they have no intention of paying my demands, and so they will pay the price for standing against me. We will not get paid today, but the next time I demand payment, and word reaches the rest of the galaxy of what I did here to those who refused me, I can assure you they will bend to my will," Jericho said. He glanced slowly around at the crew so they all knew he was speaking to them all then said, "Is that clear enough for you?"

An alarm sounded down at the front of the bridge, emanating from ops.

"Sir, I have a small ship approaching on a direct path. Should I hail them?" ops said.

"No, shoot them out of the sky," Jericho replied.

Chapter 47

"They've fired on us," Fields said.

"Don't worry, I expected as much. Get ready to make the jump," Pryde said. His calm demeanour gave absolutely no clue as to what he was feeling.

The two of them were wearing EVA suits of micro-thin material that incorporated a slim backpack that held all the equipment needed for a successful spacewalk, including a breathing unit.

"Get to the hatch now, we have to time this to the last second," he said, keeping his attention firmly on the screen that showed the approaching missile.

He could tell by how his partner was getting fidgety that the tension was beginning to get to her. The hatch was opened and they entered the airlock, closing the hatch after them. The outer hatch was opened and Pryde pushed Fields through the opening just as the missile struck.

The explosion ripped the ship apart, sending the two of them hurtling away from the blast. The shockwave from the force produced from the missile exploding gripped them both in a vice-like hold and threw them away from the ship.

Debris from the blast flew in every direction, colliding with the two figures as they were thrown about like rag dolls.

Flames from the explosion soon went out in the vacuum of space but the flying debris was the real problem. Sharp shards of shrapnel from what was left of their ship chased them through space, any one of which could penetrate the EVA suit and the person inside. Without air to cause friction, the shrapnel flew at astounding speeds which could slice through the suit and whoever was inside like a knife through butter.

The EVA suits not only held a breather unit but also a thruster pack which helped them manoeuvre in space. Once the blast threw them clear, they turned on the thruster packs to steer them where they needed to go.

Luckily, they were thrown clear of the debris, and when they fired the thruster packs their speed increased, helping them to move out of range as they headed for the Phobos.

As skin tight as the suits were, they still afforded them protection against the reduced pressure of outer space and the cold. Increased mobility was another factor that was an advantage, especially when performing difficult tasks in space. The downside to all this though was coming up—when they slammed into the starship, they would feel everything.

As the Phobos grew larger in their visors, both Fields and Pryde fired their thrusters to slow their speed. If they slammed into the ship at their present speed, they would surely be knocked unconscious, and their mission would be over.

Pryde could hear Fields grunting and muttering as she saw the ship filling her field of vision and he knew she was getting anxious about if they would decelerate enough in time.

He felt no such emotion as he had dialled down his emotional responses to almost zero. He couldn't afford anything preventing him from doing his job now—there were too many lives at stake. He remained calm as he got nearer to the ship and, as he entered the final one hundred feet, he fired his thrusters in reverse at full power to slow him down for the final touchdown on the hull of the massive behemoth of a craft.

He slammed into the beast of a ship and bounced off, then his thrusters fired once more to take him back slower this time to engage with the ship. He activated magnetic grapples on the soles of his boots to keep him in place, then looked around for his partner.

She had managed her approach without much trouble and clamped on without bouncing off like he had. She was better at this than she gave herself credit for, he observed.

"What now?" she asked, looking his way, her eyes still wide from the adrenaline rush.

"Now, we get inside," he replied calmly.

"When you say it like that, you make it sound so easy," she observed, but her sarcasm was lost on him. He reached his hand out to a panel next to him and a hatch opened.

"How the fuck did you do that? How did you even know that was there?" she said, her voice going up almost a full octave.

"On the way over I scanned for escape hatches and, when I knew their location, I directed our trajectory toward the nearest one to our approach," he replied, with mild surprise. "What did you expect, that I would try to blast our way inside?" he added.

"Never mind," she said, "let's just get inside and do what we came here to do," she added, not wanting to confirm his suspicions.

Chapter 48

"The ship has been destroyed, sir," ops said, then muttered something unintelligible.

Jericho picked up on it and looked at him.

"What?" he asked sharply.

"I picked up an anomaly, sir, just after the ship exploded—well, two actually," ops tried to explain hesitatingly.

"What does that even mean?" Jericho snapped angrily.

"I'm not exactly sure but it could mean two of the ship's crew came over to us using the explosion to cover their tracks, sir."

Jericho snapped a look at Trask, who was standing by his side. "Check this out. If two of them did make their way over here then there is only one reason why. Find them, and kill them," he said. "Do whatever it takes to stop them," he added as Trask turned to leave.

Once Pryde and Fields were inside the huge starship and closed the hatch behind them, they scanned through the schematics of the ship to locate what they needed

"How long before they detect us on board do you think?" Fields asked.

An alarm sounded, blasting out the words, "Intruder Alert," several times.

"Well, I guess that answers that question," she said.

"Come on, we have no time to waste. Now that they know we're here they will do whatever it takes to stop us and may even fire off those missiles prematurely. If that happens, we have to find a way to abort the launch," Pryde said, laying out their objective.

"What exactly are we looking for here?" Fields asked; she knew why they were there but she was a little fuzzy on all the details.

Looking around the vacant corridor, Pryde spotted a panel he needed.

Walking over to it, he took out his PIN and used it to log into the ship's computer through this access panel. Accessing the computer, he quickly scrolled through the ships' operations looking for the one thing they needed.

"Here, this is what we need. We find this," he said, indicating what was showing on the small PIN screen, "we can stop them from firing those missiles," he said.

Looking at him, she said, "Let's go then."

Trask looked at his PIN to see where the intruders were located. He'd accessed the ship's sensors and sent the readings to his device so he could track them.

This was what he was used to, tracking down problems and eliminating them. For this task, he was ideally suited, and this time would be no different from all the other times he's eradicated problems for them.

The bridge was on a higher deck than where the readings were emanating from, so he made his way to the nearest turbo lift. Once inside, he accessed the floor where the intruders were on and, as the lift began to move, a cruel smile crossed his lips as he contemplated what he was going to do to them.

He had their location and arrived on the same deck as them. The turbo lift doors opened and he exited, looking both ways, confident he would spot them soon.

Moving fast, they ran down the corridor. From somewhere up ahead Pryde heard the sound of running feet.

"Our time just ran out," he said. Bringing his Walther Q9 up, he advanced, ready to meet the oncoming threat.

The corridor they were in curved around to the right so whoever was coming was still around the bend and not yet visible. There were a few doors on both sides which led off to who knew where. Pryde had assessed how many were coming for them and knew the two of them had little chance of surviving the fight—there were simply too many.

Opening the nearest door on his right, he dragged Fields into it after him.

"What the fuck are you doing?" she said as the door closed after them.

"Saving our lives, for now at least," he said, not looking at her as he was busy scanning the room they had just entered. It appeared to be a lab of some kind, but it was deserted. All the equipment was still there and it appeared to be in good working order, but there was no sign of it being used, at least not in recent years anyway. He knew this was an old ship of the dreadnaught class, probably decommissioned at some point and then given a comprehensive refit for the new crew. Normally a ship of this size would have a crew well into a thousand, but from his recent scans of the interior he only detected a fraction of that number, possibly as few as fifty or so.

Whoever had worked on the refit, it was obvious the main criteria had been to enable it to be manned by a skeleton crew.

None of that mattered at the moment though because there were still enough crew on board to make their mission more than just difficult.

As he was looking for another way out, the door opened behind them.

Chapter 49

Acting fast, Pryde pulled Fields behind him and shot the first person he saw coming through the door.

His bullet dropped the armed crew member, making the others think twice about following.

Pryde ran for cover deeper inside the room, using the desks and the free-standing equipment as cover. Once the first shot had been fired, Fields knew what to do and followed his lead.

"There goes any chance we had of surprising them," she said as she ducked behind a large cabinet.

Ignoring her quip, Pryde concentrated on aiming his pistol at the next person he saw trying to get inside the room.

A small round object was tossed inside and Pryde looked at Fields and said, "Visor down and shut off your mic."

He hoped she understood or what happened next would completely incapacitate her.

The small round object hit the deck and rolled toward them before exploding in a brilliant white light burst accompanied by a concussive blast of sound. The Flash Bang was designed to stun anyone within range by emitting a bright light that activates all the photoreceptor cells in the eyes which causes temporary blindness of a few seconds. The accompanying bang causes temporary deafness and also disturbs the fluid in the ear which results in loss of balance.

Pryde acted fast enough and activated the helmet in his EVA suit. The visor dropped down to shield his eyes and turning the mic off prevented any sound reaching his ears. He just hoped Fields did the same in time.

As the light from the grenade dissipated, his visor lifted and his vision was still normal so when the door opened and the crewmen rushed in to capture them, he was able to perform normally.

He dropped the first man he saw and then the one at his side and it soon occurred to the others that their plan had not worked.

Pryde shot another man before the realisation hit them and, as they stopped to retreat, Fields was able to join the fight, dropping another. It seemed his message had gotten through to her in time.

"What now, we're still trapped in here?" she said, turning to snap a quick glance his way.

He checked the schematics of the ship once more on his PIN and then noticed something.

Getting up from behind his cover, he moved to the far end of the room. Hidden from sight behind a piece of equipment that resembles a hyperbaric chamber, he spotted a door.

"This way," he indicated as he opened it.

Fields backed out his way, keeping her pistol's sights locked firmly on the door they had entered before disappearing through the exit.

Closing the door quietly behind her, she looked around to see another room. Pryde was walking quickly away from her, his attention fixed on where he was going.

"How're we going to stop the missiles now?" she asked, following him.

"I'll have to figure something out," he replied.

"So, we don't have a plan B then, is that what you're saying?"

"Why are you so negative all the time?"

"That's not answering my question."

"I'm adapting to the new situation. As you should know, combat is a fluid situation and to be able to survive you have to adapt to new scenarios that come up unexpectedly."

"So I was right then, no plan B."

"The longer we argue over this means we spend less time working on the solution," Pryde pointed out, looking her in the eye.

He had stopped to face her to address this toxic situation and prevent it from developing further.

"Do you have a plan B?" he asked. When she remained silent, he continued, "why don't we stop this and work together to find a way to do what we came here to do?"

Fields nodded, keeping her eyes averted from his challenging gaze. He could tell by the way she bit her lip she felt guilty about her outburst.

"We need to find where we can access the remote firing controls and bypass them so that Jericho can't fire off those nukes," he suggested.

"What about going down to the engineering section? We should be able to access the main computer from there," Fields offered.

"I think that will be what they expect. All we need is a remote access point to the computer and then we should be able to log in from there."

Fields looked around the room they were in and pointed out something, "What about that there, it's a work station for this area. We're in the Geology Lab and they'll need access to the main computer from here—why not try that?" she said.

Pryde quickly went over to where she had indicated. "Watch the door and give me a few minutes to see if this will work," he said and Fields went to a position of cover and aimed her H and K at the door they had come through.

Pryde accessed the computer through the terminal and scrolled through the options menu, searching for the firing protocols for the launchers down on the planet's surface.

"We can't access them from here—we need a direct link from the main computer room. This only allows access to programs linked to this department and I don't have the time to hack into it. It would take hours to get inside, so we need to move," he said leaving the terminal.

He looked around for another door to exit through and saw it at the far end.

"Come on, let's move," he said, and, as Fields moved to join him, the door was blasted open.

Chapter 50

The explosion threw debris from the shattered door into the room, smashing into equipment and tables as Pryde and Fields ran for the exit.

Covering their heads with their arms, the two agents sprinted for the far side of the room in front of the shockwave that chased them. Pryde activated the door release just in time as the shockwave smashed into them, hurling them through the opening to collide with the corridor wall on the other side of the doorway.

Rolling on the floor, Pryde quickly closed the door, sealing it off from the men chasing them.

"That should hold them off for a few minutes," he said, sounding a little out of breath.

Fields helped him to his feet, her eyes wide as the adrenaline coursed through her once more.

"Which direction is the computer room?" she asked.

"One deck down and to the forward section of the ship," he told her. Despite everything that had happened, he still had a grasp on where they were and what needed to be done.

"Okay, let's go then," she said.

There was a turbo lift near where they exited. Pryde ran to it, followed by Fields, and they both entered. Pryde sent the lift down one deck and they both exited. The corridor they were in was empty at the moment, but they knew from experience that could change at any moment. They went left from the turbo lift with Pryde seemingly knowing where to go.

"Is this it?" Fields asked as Pryde stopped by a door.

"It should be," he replied, opening the door. As he entered, he saw a bank of monitors with controls on desks below them. There were people inside the room working at the desks with armed guards at either side of the door as he entered.

"Hi guys," he said, which brought everyone in the room's attention to him. As they all turned to look at him, he shot the first guard in the face at close range. Blood splashed across the wall behind his head before he dropped to the deck, dead. The other guard was shocked by the suddenness of the attack and tried to bring his rifle up to shoot, but Pryde placed a hand on top stopping him from getting it past his waist. Pressing the muzzle of his Walther against his chest, he fired twice. The guard's body shook from each bullet impact before he too fell to the deck, dead.

Fields followed him into the room then, and, as the others stood up from their work stations with their hands held high, Pryde motioned for them to move away from their consoles.

As he went to the first one to look for the missile launch controls his attention was diverted for a second. Fields also looked at what he was doing, taking her eyes off the others for just a second. A second was all that was needed though.

Three of the workers jumped on Fields holding her arms away from her sides so she couldn't use her weapons while the other struck her in the stomach, then face repeatedly.

Stunned from the barrage of blows, she was weakened to the point of almost passing out. One of the men left the others and went to attack Pryde.

Seeing it all happen in his peripheral vision, he continued to work until he saw one of them coming his way. Picking up his Walther, he shot the man in the face without looking. He was multitasking as fast as he could not wanting to divert his attention. As the man fell to the deck from being shot in the face, he saw the others emboldened and join forces to attack him also. Now he had three more coming at him which meant he had to stop what he was doing to deal with this new threat.

Swinging his Walther around to fire at one approaching from his left, he felt his hand blocked, which knocked his pistol from his grip, leaving it flying across the room.

A punch followed, catching him on the chin, rocking his head sideways. He rode the blow, blocked the next one, and returned fire with a swift jab to the throat of his attacker. It stopped any more punches coming his way, giving him time to recover from the punch he took.

Two more men came at him from either side of the desk he was standing behind. He punched the one to his left, then brought the same arm back to strike the other on his right with the point of his elbow. Both blows momentarily stopped the attackers but he knew it wouldn't last for long.

Sure enough, they soon came back at him. He assessed the way they moved and within seconds he could anticipate their next attack.

He blocked a straight right from the guy on his left and hit him with a palm strike to the nose. The blow was so accurate it shattered the soft bones in his nose, pushing some of the shards up into his brain. The shock of the blow rocked him back on his heels.

Pryde turned to the last attacker and ducked beneath a swinging punch that passed harmlessly over his head. He countered with a thunderous hook to the ribs which bent his attacker over to the side as the ribs cracked. Pryde finished him off by grabbing his head and twisting it savagely, breaking the neck.

The man with the shattered nose was still on his feet, but just until Pryde delivered a ridge hand strike to the throat, crushing the windpipe.

Turning to look at the two men still holding Fields' arms caused them to start with shock. They never expected all three of their friends to be taken out so fast, nor with such vicious savagery.

Fields reacted fast. She pulled both arms away from her attackers and slammed her fists down into the groin of the men on either side. Lifting a knee into the face of the one to her left, she felt her knee connect with his face. She felt his nose splatter on impact before the blow lifted him off his feet to land on his back.

The other man received a punch into his stomach, which bent him double. Grabbing his head, she smashed her knee into his face, then slammed the back of his head against the bulkhead. Releasing her hold, she punched him twice in the face, venting her fury on him. Blood spread across his face from the broken nose and cuts opened up by the savage punches. She threw his limp form away from her knowing all resistance from him was done.

"Thanks for the assist," she said glaring at him, her fury still coursing through her.

Calmly Pryde said, "You looked like you could handle yourself. Looks like I was right." That being said, he returned to what he had been doing before.

He stopped and turned to face his partner.

"What?" she asked as she saw his expression.

"We've been locked out of the computer. There's no way we can stop them firing the missiles now. We're too late," he said.

Chapter 51

"I'm receiving reports of gunfire down on the lower decks, sir," ops said.

Jericho looked at him as a thought occurred to him. "Where exactly were those reports from?" he asked.

"Deck fourteen, sir, midships."

"The cunning bastards, they're trying to get around the firing protocols," he said.

Sitting back in the chair, he realised there was only one way this was ever going to end. His mind made up, he said, "Access the firing controls for the missiles. Lock on target and fire all of them."

There was quiet around the bridge as the crew took in what the new orders were. Glances were exchanged between them which Jericho noticed and decided to put an end to.

"Now," he demanded.

Ops turned back to his station, as did all the others, and Jericho looked toward the weapons officer who hesitated in complying with his new order.

Jumping from his seat, Jericho stormed over to weps and slammed his hand down on the console.

"Move the fuck away, I'll do this myself," he ordered.

The man operating the station complied and moved away, looking around the bridge at the rest of the crew. His wide-eyed stare of disbelief was mirrored by everyone else present.

Jericho quickly had a firing solution loaded into the firing computer and with a satisfied smile he pressed the 'fire' control and stood back.

"Nothing can stop them now," he said.

Coalition Council HQ

"Sir, the missiles have just launched," an aide said.

President Harada looked at him, his mouth open.

"This is not the time for jokes," he replied.

"I'm not sir, take a look for yourself," the aide said and put the report up on the main monitor. The image showed the six missiles as a red dot and the path they were taking. All noise in the room was instantly silenced as all eyes turned toward the screen. Everyone had the same thought voiced by the aide.

"We're fucked."

"What was that?" Fields said as she watched Pryde running through different scenarios in his mind. His expression was blank as his total concentration was focussed on solving this seemingly impossible problem. Her words brought him out though.

He turned his attention to the screen he had been using.

"They fired the missiles," he said.

"What?! How do we stop them?!" she shouted.

"I was just working on that. The only thing I can think of is we need to get to the bridge and see if there's something up there we can use."

"How long before they reach their targets?"

Pryde looked at her, "No more than fifteen minutes."

"Let's go then, no time to waste," she said as he took her advice and ran with her to the door.

Trask reached the level where the main computer was stored just as his two targets were leaving the room.

The three of them almost collided as Trask came out of a turbo lift opposite the computer room.

Trask reacted first; he slammed the woman against the bulkhead with a hand on her chest. Then he went after the man.

Pryde saw the man come bursting through the turbo lift doors right at them. Before they could do anything, their attacker had slammed Fields against the wall, knocking the breath out of her.

Turning his attention to him, their attacker grabbed the front of Pryde's clothes and pulled him around to slam him against the opposite wall.

The impact sent stars dancing in front of his eyes, and he knew if he didn't gain control of this fight that he would lose, and it would happen fast.

He punched his attacker in the face with all the strength he could muster in the short space he had. He saw the man's head snap back a little as blood trickled from his mouth. It didn't stop him though. He felt his feet lifted off the deck again as the larger man threw him across the corridor into the opposite wall again with as much effort as if he was tossing a rag doll around.

Pryde hit the wall and bounced off. His head had slammed into the solid bulkhead and pain exploded across the back of it, which ignited another burst of stars that filled his vision.

Reaching for his Walther, he brought it up only to have it slapped out of his grip by a hand the size of a shovel.

He saw him take a step toward him but stopped mid-stride when Fields landed on his back, her arms wrapped around his neck as she tried to snap on a choke hold.

Pryde saw his advantage and kicked his attacker between his legs. His foot landed in the sweet spot, expecting it to end the fight, but that wasn't to be.

The man reached up with one hand, ripping her arm from his neck, and with his other hand he grabbed behind her, then tossed her over his head to slam her into the deck at his feet.

Pryde threw another punch at his face to prevent him from continuing his attack on his partner.

The punch caught him off guard and he staggered back a step or two, giving Fields time and room to flip herself back onto her feet.

"Who is this gorilla?" she asked, not taking her eyes off him.

"Concentrate," Pryde told her.

In a second their attacker came at them again. Pryde knew if they didn't end this now they wouldn't be able to abort the missiles in time.

Chapter 52

Coalition Council HQ

Harada was waiting for someone, anyone to give their advice. He would consider anything at this point, but all he got were startled blank expressions staring back at him.

Not one person in the room had expected this scenario; they had always bullied their way through threats of this nature. After all, no one wanted to pick a fight with one of the two superpowers in the galaxy. No one in their right mind, at least. To say they were into uncharted territory here was an understatement of epic proportions and, if they didn't take action soon, they would all die.

Not knowing what action to take, Harada chose the only option he could think of–revenge.

"Contact the battle cruisers and order them to open fire on the Phobos. Tell them to blow it out of the sky," he said through gritted teeth. If he was to die this day he was going to make damn sure that those bastards in that ship didn't live to enjoy their victory.

He looked around the room. "If we're going down today, then I'm going to make sure we take them down with us," he said which got nods of approval from the military men also present.

Time was running out, time they couldn't waste on this block of rock determined to prevent them from escaping.

Pryde braced for the next attack. Dodging beneath a punch he was sure would have caved in his skull, he delivered a fast one-two to his attacker's stomach. Pain lanced up his wrist from each blow. It felt like he had hit a brick wall and his attacker swung again as if nothing had happened.

Fields threw a few of her own punches, actually landing one on his jaw which snapped his head around. It just seemed to make him more determined to kill them though.

Pryde ducked under another series of swinging punches and he side-stepped out of range, circling around to his back. Now his attacker had to defend on two fronts, one behind and one in front.

He turned to face the most obvious threat, Pryde, which was his first mistake.

As Pryde faced him, it gave his partner time to use a weapon against him. She drew her combat knife and stabbed their attacker between his shoulder blades. At first there was no reaction so she stabbed him again and again. This brought his attention to her and he turned to swat her away with a powerful swing of his left arm.

Pryde had his own combat knife out now and, as his attacker turned he buried the blade up to the hilt into his ribs.

This brought a reaction from him. The pain from this last wound must have reached him as he threw his head back and roared in pain.

Grabbing the hand holding the knife still buried in his ribs, the giant pulled it free, twisting it away from his body, then punched Pryde in the face, knocking him flat on his back.

Fields took her chance and attacked once more, this time burying her blade several times into the shoulder area close to the neck. She was aiming for the carotid artery but he was taller than her and her aim was off. Blood arced through the air each time she pulled the blade free only to bury it once more, deeper into his flesh with each attack.

The blood loss from the attacks started to have an effect on him and his movements began to slow. He swung around to stop Fields, forcing her to back away and giving Pryde time to move in.

Stamping a foot against the back of a knee joint, Pryde collapsed his attacker's leg. As he went down on one knee, Pryde came up behind him, grabbed his head with his left hand and thrust the blade deep into the side of his attacker's neck. In one swift move he pushed the knife out away from the throat, severing the flesh and cutting his throat open, allowing his blood to drain out from a wound that could not be sealed in time.

Trask had been winning this fight until they started to use their blades. He felt desperation for the first time in his life knot his stomach as he knew if he didn't end this he would die from further wounds.

Dropping down to his knee from a blow that collapsed his leg, he felt his head grabbed and knew what was going to happen next.

He knew he was going to die; as the blade opened his throat out, and he felt blood dripping from the gaping wound, he knew it was over. The inevitability of his death was as clear to him as was his blood which flowed down his front. Falling face down onto the deck, his life faded away with every beat of his failing heart until it beat no more.

"Who was that guy? He was like a machine," Fields said as she bent forward, hands on her knees as she regained her breath.

"Who cares—come on, we've still got to stop those missiles," Pryde answered.

As she watched him run off, she muttered, "Yeah, a machine, just like you."

Composing herself, she followed Pryde down the corridor back toward the turbo lift.

Chapter 53

P ryde stopped as a thought occurred to him. Turning back around, he went back toward the computer room.

As he opened the door, he took out all the grenades he had with him, activated them, then tossed them inside.

Looking up to see Fields staring at him open mouthed, he said, "We'd better move." And ran off back in the direction he was originally heading. As the two of them sprinted off the room behind them erupted in a massive explosion from the grenades detonating.

The entire deck shuddered from the blast and the two agents almost fell off their feet as the ground beneath them shook.

"Was that necessary?" Fields asked as they ran for the turbo lift. As Pryde entered he looked at her. "Very," he said, "it might disrupt the signal from the ship's computer and the on-board computer on each missile. At least it might delay things until we can reach the master controls on the bridge."

"I just hope there isn't an army waiting for us when we get there."

Pryde declined to answer that one as he knew there would be probably more armed guards there than they could handle. It had to be done though and he was working fast to come up with a plan where they could complete this mission, and hopefully survive through to the end.

So far all he had was, kill the bad guys and stop the missiles. Not a lot to go on, but he was working toward a solution.

The turbo lift stopped at the bridge after it reached the right deck, then travelled horizontally across to where the bridge was located.

As the doors opened, they entered the bridge.

Pryde took out the nearest officer to his right with a shot to the head. Quickly moving around the room, he continued firing, hitting everything he aimed at with cold precision.

Fields followed him onto the bridge but kept her pistol trained on the man down at the front.

"Don't move, Jericho," she ordered.

The other officers stood up from their work stations, their hands held above their heads in surrender.

"How do we abort the missiles, Jericho?" Pryde asked coldly as he walked across the bridge to stand in front of him.

Placing his hands behind his back, Jericho stood up to his full height and smiled at the man in front of him as if appraising him.

"You don't," he said with an air of finality.

"Don't piss me around Nathan, there has to be a way to abort them, there's always a way," Pryde reiterated.

"Oh there's a way alright, but you'll never find it—not in time, at least," Jericho reaffirmed.

Pryde lowered his pistol and shot Jericho in the right leg. The bullet ricocheted harmlessly off the thigh much to Pryde's genuine surprise.

"Nice try, agent, but you see, attempting to force me to tell you what you want just won't work," Jericho said with a confident smile. He folded his arms across his chest, savouring the moment.

"I did not see that coming," Pryde said, looking at the leg. He could clearly see the prosthetic through the torn material where the bullet had hit. He brought his eyes up to look Jericho in the face, "Okay, let's try something else," he said, then shot him again, this time in the shoulder.

The bullet tore through the flesh and Jericho staggered back a step from the shock of the bullet hitting him.

"So, parts of you are still human then. Good, that gives me plenty to work with," he added.

Recovering remarkably fast, Jericho lashed out with his right leg, landing a kick squarely on Pryde's chest. The blow caught him unaware and sent him flying back across the bridge to land against one of the stations around the back of the bridge.

The wind knocked out of him, it took Pryde several seconds to regain his composure. Getting to his feet, he looked back at Jericho, this time with a different appreciation.

"Like I said, agent, you will never find what you're looking for from me," he said, staring back at Pryde with an almost feral grin.

Pryde ran at him, not wasting any time talking. He jumped into the air and delivered a punch as he came down. The blow never landed though. Jericho side-stepped at the last second and, when Pryde landed, Jericho pivoted and back kicked him with his left foot, propelling him across the room once more.

Bouncing off the work stations there, Pryde quickly got back to his feet. Turning to face Jericho again, he gritted his teeth, "Okay, this is going to be a little harder than we thought," he said.

He steeled himself for another attack when the massive ship was suddenly shaken by a series of explosions.

Chapter 54

S parks erupted from the work stations on the bridge as explosions around the Phobos shook the entire vessel.

"Sir, the battle cruisers have opened fire on us. We have several hull breaches from missiles and we are venting the atmosphere," Ops said.

Jericho turned to look at Pryde, "This will not help you know. I attached the firing control to my bio chip. If I die, the detonation of those missiles is sealed—not even activating the abort protocol will stop it," he said, a laugh booming from deep within him as his triumph felt good.

"If you want to stop those missiles, you can't afford to kill me! How I love the irony," he said, laughing around the words.

Pryde stared at him, his mind racing to find a solution to this new development. This definitely was a new wrinkle added to the problem, one that didn't help their cause in the slightest.

The bridge crew who were left threw frightened glances around the room as their safety now became an urgent concern for them.

"Watch out," Fields warned as a couple of the crew made a dash for the exit. Seeing as how the ship was under attack they had no incentive to remain and fight.

Fields moved to the side to allow them past—they weren't a threat to them, they just wanted out.

Pryde moved forward to face off against Jericho once more. This time he was determined to stop him.

As he stepped forward Jericho leaped into the air, aiming a punch down at his head. Pryde caught the fist just before it landed, twisted his hips and turned it into a toss. He took Jericho with him, slamming him down onto the deck.

Jericho groaned in pain as his back smashed onto the deck. Pryde flipped over onto him and rained a few blows down in rapid succession onto his face. Blood spread across his face as he opened cuts around his mouth and eyes from the blows.

Jericho tried to cover up with his arms, but to no avail; his attacker was relentless. Finally, he managed to roll over, throwing Pryde off him.

As he hit the deck Pryde rolled over away from Jericho. Getting to his feet, he lashed out with his foot at Jericho's head.

The kick was blocked on a forearm and Jericho lunged at him, barrelling him over once more. Struggling to gain the upper hand, both men fought for control. Trading blows, they rolled around on the deck until Pryde finally rolled free.

Jericho flipped himself back onto his feet and looked at his attacker.

"Time's running out," he said as more explosions shook the ship. With a skeleton crew on board and only a few people left on the bridge, there was no one able to man the weapon stations or erect the defences. The battle cruisers were free to attack at their will.

Fields hung on to a console as another explosion rocked the bridge, this one seeming too close for comfort. The sparks that had danced about the equipment now had evolved into flames and small fires began to spread across the bridge consoles.

"We don't have time for this, find the damn control and abort those fucking missiles," she shouted, hoping to grab Pryde's attention.

She needn't have worried—that had been his priority from the start, and even during his tussle with Jericho Pryde had been looking for the right control that he could use to end this.

Jericho swung a hooking right cross at Pryde's head, who ducked beneath it, allowing it to sail harmlessly overhead. Reacting fast, Pryde countered with a fast one two to the ribs, which doubled Jericho over. Pryde followed up with a series of short-range punches to his face before dropping him to go toward the correct console.

"Oh no you don't," Jericho said, grabbing Pryde's ankle as he fell to the floor. Pulling on the ankle, Jericho tripped Pryde up and he fell face first, an arm's length short of the console he was reaching for.

Snapping out his other foot, Pryde kicked Jericho in the face. Releasing his hold on the ankle, Pryde was then able to scramble away from his attacker. Getting to his feet, he moved toward the console again.

Jericho got to his feet and jumped on Pryde, grabbing him around the shoulders, trying to pull him away from the display which was showing the progress of the missiles.

Pryde elbowed him in the stomach, then again, this time in the face, forcing him to break the hold.

Jericho took a step back, then leaped straight up into the air. As Pryde watched him he looked up to see him coming back down at him, feet first.

Fields was dividing her attention with glances between the remaining crew on the bridge and the struggle between the two men. Each glance their way heightened her anxiety. It was dragging on too long, the seconds were ticking away, and, if they didn't stop the missiles soon, millions would die, leaving millions more to suffer from the radiation after the blasts.

Pryde backed away from the console just as Jericho landed in front of it. The impact cracked the deck and the console sagged into it.

Pryde struck Jericho in the side of his jaw, snapping his head around and staggering him a little. With a follow up series of blows, Pryde forced his advantage.

As Jericho fell backwards, he had the presence of mind to lash out with his legs. Both bionic limbs caught Pryde on the chest, knocking him off his feet. Flipping himself back onto his feet, Pryde made for the console, but Jericho beat him to it.

As Pryde tried to get back, Jericho kicked him again, doubling him over. Grabbing him by the shoulders, he tossed him across the room. Suddenly off his feet, Pryde was sent flying to collide with Fields. The two of them were sent tumbling across the floor.

The other crewmen returned to their stations and began to defend the ship. Bringing the weapons back online, the plasma railguns targeted the attacking battle cruisers and opened fire.

Missiles were fired and particle beam weapons sliced across the open reaches of space to slice open sections of the attacking ships.

Veering away, the battle cruisers moved into better positions to continue their attack.

More explosions rocked the Phobos as more missiles struck it, along with more rounds from their plasma railguns.

The entire bridge shook from the continuing barrages from the other starships. Minor explosions erupted across the workstations as wiring caught fire and sparks flew across from one point to the next.

Pryde got to his feet fast, turning back toward Jericho, and he picked up Fields' dropped pistol and fired. The bullet barely missed Jericho, but it did force him to dodge back from the console.

Rushing forward, Pryde kept the pistol aimed at him. "Don't move or I swear I will shoot you," he ordered.

Jericho simply smiled, "You can't, remember? You need me alive or those people on the planet's surface are all doomed," he said.

Before Pryde could argue Jericho turned and ran off to the side toward a door at the front of the bridge. He disappeared through it, laughing as he ran.

Pryde let him go and concentrated on the console where he hoped he would find the abort codes.

Chapter 55

Coalition Council HQ

Inside the room, the tension was almost at breaking point.

"Are we tracking those incoming missiles?" Harada asked. He had his jacket off and his shirt sleeves rolled up.

"Yes sir, we have every path displayed on the board."

"Activate the surface defences then. When those missiles get within range, blow them out of the sky," Harada ordered.

"Copy that, sir," the general said. After another few minutes, the general added, "Missiles will be within range of the surface defence guns in three minutes, sir."

"When they are, open fire. I want them stopped," Harada said.

"The defence guns are set to automatic, sir. When the target is acquired, they will open fire."

Leaning in closer to the general, Harada said, "Will this work General?"

"It should do, sir; these defence guns have been operational for decades."

"That's not what I meant—will they detonate the missiles if we shoot them down?"

"No sir, for the missiles to detonate they have to go through a certain procedure. You could literally set them on fire or shoot a bullet into them and they wouldn't detonate. Shooting them down now is the only way to stop them in time."

"Let's hope the guns do their jobs then," Harada said, turning to watch the screen display.

The missiles flew through the air at supersonic speeds nearing their target destination with every passing second. The destruction they were bringing with them would decimate huge areas of the planet's surface, killing millions in an instant and devastating huge cities.

The outcome was out of their hands now—they were on a pre-programmed course set into their guidance computers before they were fired. As unthinking as a lump of rock, they continued on their way with absolutely no thought of the consequences of their actions.

True harbingers of destruction.

Onboard the Phobos

Pryde searched the records for a way to abort the missiles.

Time was running out and he was no nearer to finding an answer as he was when he arrived on board the Phobos.

"He lied to us."

"What do you mean?" Fields asked, coming to stand next to him.

"There is no abort code. There's no way for us to stop those missiles from here," Pryde said, looking deeply into her eyes.

Moving away, he turned to the crew members still on board the bridge. Pointing his pistol at the crew member manning the weapons console, he said, "Target those missiles with the plasma railguns and shoot them down."

"If I refuse?" the crew member said, looking up at him defiantly.

Without looking away from him Pryde turned his pistol on to the crew member nearest to them and shot him in the head. His head distorted as the bullet smashed through, killing him instantly and painting the console red with his blood.

"That. Do I need to say anything more?" Pryde said, returning the muzzle of his pistol in line with the weapons console officer's head.

Another series of explosions rocked the massive ship.

Activating his com link, Pryde called MI7 HQ. "Sir, call off the battle cruisers; I have control of the Phobos and am trying to target the missiles before they strike their targets," he said.

"I'll do what I can Pryde, but no guarantees," C replied, then closed the call.

———

Jericho ran from the bridge through the door to the nearest turbo lift. It took him down several decks to the hanger deck where the Raptor was berthed.

He climbed inside and went into the pilot's cabin and got the engines started.

Once the engines were online, he opened the hangar bay doors and took off, leaving the Phobos behind. He didn't make the jump to hyperspace because he wanted to watch the missiles do their job. He wanted to see the aftermath of his handiwork.

Erecting the stealth cloak, he parked the Raptor in a high orbit over the planet so he could watch what was going to happen. Glancing at the chronometer on the console before him, he knew he only had a few minutes left to wait.

———

Pryde stood over the weapons controller, waiting for him to finish targeting all the missiles when a call came through from C.

"I managed to call them off and coordinate efforts between you, the defence guns and the battle cruisers to stop those missiles. It's up to you all now, so do your best and stop those bastards," Chambers said.

"You heard the man, fire the plasma railguns," Pryde said.

The next minute saw plasma railguns on all four ships fire down on the planet aiming for the missiles. The defence guns on the surface joined in the gunplay, sending thousands of rounds per minute into the sky at the same targets.

Explosions lit up the darkening sky as each of the six missiles was brought down. The threat overcame the inhabitants of the planet and they had no idea of how close they had come to destruction. All they were aware of was an impromptu firework display that lit up the sky for a few seconds and nothing more.

They would never know how close they had come for fear of inviting panic. The Council kept it from them, assigning it to the huge number of secrets governments regularly keep in order to perform their duties efficiently. No doubt there would be some people who would look for answers as to why there had been a sudden light show in the sky that day, but they would not get any official confirmation or denial, just a non-committal no comment.

When all targets had been hit Pryde returned his attention to Jericho.

"Where are you going?" Fields asked as he set off at a run.

"Jericho is still out there and I'm going to stop him. You finish off here; reinforcements will be along shortly from one of the battle cruisers," he replied over his shoulder as he left the bridge, not giving her time to argue.

"Time to finish this," he said as he ran down the corridor.

Chapter 56

S itting in the pilot's seat on the Raptor, Jericho watched as all six of the missiles were shot down.

"You sure are a resourceful sonofabitch," he muttered. He knew what must have happened—the agent he had fought must have somehow gained control of the Phobos and co-ordinated with the Coalition forces to shoot the missiles down. The notion that he had attached the firing configuration to his bio-chip had been a total bluff, one that had been designed to prevent his death at the hands of those agents. It had worked in as much as it had allowed him to escape.

His plan had failed and he was alone. All his men who had followed him were on that ship, so they were either dead or captured.

Like this, there was nothing he could do of significance. If he wanted to gain anything from this, he would have to leave here with his skin intact so he could regroup and fight another day.

Before he even considered that though, there was just one more thing he had to do.

As Pryde reached the hangar bay he chose a small one-man fighter, the predecessor of the Raptor, and got inside. Within minutes of him leaving the bridge he was airborne leaving the Phobos.

"Pryde to Fields—is there any sign of the Raptor on your sensors?" he said through the comm link on board.

"There was a trace of something nearby that headed down toward the surface of the planet. We can't be certain if it was him, but the odds seem to be leading that way," she replied.

"Where are you going Nathan?" he muttered to himself.

"What, I didn't catch that?" Fields asked.

"Send me the trace you picked up and the direction it was headed; I'll go take a look," Pryde said, setting course for the planet's surface.

The data displayed over his nav screen and he realised there was only one place he would be going now. His endgame had been stopped, his objective prevented, and he supposed there was only one thing left for him to do. The people responsible for his failure would have to pay. His narcissism wouldn't allow him to accept he had done anything wrong. He wouldn't even consider Pryde and Fields to be the ones responsible for his failure, even though they were at the forefront, no they were simply acting under orders. No, the real people responsible were those who made the decisions.

Knowing that, Pryde now knew where Jericho was heading and he increased speed on his ship to maximum thrust and hoped he would be in time to prevent what he knew was going to happen.

Coalition Council HQ

Cheers of congratulations and relief travelled around the room. Hive fives were slapped, as were fist pumps at the outcome.

"We did it, sir. We stopped them," said General Wallace, smiling broadly.

Harada was not so pleased. He looked around the room at all the smiling faces and the signs of celebration and couldn't help but think of how close they had come to witnessing the deaths of so many millions and the destruction of six cities. Considering it as a political situation, it would have been the singular event that would be remembered throughout history. No other event throughout history would be regarded with such revulsion.

His relief at having averted such a disaster was almost overwhelming and he had to take a seat to steady his legs from collapsing under him.

"Are you alright, sir?" Wallace asked, with concern causing his brow to crease.

"Just a little shaky General, nothing more."

As the cheering and congratulations continued, Harada heard a call come through.

"President Harada, we have reason to believe that Nathan Jericho is on his way to you. You and everyone at the headquarters are in danger, sir," said Chambers.

"Thank you, C, I'll alert the security teams," Harada replied, which brought looks from everyone in the room, bringing a sudden halt to their celebrations.

As Wallace looked his way, Harada said, "It seems this isn't over just yet."

Chapter 57

Jericho knew he probably shouldn't do this, but he felt compelled to do it anyway.

As the Raptor came down over the Council Headquarters building, he armed the weapons systems.

A flight of Talon swing wing fighter jets flew over the rooftops of the area keeping guard over the building. On the ground he saw several armed guards dressed in combat gear holding ARX rifles ready to fire. An anti-aircraft gun was placed at each corner of the building and one on the roof as well to provide complete defensive coverage. Approaching it would not be easy, but, then again, he had no intention of approaching it. With the Raptor F95 he could attack from afar with almost total impunity.

Approaching in an attack run, he fired off missiles aimed at the anti-aircraft gun emplacements. The first missiles struck one of the guns and blew it apart in a loud explosion that sent pieces of it flying into the air. All the other guns began tracking the incoming aircraft and fired as it passed overhead.

Tracer rounds lanced through the air trying to hit the Raptor. Unable to lock onto the unusual radar signature of the revolutionary craft, all they did was fill the air with thousands of rounds of hot metal.

Jericho turned around for another pass and fired more missiles as his turn was made.

The missiles hit another gun emplacement, blowing it apart like the first, and then Jericho fired his particle beam weapon, slicing apart the building.

Laughing as he flew past, he was beginning to enjoy himself.

Inside the building, it became obvious that Jericho was winning this assault.

"General Wallace, I would like to know what you intend on doing to stop this assault before we all die," Harada said, clinging onto the back of one of the chairs.

Rubble had started to fall from the roof after the building was hit by the particle beam weapon. Their defences seemed to be incapable of stopping his attack and everyone in the room was fearing for their lives.

"My men are doing everything they can, sir," Adams replied.

"Somehow that doesn't reassure me, General," Harada told him. "Perhaps we should consider asking for help from outside?" he added.

"I agree sir, and I would also suggest we retreat to the bunker below."

Harada didn't need much convincing about his own safety so he agreed quickly.

"Do what you have to, General, we need to stop this attack before he does something more drastic. He's obviously at the end of his tether and feels he has nothing left to live for. There is probably nothing he won't do to finish what he thinks this is," he said as he was led away by his security detail.

"Copy that sir."

As they all left the Council Chambers Wallace was already making the call.

Pryde saw the Council building in the distance and saw the Raptor swooping in on an attack run. There was already quite a bit of destruction around the building. Gun emplacements had been destroyed, the building itself had been hit by what he supposed was the particle beam weapon, and Jericho was coming in to deliver another telling blow.

He was within range of his weapons on board, so he attempted to lock on but found the sensors were unable to give him a stable signal.

Instead, he fired the mini gatling guns placed on each wing hoping to get his attention.

The mini guns spewed out shells at an astounding rate and Pryde watched as they neared their target only to miss at the last second. The Raptor began another manoeuvre, taking it back around for another run at the building.

As the two aircraft faced each other, Pryde fired off another salvo from his mini guns hoping to hit the target this time.

They were too far apart to look each other in the eye, but Pryde knew Jericho knew who was facing him.

Particle beams lanced across, which Pryde had anticipated and was moving out of the way from as they were fired. The twin beams passed by harmlessly over the port wing of his fighter.

Bringing her back up on target, Pryde fired his guns once more followed by two missiles. Seeing the approach of the two missiles, Jericho jinked the Raptor away and down into a looping turn.

The missiles blew up far away over the city.

Pryde knew he needed to get closer to get a secure lock on this amazing craft. Just as he was coming around to attack once more, he turned and the missile lock warning sounded on his flight controls. He saw the Raptor coming up behind him and just had time to see them fired.

Boosting his engines to maximum thrust, he turned to port, boosting his speed up to Mach eight or nine. The pressure on his body was enough to make him almost black out as he desperately tried to evade being blown out of the sky.

His instruments kept him aware of how close the missiles were with a countdown to impact. Twisting and turning, he threw the fighter through some desperate manoeuvres—at one point he skirted the ground between a row of buildings, forcing the bystanders to run for cover. As he pulled her up into an almost vertical ascent, he glanced over his shoulder to see the missiles closing in on him.

Dipping his starboard wing at the last second, he saw the missiles pass over, accelerating past him only to turn around in front of him as they re-acquired their target lock.

Pryde dived for the ground after the narrow miss but was chased once more by the missiles, reluctant to give up their prize.

As he turned back to ascend once more, the missiles had again locked on. This time they were too close for him to evade.

At the last second he attempted the same trick but his wing was clipped by one of the missiles. The explosion tore off his entire wing and exploded the accompanying missile. The loss of the wing and the shockwave it came with sent his fighter into a devastating tailspin heading for the ground.

Struggling to right the aircraft, Pryde could do nothing. Seeing the ground approaching at top speed, he tried everything he could to prevent the inevitable.

Firing thrusters, he was able to regain some semblance of control. His spin slowed and he was able to steer the craft into a horizontal flight path, but it clipped the rooftop of a building and started to break up.

Ejecting was his only option now, so he yanked back on the release handle and was sent flying free of the craft and high into the air. His chute opened, slowing his descent and giving him time to see his plane crash into another building. The explosion took out the top three floors in a fireball that scattered fiery debris over the street below.

As he looked around him he saw the Raptor turn back toward the Council building—clearly he was not finished. Pryde watched as the Raptor attacked the ground forces with guns and particle beams and, within seconds, it had destroyed every last resistance.

Floating to the ground, Pryde saw Jericho bring the Raptor in for a landing at the front of the Coalition Council Headquarters.

Chapter 58

Jericho took an ARX rifle from the rack behind the pilot's cabin, as well as a Sig P9000 pistol. In his ammo belt he placed several grenades, then picked up his backpack and left the Raptor.

All the guards who had been on duty were dead and lying where they died, littering the ground outside the building.

The entrance was clear, giving him free access to the building. He had ensured that, although the building had been put into lockdown mode with all doors and windows barricaded, he had made sure to target the front by blowing a hole through the entrance.

Stepping through into the lobby, he noticed that it was empty. Everyone must have run for cover or evacuated as soon as the shooting started. That was good; it meant there would be less interference to what he was about to do.

As Pryde made his way toward the Council building, a call was routed through to him from headquarters.

"Pryde, we have some interesting and rather disturbing news about those missiles," Chambers said.

"I don't like the sound of that sir, and I'm a bit pushed for time here, so can we jump to the part where you get to the point?" he replied knowing he wasn't going to like what he was about to hear.

"Calculations have been completed on the amount of nuclear material Jericho had and put against how much was used in weaponizing the missiles. There was a discrepancy," C said.

Pryde stopped walking as he tried to wrap his thoughts around what this meant.

There was only one conclusion he could come up with.

"He kept some back for another fail-safe, in case his strike failed. That's why he's headed for the council building. He's planning to blow them all up and destroy the entire city along with himself," Pryde said.

"That's the same conclusion we came to. Pryde, you're the only one who can stop him now."

"Copy that sir," he said and continued running, this time at an increased pace. Time really was running out.

Jericho stormed through the building, searching for the Situation Room. He knew the council members would all be there, including his prime target, Harada.

The only other place they would be would be the bunker and, if things went as predicted, protocol would demand they all retreat there for safety.

The bunker was built to withstand a direct missile strike from a bunker buster missile but, seeing as how nuclear warfare was a thing of the past and had been made illegal, the builders had not deemed it relevant to reinforce the bunker to withstand a nuclear strike. Why would they? After all, nuclear missiles were a thing of the past and no one in their right mind would ever think to use one of those.

This thinking had played right into Jericho's plan. He never expected them to pay him what he had demanded. His experience in the Special Forces had taught him they never negotiated with terrorists or extortionists. He knew they would do everything they could to delay and track him and his group down. He knew they would attempt to stop the missile strike, which they had, which left him one last tactic to play.

It had all led to this moment. The last confrontation with the one man he had deemed his target in the first place. President Harada, a man so self-important he always placed his own needs, his own self-image above all else.

It had been because of him that Jericho had left the Special Forces. It had been over something as trivial as pay grades. Harada and his budgetary requirements had meant that funding to Jericho's group had been cut, which proved disastrous on his last mission. The cuts to their funding meant they hadn't had the correct equipment, nor the back up they had needed when going up against a terrorist cell, and it had failed. Not only that, but half of his team had died trying to reach the exfil point where they were supposed to have been picked up. Because of the cuts, the ship sent wasn't adequate for the task, and it was shot down. By a miracle Jericho survived the crash and somehow made his way to safety. Badly wounded, he was finally picked up and taken to hospital where his injuries were taken care of, but the mission and all data pertaining to it was wiped from all records.

When Jericho learned of this, he resigned and formed ICE with the single objective of bringing Harada to his knees.

His hatred of the man was like a thing alive, burning inside of him, a raging inferno of hate that would only be extinguished with his death.

A death he was about to deliver today.

———

Pryde reached the building and entered, his senses on high alert.

Another call came in from headquarters.

"Pryde, there's something you might need to know," C said.

"I'm not sure I understand, sir,"

"We did some more digging on Jericho and we found something that might give us a better understanding about him and his motivations."

"Go ahead, I'm listening."

C told him everything they had uncovered about Jericho's last mission, about how it was wiped from the record and why. Filling in as much detail as they had found out, they painted a fuller picture of the man and what he was about.

When he was done Chambers said, "So what do you think?"

"I think this could've been his objective all along, sir. It always bothered me why he would try to extort the government like this, knowing what he did about how they deal with situations like this. He would know that they never negotiate with threats of this nature and he would know that better than most. I think he's been giving us the run around to get to this point. If he harbours a grudge against the President, then that's who he's going after, and if he has a nuke with him and considering his skill set and how determined he seems to be, then the President is in very real danger."

"That was our thought as well."

"I suggest you get in touch—inform them of what's coming their way and to take precautions. If I don't get to him in time, I would order the security detail guarding the President to shoot on sight and shoot to kill. We cannot take any chances with him."

"Already done, Pryde, just make sure you get to him before they have to implement that order. I don't trust they will act in time, whereas I know you'll have no qualms about putting a bullet through his skull."

"Copy that sir, no qualms."

$$\rule{6cm}{0.4pt}$$

Chapter 59

$$\rule{6cm}{0.4pt}$$

I nside the bunker the atmosphere was a little calmer. Harada relaxed a little when he heard the three-foot-thick steel door closing them inside. The seal was the finishing touch, making the entrance airtight.

The air conditioning kicked in the moment the door sealed them in, supplying them with enough clean air to breath for the duration of their stay inside.

When the call came through from Chambers the atmosphere altered immediately.

"You have no need to worry about the President; we are secure inside here—he can't get inside," General Wallace said in an effort to reassure him.

Harada wasn't comforted by that though, and he began pacing the room, then turned to Wallace. "Safe inside, you say, but what about the nuclear device they say he might have. This thing won't withstand a direct hit from something like that, and you know that," he said, his eyes darting around the room taking in every detail of what he thought was to become his coffin.

"Sir, I've placed some of the security detail at strategic points outside this shelter. They'll take him out before he even gets close. Trust me sir, you're in the safest place possible."

"I wish I had your confidence, General."

"Trust in the system, Mister President. This is what we train for sir."

"I don't think anyone can train for this," Harada said, and by the look in the general's eyes he knew he held the same belief.

Jericho got deeper into the building. He pulled up the schematics of the building just to refresh his memory. It had been a long time since he'd been there and so he wanted to be sure.

The schematics displayed from the computer onto the screen of his PIN and he traced his path from where he was at present to where he needed to be.

Finding the route he needed, he set off toward the elevator that would take him to the level where the bunker was.

Pryde was in the building. He knew where the bunker was situated and he knew that's where Jericho would be heading, so he gave chase.

Running down the corridor to the elevator he was aware of the way the clock was running against him.

The elevator took him down to the level he wanted and, as he exited, he looked right and left to see if anyone was about. The bunker was on this level, but he still had some distance to cover before he reached it.

Gunfire sounded somewhere close by, and he reckoned Jericho had engaged whatever security detail was guarding the President's location.

Picking up his pace, he sprinted toward the sound hoping to get there in time.

Jericho rounded a corner and was greeted by the sight of three armed security personnel. He reacted first and shot the first one with his rifle. The bullet slammed into the man's chest, knocking him back a step or two.

The other two men returned fire. Bullets from their pistols peppered the walls around him as Jericho ducked down onto one knee. He picked his next targets carefully and picked them off with two more shots, dropping them where they stood.

He knew the others would be alerted to him coming for them now as he got to his feet. Looking around, he made sure he was alone before continuing.

The corridors looped around toward the far end where the bunker was, the deepest area in the building. There was nowhere else for them to hide from him now and, consequently, nowhere to run to.

The last stretch approached and he looked around it. The door to the bunker was there and standing guard were three guards, all aiming their rifles at the corridor in front of them, all ready for anything.

He took out a grenade, primed it, and then tossed it around the curve in their direction.

He heard the consternation from the guards as they saw the small round object hurtling toward them.

The explosion flung body parts toward where Jericho was hiding. The noise from the blast was deafening, made louder by the confines of the corridor.

Smoke billowed out from the blast site, filling the corridor and making it almost impossible to see through.

Jericho waited until the air conditioning took most of the smoke out through the vents in the wall. As soon as he could see he moved toward the bunker door,

The sound of the explosion stopped Pryde in his tracks. He knew the sound of a grenade going off well enough to know that's what it was. For a second though, he thought it was the nuke detonating and he waited for the blast to reach him. As he waited for what he thought would come he held his breath, tensing every muscle.

It had been an involuntary act, and ,when his brain registered that it was nothing more than a grenade, he relaxed.

Breathing under control once more, he continued, but this time he had more of an incentive to reach the bunker. His thought was that Jericho had reached the bunker and was preparing the nuke. He couldn't allow that to happen.

He was almost out of breath when he reached the last stretch. In front of him was Jericho, kneeling down and peering into a small backpack.

"Stop what you're doing right now Jericho and stand up," he shouted.

Looking over his shoulder, Jericho looked at him and smiled.

"You're too late," he said.

Pryde looked at him and raised his pistol.

"You don't want to do that," Jericho told him, holding up a hand to halt him.

"Why not?"

"The bio chip, remember. I linked mine to this bomb, and if you kill me it detonates and you won't be able to stop it," Jericho said with a smug smile.

He got to his feet slowly to not give the agent any need to fire.

"Okay then, I'll tell you what you're going to do. You're going to turn that bomb off and then you're going to surrender. It's finished Nathan, it's over, and there's no escape for you here," Pryde said.

Jericho simply looked at him and his smile faded. "Why would you think I want to escape?" he asked.

Pryde saw it all then. This was his endgame, his final play, and he never expected to come out of this alive. His one purpose here was to see the death of the President. As soon as he knew that it sent a chill through him.

There may be no way to prevent this bomb from detonating, there may be no abort code for this bomb, and if that was true then there was no way to prevent this from happening.

Jericho started walking toward him.

"It's over Agent Man. You lost, so you might as well get out while you still can." Looking at his chronometer, he added, "Oh, sorry, there's not enough time."

Chapter 60

"Well, if you're not going to leave, then that's okay too. We'll just have to do this the old-fashioned way," Pryde said, putting his pistol away in its holster.

He balled his hands into fists and stepped forward to engage Jericho. He was going to beat the answer out of him.

Jericho smiled, "This should be fun," he said.

They faced each other and Pryde saw in his opponent's face that he was enjoying this. He considered the upper hand was his, something that Pryde intended to prove was wrong.

Taking the fight to Jericho, he threw a series of punches at his face. Jericho blocked a few on his arms as he covered up and retaliated with a few short-range hooks to Pryde's ribs when the opportunity presented itself.

A snap kick from Jericho aimed at his thigh was blocked by bringing up his leg. A right cross to the head was blocked by Jericho, who caught it on his arm. Rushing forward, Jericho grabbed Pryde and slammed him against the wall.

The impact knocked the wind out of him and, for a second, he saw stars burst in front of his eyes as his head slammed into the wall.

Jericho took advantage and grabbed Pryde's hair and slammed his head back again, then with his other arm placed it across his throat and tried to choke him.

Pryde felt his air waves blocked as his throat was being constricted. His emotions were under control, but he felt panic begin to bubble up as he was finding it difficult to breathe. Using a supreme effort of will, he pushed the panic back down where he could control it better.

Forcing his hands up, he grabbed the arm and pushed it away, far enough to be able to drag some air into his lungs.

He brought up his knee and forced it in between him and Jericho to open the gap between the two of them.

Jericho withdrew his arm from Pryde's throat, which gave the latter time to punch him in the face. Blood spread across his mouth from the blow and he spat a glob of red sputum at the floor as he took a step back out of range.

Taking a couple of deep breaths to fill his lungs, Pryde readied himself for the next attack.

Reacting faster than he anticipated, he was knocked back against the wall by a kick from Jericho's right bionic leg. The force of the blow almost knocked him out. As he slumped forward, out of breath once more, he saw his attacker getting ready to deliver another blow. If this one landed, it would cave in his chest and no doubt kill him.

The kick sailed over his head as he dropped to the floor. The foot landed above him, sending pumice dropping into his upturned face from the huge dent in the wall. Cracks spider webbed outward from the impact crater in the wall.

Jericho brought his foot back out and stamped down on Pryde's chest.

Crying out in pain, Pryde knew at least one rib had cracked from the blow. Before he knew it, the pressure had been lifted and the foot was being replaced, this time on his throat. In seconds he would be dead if he didn't do something.

"It's over, Agent Man, you lost," Jericho sneered at him through a cruel smile.

Pryde could feel his throat being crushed and knew he didn't have long left.

Any normal person would have struggled in panic with the foot, pulling and tearing at it in a desperate attempt to lift the pressure from their throat, but not Pryde. His mind was still coldly calculating what to do, running through various scenarios on how to deal with this situation. He knew he didn't have the leverage, nor the strength to force the foot from his neck, so he turned his thoughts to other solutions, searching through various ways until he came up with the only one left to him.

Reaching into his holster he withdrew his Walther Q9 and placed the muzzle against the side of the knee on Jericho's leg that he had pressed down, choking him. Pulling the trigger, he fired three times, destroying the joint and collapsing the leg. As Jericho collapsed sideways, Pryde rolled free, pushing himself away from his attacker, who was also on the floor.

As fast as he could he brought his Walther around and fired. The bullet hit Jericho in the centre of his forehead, exploding out through the back of his skull painting the floor behind in red.

Scrambling to his feet, he rushed over to the back pack. Ripping it open, he saw the device inside. He didn't recognise it other than that it was rigged to explode and that it had a small amount of radioactive material inside. He did recognise the housing it was contained inside, but the design was so old that he had no idea how it worked beyond the basic principle behind it, nor did he know what was more important, how to disarm it.

There was a counter set in the device which had started to count down toward zero. Clearly Jericho hadn't been lying about that part—it was connected to his biochip and now he was dead it was set to explode.

Chapter 61

Pryde called MI7 HQ when he saw what he was up against.

"Sir, listen, I have a mini nuke here outside the door to the bunker. It was set to Jericho's bio chip and when he died it was set to explode. I need options as I have no clue how to disarm it," he said. All he was met with was silence.

"Sir, I could do with some input here," he urged, beginning to wonder what the delay was.

"I've consulted several advisors Pryde, and it seems there's not a lot you can do, I'm sorry," C said, sounding genuinely upset.

"I'm sorry too, sir, but I can't accept that. There must be something. Is there anywhere I can place the bomb to minimise its effects?" he said, clamping his teeth together in determination.

"Wait, I'll check."

Pryde looked at the countdown timer and he felt sweat start to bead on his forehead as he knew he didn't really have time to wait. He accepted it though because there was nothing else he could do.

"I think we may have something Pryde. When the building was built and the bunker put in place there was a failsafe built in case of something like this. You have to place the bomb into the bunker and activate the fail-safe function, which will drop the entire bunker down into a shaft three miles down."

"How do I get inside sir?"

"The President has been informed and should be coming out any moment."

The door behind Pryde began to swing open. Pryde gathered up the back pack and rushed inside.

"Get out, get everyone out now!" he shouted. Grabbing one of the officials he said, "Show me how to activate the fail-safe function?"

The two of them ran over to the control panel that operated the monitors and computer. Once Pryde knew how to operate the fail-safe he said, "Go, get out now."

Placing the backpack down on the floor, he started the fail-safe, then made a run for the door. He got through the opening as it was closing and was through just in time. He saw it shut and heard the seal slam into place as it was made airtight.

The entire corridor began to shake and rumble as the entire bunker began to move, slowly at first until it gathered speed, dropping into a huge shaft. A solid looking slab slid into place, covering the massive hole.

Pryde turned and ran for the exit, retracing his steps down the corridor to the elevator. It had already gone, taking the President and his Council members up to the ground floor.

There was a door at the side of the elevator which he opened quickly, then started running up the staircase which the door opened onto.

His arms pumping as he ran up the stairs to the floor above, he kept his breathing under control. His heart beating like a trip hammer, he was getting more breathless the faster he ran. Not giving up, he forced himself on to greater efforts.

Finally, he reached the top and the ground floor. As he ran for the exit, he felt the ground beneath his feet shake as the bomb detonated underground.

Outside the building he saw the President and the others taking off in a jet copter that had been waiting on standby.

The explosion lifted the building off its foundations as it burst outward like a bubble bursting, throwing debris up into the air.

Pryde was caught in the shockwave and hurled off his feet into the air to land over fifty feet from the entrance.

The building collapsed into itself after the initial blast, the majority of it contained by the depth of the fail-safe shaft.

Pryde rolled around on the ground, pain exploding in his body. His ribs and chest already hurt like hell from the pounding they'd taken during the fight, but now the rest of him had joined in too.

As he lifted his head to look back at what was left of the Council building, he realised how lucky he'd been to escape the blast. He had completed his mission, stopped the missiles from destroying several cities, and had prevented the President from being killed. All in all, a good day's work.

He was just congratulating himself for that when his vision began to fade as darkness came in to protect him from the all-consuming pain and he blacked out.

Chapter 62

Pryde came awake slowly. His head seemed foggy and, when he looked around, he knew why.

The room he was in was pristine and white with a bank of monitors over the bed he was lying on. He heard signals as the attached pads read his vital signs.

The pain returned then, and his chest felt tight from the bindings that were laced with medication to help the healing process of his damaged ribs and the rest of his body was a dull ache. It was difficult to know which part hurt the most; it might have been easier to see which part didn't hurt.

"Good, you're awake," C said from his side. He tried to turn his head to look his way, which sent a sharp pain lancing through his ribs. Groaning, he said, "How long have I been here sir?"

"We brought you here yesterday. You had quite a few injuries, three broken ribs, and several large contusions, lacerations and assorted bruises. It seems you were in quite a fight."

"I'd like to say it was just another day at the office, sir, but this was nothing like that."

"Well, I would tend to agree, and that's why you are being given all the time you need to recover. By that I mean once you are discharged from here you can take as many weeks as you need to recuperate fully. I need you back at work Duncan, but I want you fully fit. Is that understood?"

"Fully sir, and thank you."

Chambers nodded his understanding then said, "Good, now you get some rest and allow your body to heal."

Pryde watched his boss leave the room and he relaxed into his pillow, his mind returning to the last few things he remembered about the mission.

There was something playing on his mind, something that had been tickling his conscious mind trying to get his attention. Now maybe he could allow it to surface so he could find out what it was. Had he missed something? Was it some detail that needed to be brought into the light? Was it something that pertained to the mission? At the moment, he couldn't quite grasp at it, but he knew he would. He just needed time and this was the best time to do it. He relaxed his mind and cleared it of everything that his surface mind was thinking about.

Closing his eyes and relaxing, he focussed on the thread that was beginning to wriggle free. Seeing it in his mind, he reached out to grasp it. Once he had it, he carefully began to reel it in. If he pulled at it too aggressively, it would retreat and he could lose it.

Gently he pulled it in, slowly gathering it together and as he did he began to understand it more.

The more he gathered it in, the more his face darkened.

"How did I miss that?" he said when he finally had it all.

<hr>

Coalition Intelligence Agency HQ

Director Yusef was disappointed. "What went wrong? Fields, I put you into the mission so you could gather me the intel to close down MI7. You failed me, so please, tell me why I should even entertain continuing your employment here?" he said, trying to keep his anger from showing.

Fields stood in front of his large dark oak desk. His private office inside of the headquarters was surrounded by security measures such as privacy shields and a contingent of armed agents acting as guards.

"I am sorry, sir. Perhaps you were a little presumptuous to jump the gun as it were," she replied, keeping the smile hidden, "I have with me a data chip that has all the information you require to finish off that organisation, sir," she finished off holding out her right hand with the small device inside.

Yusef's eyes darted from the small data drive to her face. "It seems you may have redeemed yourself," he said. "I'll take care of that and you can get on with your leave. You have a two-week vacation coming to you if I'm not mistaken," he said.

"Thank you, sir," she said, handing over the small device. With a smile she turned and left the office.

She returned to her apartment and was about to make herself a drink when something alerted her to a presence nearby.

"Hello Jasmine, nice to see you again," Pryde said. He was sitting on a chair in a darkened corner of her lounge.

"Jesus Pryde, you scared the crap out of me!" she said a little breathlessly. "Shouldn't you still be in the hospital?" she said, looking at him with concern narrowing her eyes.

"I'm not too bad, just a little tired that's all," he replied.

"What're you doing here?"

"I came to see you."

"Really? I didn't think I made that much of an impression on you."

"You didn't."

"Then why are you here?"

"To ask you—why?"

"Why what?" she said, stalling. She was moving slowly toward the side of the room. On the wall there was a panel that controlled the security system she had installed in her apartment.

"I wouldn't try to do that, Jasmine. I already dismantled the system so the silent alarm you're trying to raise won't have any effect," he said. He knew exactly what she was doing and had anticipated it.

Turning her head to look at him, she said, "What is it you want to know Duncan?"

"Why you sold us out. Every step of the way you were informing Jericho about our movements. How long have you been working for him?" he asked. He didn't get the reaction he expected though. Fields was genuinely surprised by his accusation, shaking her head in disbelief. "The only person I reported to was Ibrahim, the head of the CIA," she said.

"Oh you're good," he said, "you probably think because I damp down my emotions that I miss things, simple things like tells. You see, when we challenged you about your loyalty you were about to say something about what we wanted you to do violating your mission orders. When I asked what those were you brushed it aside."

"That was just..." she started to say but Pryde held up a hand, halting her.

"Don't bother lying," he said.

"Okay, you got me. So what now?" she said with a smile.

"Now I take you in–to HQ."

"I don't think so, Duncan," she replied, dropping the smile. Her expression hardened, her jaw set in determination, and he knew this was not going to end without a fight. He immediately went into combat mode, dialling down his emotions, shutting off everything that would conflict with what he knew he had to do. In seconds he would be completely under control, but he didn't have seconds as Fields made her run at him.

Her head down, she tackled him around the waist. Slamming into him, she took him off his feet and the two of them crashed onto the floor.

Pain exploded across Pryde's chest and he cried out in agony. The distraction of pain delayed his ability to dial down his emotions and he struggled as he had to fight off a vicious series of blows from his former partner.

He brought his right knee up into the back of the woman sitting on him. A second and third knee strike finally knocked her off him and he was able to roll free.

Getting to his feet, he backed away from her as he recovered from her first attack. Taking deep breaths, he brought himself back under control, and then he had shut down all emotions. Going deeper than he had ever gone before, he even cut off his pain responses.

His face hardened, devoid of any emotion, totally focussed now on the task at hand.

Looking into her eyes as she weighed up her chances against him, he saw her eyes narrow as she knew things had altered.

 Rushing at him again she threw a flurry of punches at his head, forcing him to cover up with his hands. Combining a kick to her attack, she lashed out with a low roundhouse aimed at his injured ribs. Dropping an elbow, he caught the kick on his bicep, but left that side of his head unprotected. Dropping the foot, she tried a high roundhouse to the side of the head.

He ducked under the kick and swept the grounded foot with a low sweep. Her leg went up and she fell hard onto her back.

Standing up, he stepped back as Fields flipped herself back onto her feet. Facing each other, they weighed each other up once more.

Conserving his strength, he allowed her to come at him first.

"You're not going to come easy, are you?" he said, already knowing the answer. If he had any doubt at all it was destroyed by the way she set her jaw in determination before telling him, "I'm not coming at all, not with you at least.

Only one of us leaves this room alive, and it's not going to be you."

Pryde gave a nod of understanding. This was a fight to the death, something he had anticipated before setting off to challenge her.

Fields made a dash for him, arms reaching out to destroy him. He dropped his right hand to his side, activating the quick release mechanism that held his knife up his sleeve. He blocked both arms reaching out, knocking them aside and grabbed her head with his left hand then rammed the blade up through the underside of her jaw and into her open mouth. Her eyes went wide in horror as the realisation dawned on her that she'd fucked up by underestimating him. Blood pooled inside of her open mouth and Pryde could see the blood-soaked blade between her teeth.

With a final push he forced the blade up through her upper palette and into her brain, slamming her mouth shut. Her eyes rolled back in her head as her brain shut down. Pulling the blade free, he released her to fall on the floor. She was dead before she hit the ground.

He knelt down to check her carotid artery, already knowing what he'd find; then he wiped his blade clean on her clothes before retracting it into the sheath up his sleeve.

He got to his feet and left the room, this part of it finished.

Chapter 63

MI7 SecOps HQ

Pryde made his way to headquarters and, once he was checked in, he went through to C's office. On the way through the building he noticed concerned glances from the personnel, which was highlighted when he met Goodchild.

"Duncan, what the hell are you doing out of the hospital? You look like hell—are you alright?" she said, placing a consoling hand on his arm.

"I'm fine," he replied, wondering what all the fuss was about.

"What are you doing here Pryde, I thought you were supposed to be in hospital?" another voice joined the conversation. Pryde turned to see C standing there.

"I thought I'd better report to you a development, sir," Pryde said.

"Good God man, you look like death warmed over! Why aren't you resting?"

"What is all the concern over my health about?"

"Come over here," C said, directing him over to a mirror where he looked at himself. As soon as he saw his image he understood what all the concerned glances were for. His face was bruised and had cuts over his right eye and cheek. His lips were slightly swollen and blood trickled from the corner of his mouth. His skin pallor was ashen, showing signs of exhaustion which he had masked, including the pain he had endured. Now that he saw it, he had to agree—he didn't look well at all.

"Point taken, sir. As soon as I deliver my report I'll return to the hospital," he said.

"What report are you talking about? The mission is over Pryde; what else is there to learn?"

"Fields, sir. She was working for the CIA all along. We suspected that she had a hidden agenda and we attempted to use her to allow misinformation to trickle through to her boss. She played along, or so we thought, but she was still working for them as her priority. I challenged her about it just now and she tried to kill me. Why was that, do you think?"

Chambers narrowed his eyes as his brow dipped over them. "Did she now? I suppose she didn't survive the encounter?"

"No sir, I'm afraid not. I fear she may have passed on sensitive data about the operation though, data that might be used against this organisation. It would be easy to manipulate the facts to make them fit a certain biased agenda, should they consider it necessary."

"Leave it with me, I'll handle this. You need to take some time to recover. If what you say is true, and I see no reason to doubt you, then I think you'd be safer at home rather than at the hospital. I can have your place watched much easier than if you were at the hospital," C said.

Just then someone joined them holding a small bag, from which they took out an injector gun.

Before Pryde knew what was happening the gun was placed against his right arm and fired.

"That should help your healing process, sir," the med tech said.

"What was in that?" Pryde asked.

"A broad spectrum of antibiotics with pain relief along with a selection of other meds that should help speed up your recovery, sir," the tech told him before leaving.

"I feel better already," he said.

"Jokes? That's something new from you, Pryde. I never thought you had it in you," Chambers observed.

"Just trying something new, sir."

"Okay, now you can return to your apartment to get some rest while I handle this other matter. I think the Director of the CIA and I need to have a little talk."

Alarm bells warned of an incoming threat before Pryde could comment.

On the main monitor screen in the main hall displayed the image from outside. The HQ was situated close to the river and coming at them from on the water were three small attack boats.

"I think he's taking a more direct approach sir," Pryde said.

Ibrahim Yusef's hatred for MI7 was such that he wanted nothing more than total destruction of the organisation.

He had planted Fields inside their operation to find the missiles and Jericho under the assumption that she would gather information that would damn their organisation so that he could shut them down once and for all. He knew about the missiles being stolen, he had allowed the information about them to be leaked to the right people, he knew Jericho was desperate to bring down the President after the last mission he was on that saw the deaths of his entire team, and he knew because it was intel from his department they had acted upon. It had been a sacrifice he was willing to make to bring about the destruction of his hated rival.

The information brought to him by his agent had been good; it had included the location of their headquarters, which was all he really needed. Sending a fleet of boats to strike at them had always been his intent, and all he had needed was a location. Now he had it and he was about to watch their destruction first hand.

Standing on the bridge deck of the flagship of his small fleet, he watched the other two attack boats prepare to fire on the disguised boathouse.

As he watched the missiles fire off he said, "Knock knock."

Chapter 64

"Incoming!" shouted someone inside the main room of the boathouse.

"Brace for impact," Chambers said as he knew there was nothing they could do to stop the missiles, as they were inside the defence perimeter. The close quarter combat guns wouldn't be able to lock on target in time.

Pryde moved fast toward the exit. He had to do something to stop this.

Outside the boathouse were several boats moored up alongside the jetty. Picking the nearest one, he dropped down into it after untying the ropes. He soon had the engines purring like a big cat and he steered the small sleek craft out into the river.

Activating the weapons systems on board the speedboat he targeted the incoming missiles, then fired off a salvo of rockets. The explosions destroyed not only the missiles but the shock wave blew out all the windows in the boat house, as well as damaging some of the structure. Better that than the alternative though.

Increasing speed, Pryde prepared to engage the enemy. Firing a couple of missiles at the lead ship, he blew it out of the water, leaving just the second attack ship and the flag ship.

"That was too close for comfort," Chambers said, then he began to rally the defence troops.

"Man the guns, and I want people out there with rifles. Come on people, Pryde can't do this all on his own—get out there and give the man a hand," he shouted.

The weapons systems were activated and a series of gatling guns popped up from hidden recesses on the dock side and began firing at the last remaining ship that was swerving and weaving around, firing guns of their own at the boathouse.

The air between the shore and the attack boat was filled with flying shells fired from weapons that only had one purpose, to kill. Anything that stood in their way was shredded by the sheer volume of ammunition fired.

Pryde saw his chance and went after the flag ship. Weaving away, out of the line of fire between the two combatants he headed for the ship farther out in the river.

"Why are we not firing on that ship, and tell me who is on it please?" Yusef said, his voice dripping with contempt for the crew.

"Scanning now, sir," said ops. "One life sign and from his ID it appears he is an agent of MI7."

"Track it and shoot it," Yusef said, his voice rising as his anger rose within him.

The weapons systems were already online and the gatling guns on deck started to track the small craft. Struggling to lock on to the target, they moved left, then right as their sensors searched for a signal.

"The boat is moving fast, sir; it'll take a little longer for the guns to lock on," the weapons officer said as Yusef went to stand over him.

"Take a shot now, and if you miss then the agents on board will get him when he tries to board," Yusef said, then walked away, expecting his orders to be carried out.

The guns were fired but, without a secure signal to lock on to, they fired blindly, strafing the water and churning it into white foam.

The speedboat seemed able to evade them with ease and within moments was pulling near the flag ship.

Pryde had his pistol already out and ready to fire when he came close enough to the ship in charge.

Men started to line the deck with rifles getting ready to aim at him. Taking the initiative, he fired first, dropping two of them into the water before they even had time to aim. Seeing two of their numbers fall so fast, they started firing in panic. Their aim was not as steady as it should have been and the nearest any of them came to hitting him was a few shots that hit the deck at the side and one that shattered the windshield near where he was standing.

Pryde had no such inability and he continued to calmly aim and fire, dropping three more before the last two retreated back to find shelter from his unerringly accurate shooting.

He swooped around the other side of the ship and came in at the rear where a divers ledge was fitted. Jumping from his boat onto this, he grabbed hold of some ropes tied to the side and pulled himself up. He was over the side of the boat in a second or two, planting his feet on the deck.

The two agents who had dived for cover could be seen in the wheelhouse just aft of the flying bridge where Yusef was controlling the action from.

The two men turned their attention to him and were about to fire when two bullets were fired, one for each of them. Each shell hit its target, dropping them each with a headshot.

Pryde ran forward and up the steps to the flying bridge. An agent at the top tried to stop him but a punch to the groin changed his mind. Pryde pulled him past him to fall in a tumble of flailing arms and legs down the stairs.

At the top he saw the stations at work. There was a captain's chair, helm, operations and weapons station–very similar in layout to a starship bridge except for size.

Yusef turned his head to look at him and scowled. "Why won't you just die?" he said, blowing out his cheeks in exasperation.

Pryde lifted his Walther and was about to fire when he was tackled from both sides by two more men.

Grabbed by his arms, the two men slammed him against the bulkhead and the side of the flying bridge. Pain raced across his back from the impact and he desperately tried to close his mind to it. Yanking his right arm free, he elbowed one man in the face, smashing his nose in a bloody burst. With the same hand, he struck the other man across the bridge of his nose with a ridge hand strike. The snap of the bone shattering gave him some sadistic comfort as the grip loosened on his arm, freeing him. A knee to the stomach followed by an elbow to the back of the neck finished him, leaving just the one who had been given the elbow to the face.

Swinging a looping right hand, he tried to take Pryde's head off his shoulders. Blocking the blow on his forearm held high against the side of his head, Pryde countered with a straight right to the face followed by a left cross to the jaw, which snapped his head around. Pryde finished it off with a knee to his face which took him off his feet to land on his back.

He was breathing hard now after all his exertions and he felt weak still from his injuries.

A wave of vertigo washed over him and he had to steady himself against the bulkhead rather than fall over. His head spinning, he saw Yusef leave the command chair and come to face him.

"Look at you man, you're out on your feet," he said. "You can't win, you know. I'll destroy MI7 and everyone in that building and there's not a thing you can do to prevent it. The only good thing about it for you, is you won't be around to see it."

Pryde was bent over with one hand on his thigh as he tried to gather his thoughts. A pistol was levelled at his face in preparation of ending his too short of a life, a life he wasn't ready to let go of just yet.

Marshalling his last reserves of strength, he stood up and thrust out his right-hand fingers, stiff as they connected with Yusef's throat. The blow collapsed the older man's oesophagus and he dropped the weapon as both hands clutched at his throat, his eyes widening in realisation and horror at the knowledge of what was to come.

His face turned blue as his airwaves were blocked and his throat started to swell from the bruising from the strike. He was dying and he knew it. No matter how much he clawed at his throat he could not drag enough air into his lungs to save his life.

Dropping to his knees, his eyes locked on Pryde's, begging for help. All he got back was a cold unrelenting hard stare of indifference.

"Not today Director, and not before you," he said just as he saw the light go out in his eyes and he fell over to the side, dead.

The three at the front were all facing him, so he held up his pistol. "Don't even think of moving," he said.

Epilogue

C ouncil HQ

President Harada was sitting behind his desk in his office when Chambers walked in.

It had been a few days since the attack on the boathouse and things were finally returning to normal, something anyone in the intelligence community knew could change at a moment's notice.

Getting to his feet, Harada came from around his desk to greet his visitor. Warmly shaking his hand, he said, "I'm glad I could say thank you in person, William. If it hadn't been for you and your people working so hard, I don't like to think what the outcome would have been," he said, showing signs of sincerity in his eyes and voice.

Chambers could see through the façade though, for he knew Harada for what he was–a self-serving politician, nothing more. He was willing to play the game though, for now.

"Thank you, Mister President, they were just doing their job, same as always," he said.

"Come, sit," Harada said, indicating the white leather sofas at the other end of the office, each large enough to accommodate three people. They were arranged facing each other with a walnut coffee table placed in between. This was where informal talks were held.

Chambers sat in one as Harada took the one opposite him. "Now then, what was it you wanted to talk to me about—you said it was important?" he said to kick off the conversation.

"It's about Director Ibrahim Yusef, sir. I understand you know of his disappearance."

"Only that he disappeared, but everything else is still a mystery. I have tasked the Agency into looking for him, but I fear he may have been taken hostage by remnants of ICE."

"No sir, that's not the case at all. In fact he was working with them all along."

Harada sat forward almost as if he hadn't heard correctly. His eyes narrowed in suspicion as he said, "What are you basing that on William?"

"After the attack on my headquarters, I ordered a deep dive into Yusef's affairs. I'd known of his jealousy of myself and my organisation, which stemmed from the fact he thought you considered us your 'private little army' and in doing so believed we received preferential treatment. That's not the case as we both know, but he was convinced of it."

"Why would he think that?"

"That's not important now, but what is important is that he instigated a plan to bring MI7 down no matter what. He knew about the missile testing program. In fact, he was on the board that investigated the validity of such a weapon. He had intimate knowledge of them and what they could do–their entire potential. What's more, he knew about where they were being shipped to and by whom. He leaked that data to Nathan Jericho who had been the leader of a Special Forces mission that failed, causing the loss of his entire team. They had been acting on intel from his agency so the mission would fail."

"Why would he do that?" Harada asked, confused by all the machinations of this story.

"It was all engineered so that Jericho could be guided into doing Yusef's bidding while he thought he was acting independently. He led Jericho to believe that the failure of the mission was down to your political decisions, budget cuts in military spending, and others, which was untrue. Jericho hijacked the missile convoy after being gifted the Raptor F95, another test platform Yusef had intimate knowledge of from his dealings with the Haynes Corporation. Jericho knew you would never negotiate with terrorists—it is government policy and has been for centuries, something he was well aware of from his time in the military. He knew you would task someone to investigate, and Yusef thought it would be us, something that turned out to be correct. Jericho's endgame was always to come after you, sir. You were his focus through the entire operation, guided along by Yusef. Yusef hoped we would fail and, in doing so, you would be killed, which would eradicate his two main obstacles in front of him for his grab for power. With you dead, he assumed MI7 would be terminated, so when Jericho's attempt on your life failed, he came after us directly."

"And you have evidence of this?" Harada asked, still not believing it all.

"I do, sir, it is all documented and can be produced as evidence."

"I'll look into it, and I will have Yusef brought in for trial as soon as he's found."

"No need, sir; he has already faced justice. My man killed him on board the ship he had commandeered to attack my headquarters. We also have in custody three operatives who took part in the attack who will all attest to Yusef ordering the attack."

Leaning back on the sofa, Harada looked at Chambers, assessing him through eyes that had narrowed in suspicion. He wondered what his old friend wanted out of this.

"So, what do you want from me?" he asked.

Chambers paused before answering, smiled a little, then said, "Nothing sir, seeing as how Director Yusef is deceased there seems no need for further action against him. I will, of course, keep all the evidence against him in a safe place. I think you would agree that, should knowledge ever reach the media, it could raise certain questions. We wouldn't want others to be tainted with the same brush as it were. After all sir, Yusef was a personal appointee of yours, and he was given the position on your personal and specific recommendation."

Harada saw it then for what it was, subtle blackmail. "Quite," he said, "we wouldn't want that to happen, and as a show of gratitude for all the good work, you and your department have done over the last few years, and specifically, on this last operation, I think it's time I increase your budget."

"You are too kind sir," Chambers replied with a smile.

Getting to his feet Chambers said, "Well, sir, I'll leave you to get on, I'm sure you have a busy day ahead of you."

With a slight bow he left the office. He had accomplished what he'd come to do, and now he could get on with his job, but he still had one more stop to make before getting back to the office.

Pryde was getting bored. He'd done as ordered and returned to the hospital to continue his recovery. The doctor who was looking after him had been furious about him signing himself out. He gave him a serious talking to when he returned, pointing out that he was lucky to be alive, the damage he could have done to his injuries, and finally pointing out how far back he had put his recovery time.

Pryde had taken it all on the chin, for he knew what the doctor had said was, in essence, correct. The situation had demanded his taking action though and, as it had turned out, he had been proven right.

He was just wondering when he would be able to return to work as he lay on his bio-bed when the door opened.

"Sir, it's good to see you. Are you here to order me back to work?" he said, sitting upright.

"I'm afraid not, quite the opposite in fact. Yes, I do need you back at work, but I want you at one hundred percent efficiency, nothing else shall suffice. So, you will remain here until the doctors are satisfied and you have recovered fully, is that understood?" Chamber said.

"Perfectly sir," he replied, his shoulders slumping a little with his disappointment.

"I just dropped by to see how you were doing and to inform you I delivered the evidence against Director Yusef to the President," Chambers said.

"How did he take it?"

"About as well as we expected. He tried to play it as if he had no knowledge of it."

"It must have hurt a little when he found out Jericho was gunning for him, especially considering how Yusef had turned Jericho against him. Just shows that Yusef wasn't as good a friend as Harada thought after all."

"Agreed, I told him I was keeping the evidence in a safe place in case such a thing would happen again. He doesn't want it getting out to the media any more than I do, but he has more to lose. We got an increase of our budget for our endeavours though, so it's not all bad news. Harada has been put on notice that we know about his involvement—well, not so much involvement, but knowledge of it all. I suspect he considered that we were getting too successful and thought it time to bring us down a peg or two. He couldn't justify it as a political decision, so he allowed Yusef to set us up to fail."

"Big mistake," Pryde said.

"Yes, well you get some rest and I'll see you back in the office when you've recovered."

"Yes, sir, can't wait, sir."

"Enjoy the rest Pryde, I've a feeling you're going to need it."

Pryde watched as his boss left his room and he lay back down on his bed. The anticipation of getting back to work was all that was keeping him sane. Chambers had meant it as a warning, about worse things to come, but he relished the challenge. In fact he looked, forward to it.

The end,

for now,

Duncan Pryde will return.

About the Author

Jan Domagala was born in Staffordshire, England to a working class family where at school he discovered the joys of reading. Jan was a big fan of sci-fi books but would read almost anything he could get his hands on. His mother took him to join the local library as soon as he could read and from that day on, if it had words on it, he'd read it.

In the early 70's there wasn't much choice for employment where Jan lived so he ended up in an apprenticeship in screen printing for the ceramic industry. In the early years of his apprenticeship he had the pleasure of a trip on the schooner Captain Scott, a training ship as part of the crew. They sailed around Scotland and even up as far as Stornoway in the Outer Hebrides.

Jan is still in the same trade after a forty year career, but his passion is and has always been writing. After several abortive attempts, he started the Col Sec series, which is an action-adventure series set in the twenty fifth century.

Jan is currently working on the next book in the series.

Join Jan by subscribing today!

http://eepurl.com/dLM3gk

Follow me on BookBub! https://www.bookbub.com/authors/jan-domagala

And on Facebook: https://www.facebook.com/ColSecSeries

Also by Jan Domagala

The Col Sec Series

Ronin

Omega

Discovery